MW01657151

# Journey from Frog Creek

Copyright © 2006 Valerie Guimaraes
All rights reserved.
ISBN: 1-4196-4721-0

To order additional copies, please contact us.
BookSurge, LLC
www.booksurge.com
1-866-308-6235
orders@booksurge.com

VALERIE
GUIMARAES

# JOURNEY FROM FROG CREEK

2006

# Journey from Frog Creek

# CHAPTERS 1-4 PLAGUES

# CHAPTER 1

*Where did I put my bags? Stay by mama. Hurry. Why can't I find my clothes? It's too late. Where are my bags? Where can I hide them? Was that the door? I can't breathe. I'm going to give myself away. I can't do this now. Put everything away. Don't say a word. Oh please, baby. We're playing a game. What's wrong with this old phone?*

*What the Sam Hill are you doing? Breathe! Oh, nothing. I'm just cleaning and playing with baby.*

I was awake. I hollered out in my sleep. Did I wake up my angel? Was he all right? I better check him and the doors. My heart was poundin'. I was soaked again. The dreams were gettin' closer and closer. I gazed out the window curtain. There was no one was there. I checked all of the windows and doors. My angel was sleepin' like an angel. I put my hand on his chest and covered him up. Thankfully Sula's twin home was cool at night. I was so hot.

What was I doin'? How could I get away with this? He was right. I couldn't do nothin' right. He was always right. After all, He went to that high fangled school and got a good job. At least we had food on the table. I hoped Granny was okay. I hoped she could see her way through to forgive me for what I had done. I just had to keep on and have some faith in my baby. I was doin' this for him. It seemed like I didn't matter none.

The next morning I woke, and I was all wore out. Hopefully those dreams would stop a while soon enough. The knock on the door scared me at first. Thankfully Sula always liked to say "hello" after she knocked.

"Where's my little man?"

Sula always greeted him that a way. Jay came out all sleepy-eyed and came right to me. He was my savin' grace. *Good Lord, was it good to put so much on a youngin'?*

"I got oatmeal and toast this mornin', my sleepy one. I think I can even find some sugar and cin'mon for ya."

I gathered the food 'round the table. I bess keep buyin' in small quantities. Never knew when a body was goin' to have to pick up and go. Jay looked a might happy at the talk of sugar and cin'mon. It was his favorite.

"What are ya'll goin' to do today? I got some lamps and some towels I found. I ain't used them in a long time. I think you need to get this place fixed up, if'n you're goin' to stay a while?"

I knew Sula wanted to know more 'bout me and my plans, but I just couldn't say on.

"You ain't answered me. I can see you're still all bottled up inside and ... well, I ain't tried to wheedle it out of you. No sir. You seem tighter than a drum some days. Did you have a bad night?"

"Yes'm."

It had been almost two weeks since we'd been in Chatfield. I remember givin' Jay the map I drawed. We were standin' outside of the public library. I traced the map as best I could from the one in the library. I remember I held out the map and knew Jay would know where we should go.

"Jay, you're a man, though you're only three. I reckon you'll know where we need to go. It's got to be safe for us'n. Can you point out on the map I drew up and tell mama where we need to be?"

His little finger was right on Chatfield. I hadn't ever heard of it before and maybe He hadn't either?

"Cinda! You got plans today?"

"No Ma'am, I don't reckon I do."

"Stop calling me ma'am. I ain't so old, and we ain't so formal. You understand?"

"Yes'm, I understand."

The fact was I was so used to playin' dumb, sometimes I just plain forgot m'self. I did understand a lot of things. It might take me a while but when I figure it out— look out!

Sula was playin' a might with Jay, and I took that opportunity to clean up a bit. First I did the dishes. Old habits, I guess. It seemed like once the kitchen was clean, I could relax. It was time for a nice warm bath. What a "luxury!" See Sula, I can use words too. I weren't much good in school. I was good with figurin'. That's what Miss Dawling said, anyway. As soon as He put His sights on me, He said book learnin' wouldn't help me very much. What I needed was a man to care for me. Since He was all graduated, I figured He knew what I needed.

I started thinkin' again. How long could we get away with this? What if they found me? I wished I could talk to Granny again. I wished I could just hear her voice. I could say I was okay, Jay too. *Lord, help her to know we were okay.* I didn't rightly know if I could call upon the Lord, but I would anyway. I knew a phone call was too chancy right now. Sittin' in the bear claw tub felt good. I could think for a bit. I dried my hands, climbed out of the tub and reached for my map. I put it in a safe place.

The first night we were there I spied a little place right under the sink. It was curious. A tiny makeshift cabinet with linoleum clean up onto the floorboard around it. The cabinet had glass knobs on the outside of it. I looked inside and saw all kinds of balms, half-used soaps, lye, salves and whatnot. I felt all around inside and found a loose board behind some soap and a bottle of bluing. It was plum dry with lots of space behind it. It was His secret spot that gave me the idea. I placed all my important stuff in that cabinet that night, and it'd been there ever since. My map, money, His watch, a pen and some papers I found tucked away inside of His secret spot. I smiled at the thought of it. Oh, and the number, in case I needed help.

From what I remembered from the County Library's big state map, Chatfield was nary four counties away from Rondo Township. If I marked the scale of miles right, I was nary 100 miles away from home 'crossed the State line. Nobody would ever 'spect someone like me to get this far on m' own. It seemed safe enough for now. I didn't have any definite plans. I needed time to think. What if my past came all down on me? What would happen to Jay? Jay couldn't go back to Him or His family. Why, they'd try to...NO! I wouldn't think 'bout it at all. If'n I kept thinkin' those kinda thoughts it just might happen. I couldn't let that happen to my angel. No sir!

When I came out of my room Jay smiled and came a runnin'. I ain't never had a room of my own 'fore, and it seemed nice. Even though there was a little bitty room offin' the kitchen where Sula said I could put Jay, I kept 'im close by. As we hugged, Sula went off on one of her lectures.

"You know, Cinda. I ain't forced you to tell me nothin'

'bout nothin'. I think if you're gonna be stayin' it's high time we talked turkey with one 'nother. Listen to me, I sound like one of them country people down near Rondo way..."

I gasped! How did she know 'bout Rondo?

"What's wrong, child?"

Before I knew it and could help it, I was cryin'. I was flat out bawlin'. Just hearin' her say my hometown sent a chill through me, and I think I was cryin' before I knew it.

"See, you're all bottled up and ready to burst. I knew it! It's time you trust old Sula now. Why, look at Jay. I'd say he's used to seein' you cry. Is that right?"

She was right 'bout that. Jay come up to me and just stood near by me. He was waitin' for me to say "it's alright baby, Mama's gonna be just fine." And that's what I said. He smiled at me and went on a playin' with some old toys Sula give us the day we came to her twin house.

"I guess you're right, Sula. It's time I told you a few things 'bout m'self. I rightly don't know where to begin."

Just as I was 'bout to say somethin', and I really didn't know what I was gonna say, there was a loud knock on Sula's front door.

"Dang blame it! Just as we were gonna get real comfy, too. I'll be back later. I think it's a fella about one of my ads."

Off Sula went. I don't mind sayin' that I was relieved. I ran to the little window by my front door. Cranin' my neck I could see an older fella with a suit on...was that a badge? Oh Lord, no! I ran to Jay and held him close. I ran into the kitchen where me and Sula's doors met one 'nother to see if I could pick up on anything. I was used to this. When He and Granny would talk at night, I would sneak down the hall and listen. I listened out of fear, I guess.

What were they sayin'? I told Jay that we needed to run.

Poor baby, he picked up his bear and blankie and came back to me, just like we practiced. I went under the sink and found my important stuff and headed for the back door. Heck with the clothes. There I went again. My, how my language went to pot when I was mad or scared. As we slipped out the back door, I wanted to leave Sula a note or somethin', but I didn't. There was no time.

We got to a park aways from Sula's, and we set down a bit. I had to think. Jay went right over to the little sandbox. Someone had left a pail and shovel. I guess they know'd a needy soul would come by and want to play. I collected on my thoughts. If it were the sheriff, then Sula wouldn't know much 'bout me, not even where I was from. Now I was glad I nary said a word 'bout m'self. What if he weren't a sheriff? There I run off and what would Sula think? I figured I had to know who the man was.

I told Jay we were bein' spies like on the old movies we had seen on Granny's old TV. He smiled but I don't believe he know'd what I meant. He was just happy holdin' my hand. I stopped at the gas station near the edge a town. This was where the red eye brought me my first night in Chatfield. The gas station was a familiar place to me even though I hadn't ever been there afore. It was white washed with green gas pumps. There were chairs just for anybody to sit on near the front door. There was an outhouse 'round the back. The Coca Cola machine was a sight for sore eyes now just like it was that night. I got us an Orange Crush. My, I loved that soda pop! Jay, too. That night we arrived, an older fella come out and greeted us after we got off the bus. He was wearin' overalls just a covered with grease and oil. He had tools all on himself. He looked like he could fix anything. He directed us to the café across the street. That was where we first met Sula. The gas station man said

Maude's Café stayed open extra late on Friday nights 'cause that's where the next bus came 'bout 10 o'clock, headed on to Mantorville, Osage and all points north.

Jay and I sipped on that Orange Crush like it was the first soda pop we ever had. We went on a walkin'. There was a car smack dab in front of Sula's. In all my rush to get out of the house, I didn't look to see for anything else. Boy that was dumb! He always said I was dumb, not checkin' for anything 'round me. Once He stopped me when I stepped off a curb 'cause I nary got hit by a big old bus! I 'member thinkin' that maybe He did care some for me.

I tried to look all ord'nary like. I held Jay's hand extra tight as we walked down the street. I tried to think and calm down, but I had to keep movin'. I thought 'bout the red eye that came by every Friday night at the gas station. One of the first things I checked on was to see how I had to get out of this town, if'n I needed to— fast. Too bad it was Tuesday. I hadn't never really cared about the days of the week afore. The days would just melt into another down home. Fridays were special. Well, kinda, I guess. I caught sight of a pretty little white house with flowers all 'round. I told Jay to just take a look at all the pretty flowers. We stopped to look on, sippin' Orange Crush, just like we had no cares at all. The flowers were pretty. They were all just standin' tall and each one looked different in its own way. Bees just buzzin' 'round them. I sure didn't like bees. Too bad you needed bees to have flowers. How could something so mean help things grow? The houses looked mighty big and the world seemed mighty small when you walked 'round like this. Just think, people had lives and family all tucked inside four walls. No one could really know what went on inside. I looked up at the house and saw that the sheer curtain moved just a bit. I guessed someone was watchin' out for their flowers.

A feelin' a dread came all on me. For a moment I was all caught up in my thoughts. "Life will pass you by!" That's what Maw would say anytime I was day dreamin'. I glanced down the street and saw that the car was gone now. I had to make a decision. I turned us 'round and came back the way we came. I walked slowly toward Sula's backyard. It seemed right quiet. I decided to go in. I was plum tired of runnin'. Sula seemed nice and all. She gave me m'space all this time. What would I say to her? Why did we run off? I got used to thinkin' 'bout stuff afore someone might ask so as to look like I was up to nothin' at all. Why, I could even look like I was thinkin' of nothin'. I practiced it so I wouldn't get beat. First by Maw and then by Him.

Sula didn't open the door to her place. That was a good omen. I knew she must a heard us come in. If'n that man was from the law; there would be more 'citement 'round. I decided it was safe to go in. I kept Jay and me real quiet-like, just in case.

"Can't talk now, Cinda. The man that came by wants me to find some important papers about my house. I'll have to talk to you about this later. You alright, child?"

"Yes'm, I am. Don't worry 'bout us none. Jay will take a nap and I just might join him."

Safe for another day.

# CHAPTER 2

*How can I hide these clothes? I can't take this much stuff. I have to put everything together so I can grab them and run. I could hide them outside by the old tree. He could come home any time now. What'll I do? Where will I go? I need money don't I? He'll find it. He'll take it. I could call ... please someone answer. He's home!*

*What are you doing? You're just a nut! Why do you have a suitcase? Just playin' with the baby is all. What's for supper?*

I woke m'self up by my sobbin'. I looked around, dazed for a sec 'cause I didn't know where I was. Then I remembered I was at Sula's and I was okay. Jay!? I wiped my eyes as I looked around and saw him through the dark light. Breathin' like a baby. I reached to touch him just to be sure. I loved the darkness. Nobody could see me, case my thoughts betrayed me. No one could see my tears or know that I was scared silly. How could darkness be a blessin' and a curse all at the same time? One of life's mysteries, as Granny would say. Quietly, I got up. I was all sweaty again. How long could those dreams go on? Guilt? Water would taste good 'bout now. I grabbed a cool drink and held it to my head. I moved toward the back curtains overlookin' the backyard. There was nothin' there. I checked the front door— locked. No way to live. Not at all!

How long had I been away now? It'd be comin' up on two weeks. Granny said someone's past can come crashin' down on them in one afternoon with family. I lasted longer than that. But I don't have any family 'round. *Please, God, I missed Granny.* He always did say that I would never last anywhere without Him and I bess 'member that. No one would ever want me or like me 'ceptin' Him. Sula liked me. She seemed to have takin' a likin' to Jay too. I couldn't go back now. Nope, there was no turnin' back. Not now, after what I had done.

Was that a car I heard? At this hour a night? Just like home. I could see pretty well at night. There was no need to turn a light on at all. A station wagon?! I couldn't tell if I was a screamin' out loud or not. I sank to the floor. I was gonna hurl right here! I had to see. They couldn't a found me?! Sure enough, I'd recognize that old funny station wagon anywhere, anytime. My heart was a poundin'. I was fully awake. It couldn't be a dream. *Please God.* What were they droppin'? Wood? I was gonna hurl. Hurlin' and bein' quiet just ain't possible. I was crawlin' on the floor like someone with a guilty soul. I couldn't be seen. I just had to calm down. I ran cool water over my face and took in some air. I had to see. I was scramblin' to the kitchen window; I could see the wagon go slowly down the street. They knew I was here!

Mornin' came early, and I started right in. I was just gonna' tell Sula that somethin' came up down to home. I was pacin' just like in my dreams. What was the name of the town I picked last night...Stanton? Sorry baby, mama's gonna have to be more bold. Jay, just a playin' away. Yeah, Stanton, it was off in a whole 'nother direction. But she'd ask me how I heard from them. I made a call on the pay phone at the gas station and found out that I'm needed to home. Jay slept late this mornin'. I hoped he could sleep on the bus. That red eye would be packed up, I suspect. I had to make sandwiches, buy soda pop...

*Bang! Thud!* Oh, no! It was Him! He was at the front door!

"Cinda, you there, girl?"

Why, that was the back door. What was goin' on?

"Did you get your phone book? Isn't it a marvel? We can get a listing of all the people in the town— who's got phones, that is. People from all around the county. People we don't even know. Mornin', Jay. Come to Sula, now. Jay ran to Sula, blankie in tow.

"Cinda, my, you look worn. Did you have a bad night?"

I was numb, but I went to the front door and opened it ever so slowly. *Plop.* It was a phone book. They were droppin' phone books? How could that be? Why? How long they been doin' this? Was this where they went on those long trips? Why didn't I know? As I thought on it, I knew why I wouldn't know none 'bout this. They clean made fun of the Gaye's when they done it. Sherm was just tryin' to put food on the table like everybody else in those hard times. He had six kids, a wife and what not. I musta looked strange 'cause Sula asked me if I had seen a ghost or somethin'.

"No Ma'am, no ghost. I'm just curious is all. How did they get here? The books, I mean."

"The phone books? Why, the phone company just finds people who got a car and some time on their hands. They pay them a few dollars, money for gas and food. The phone companies need people to go to the country folks. There is not much call to go to places other than that. Why do you ask?"

"Just wonderin'."

I wondered if she could tell that I was lyin'. *Lord Almighty, please, I hate lyin'.*

"Now look, Cinda. I gotta talk to you about a serious matter. You know that man that came by the house earlier this week? Well, he was an inspector from the county. If I plan to rent out this place again, why I gotta file papers and come clean. I guess some folks 'round here got their dander up and reported me. They say I got someone livin' here and makin' all kinds of money. I kinda told 'em a little tiny lie to help us both."

I looked on at Jay whilst Sula told me her little tiny lie. That's what I need to do, come clean. If'n I help Sula, maybe she would help me. Lyin' 'bout a house or 'bout bein' kin didn't seem even though.

"Cinda?

"A lie. Why Sula, I never…"

"I'm no liar. I'm no crook either. That's what I told him. Mr. Parsons is his name. He's a new fella in town. I told him that you were my sister's daughter come for a visit. Fact is, if you stay here for more than a month, well, I gotta charge you rent; kin or no kin. That'll mean I have to file papers with the county. He has to inspect the place for cleanliness, and I have to pay some kind of fool tax. I told you I used to rent the place out by the week a few years ago."

All the while Sula was talkin' my mind was thinkin'. What if they wanted to know who I was? What if they wanted proof or somethin'? Like some kind of paper. Like I had to show the manager of the bank at Rondo. *Oh Lord, I was in trouble.*

"So, you see Cinda, we have to talk turkey. Are you plannin' on stayin' here for a while? You know, that night when I met you at the café I could tell you were runnin' from something, and it didn't matter to me from what. I took one look at you and that tired little boy of yours and I could tell you was good people. I figured you were from the country and..."

I had to say somethin' before she said anymore.

"I would like very much to stay here a while. I will be your sister's daughter come for a visit."

All her talk 'bout the phone books set me at ease 'bout Them knowin' where I was.

"But I may have to go back home...to Stanton."

My heart was poundin', and my head hurt.

"I could be needed down to home and would have to go back. I called home yesterday."

I felt so hot and down right sick now.

"I needed just a break from things. Jay's daddy is dead. He took sick. We're alone and I needed to get away from His family tellin' me what to do."

Boy oh boy, once I started a lyin' I just couldn't quit. Before I knew it, I said some mighty things.

"I'm an only child."

This was partially true.

"I got married at 14 and lived with Jay's daddy's family."

This was kinda true too.

"I was tired of bein' bossed 'round by family who knew what was best for me, and I needed a break from Them."

That was true enough.

"I'll be your sister's daughter. I'm all talked out, Sula. Oh, what's my name?"

Sula looked a might shocked at all my words. Even Jay was by my side as I went on and on. I felt different too. It's a funny thing. I always heard that the truth shall set you free, but here I was lyin' up a storm and I felt free. Granny would be down right shamed.

"My sister does have a daughter. She's married to a man who's in the army. They got a boy about Jay's age. They're livin' down south somewhere. My sister Stella lives in Hixton. She had but one child, Myrna. She died young but not before she had Marilyn. Marilyn married Eugene, the one in the army. Eugene Houghton's his name. Last I heard, Eugene entered the army, and they had a little boy and they're doin' just fine. Stella raised Marilyn just like her own daughter. It's kinda nice, you know. She always wanted more children and well, through a tragedy, she got her wish. That's the way it works you know, life. One person's tragedy is another's blessing, 'cept when both happen to the same person at the same time. That's refining. You know, like it says in the Bible?"

*Cinda Houghton from Hixton.* I liked that! My mom's name was Stella. I ain't much thought 'bout my Maw in a while. I bet Stella was as nice as Sula. Maw always said I'd turn out no better than m'dad. I never did know him, though. All I was fixed to do was turn out kids and do housework. It seemed okay to me, but the way Maw said it, I knew it was a knock 'gainst me.

"Is $40.00 a month too much for you, Cinda?"

"No Ma'am. It seems right fair."

I thought about m'money. I didn't like to think 'bout money. It's all I got in the world, and I didn't know where I could come upon more. Granny would help if'n she knew where I was. They could find me for sure if I called to home. I'd better save that for a real emergency. Like if Jay took sick or somethin'. Sure hoped I didn't have to pay for that lie I told 'bout Him. Seemed like I just kept a payin' and payin' for Him.

"It's settled! I'll file the papers next week. Let's go to the town's picnic tomorrow. It's high time you met some of the folks 'round here. Most of the folks worth meetin' will be at the picnic. There will be church folks, farmin' folks, some of the business folks and Lord, lots of little kids Jay's age. The Chatfield Town Celebration and Picnic draws lots of people. You okay with that?"

# CHAPTER 3

*Come on Jay baby, run. If we don't get to town we'll miss our bus. We have to get off the grass and take to the road. We'll make better time. Come on, baby! Where did I put our bags? Someone musta took the bags I hid. Oh, no! There's a car a comin'.*

*Hey! What are you doing out on the road? What are you doing? Lookin' for bottles for money. We do this now and then. Oh yeah, well where are the bottles and where's the money? Slap. Slap. Where's Jay? Jay?*

I woke up to Jay screamin'. My heart was poundin'. I couldn't move.

"Jay, mama's comin'. Mama just had a bad dream. Its okay, baby. It's just fine now."

Rockin' the baby back and forth comforted us both. Land sakes, I was all sweaty 'gain. I musta hollered out Jay's name for him to be screamin' like this. I started singin' the lullaby I heard Maw sing to my little brother afore she left with him. I didn't rightly like it, but it was the only lullaby I knew. Jay relaxed in my arms. He was breathin' real heavy. I didn't know too many sweet sounds, but this was surely one of them. That and baby feet hittin' the floor as they came a runnin'.

Seein' the doors locked and no one in the street, I could rest a might. I thought about Granny and my heart started a achin'. It was like I could even hold it in my hand. I sure wished I could talk to her 'gain. *Please Lord, I hope she's all right. Help her to know I'm okay and Jay too. Amen.*

Granny didn't take to Jay right off. It was mainly because of the family He came from. She said it was a bad family. They drank, took up with one 'nother, why even the Grandmammy herself took up with her own kin. She never said which one, but I had my hunches. I heard tell that one of the girls even skedaddled off with one of her kin too. I had my hunches on that one too. In time Granny warmed up to Jay. I was real glad 'bout that. I didn't rightly know what I was gonna' do if'n the two people I loved the most didn't get along.

Sula packed us all a fine lunch for the picnic. I didn't bring anything 'cept two bottles of Orange Crush soda pop. We started walkin'. Sula said it was only a few blocks. Shoot, it was close to a mile if you asked me. Jay was just a clingin' to m'arm. Sula would point out different houses. He lived here, and she lived there. They were snooty. They were good folks. Why, the way Sula said it, some of these folks would take you right in like you was kin. I made sure to look hard on those houses, 'case I needed to run for help.

As we were walkin' on, I thought how Jay picked us a right nice town to run to. All these houses were so nice and kept up. There weren't like the ones in Frog Creek. No, sir! Why, each house had a porch and some had a swing built up in them. Most homes had a flowerbed or two and lots of trees. Why, if you stood in the middle of the road, it looked like there was a coverin' of trees directly over you and it went on for as far as you could see.

The town square, as Sula called it, was so nicely decorated. There was a pavilion right in the center of the square. It was white. It was just painted accordin' to Sula. There were banners strung out from each post of the pavilion. I never saw so many happy people in one place in m'life! The entire town square was all decorated with banners and flowers. There were such pretty colors all 'round. The people were millin' all 'round talkin' and laughin' real friendly like. There was a man in a top hat and gloves. He was talkin' all loud and important like. Sula said he was the Mayor of the town of Chatfield. I pointed him right out to Jay. I wanted him to see, first hand, a real important man. There was food at a big table. That's where we were headin'. Sula put our picnic lunch right on the table, and she led us to a nice wooden bench to see the sights.

The ladies were all so pretty, too. Some had on hats and pretty dresses. Some ladies showin' a might too much skin on top. I know'd He'd a liked me to look like that. It didn't seem right to me to be showin' all what God give ya to please anyone. But He liked that. I remember He would talk on and on 'bout women half His age. I got a sick feelin' in the pit of my stomach when He talked 'bout younger girls, even younger than me. Sayin' "She'll be a winner" or "No one will even come close to her when she's older." What made me feel the most scared was when He was teasin' about His male kin. Talkin' 'bout things that ain't fit for human beings. I hugged Jay. He was enjoyin' the sights as much as I was. It was my thoughts that plagued me.

For the first time in a long while I looked down at m'self. I had on a gingham jumper and white blouse, with white socks and saddle shoes. My hair was all pulled back. I brushed it 100 times most every night. That was me, simple. I was not gussied up at all. Granny would be proud. Granny and Sula were the only ones who said I was pretty.

The pie eatin' contest was a hoot. A man by the name of Little Mannie won it easy enough. If'n I heard right, he done ate eight whole pies! Some lady Sula didn't take too kindly to, Nelda won some flower contest. Tug o' war, three-legged race, and races just to race were all about us. I had to admit, I felt down right gay.

"Mrs. Graw, I'd like you to meet my niece, Sandra. She's from Rondo and this is her mother..."

I stood up like a shot! Rondo? The talk came from behind us. My head was spinnin'. It was a good thing Sula was holdin' Jay tryin' to get him to look at the tiny dancin' dogs. I turned my head, but I just had to see. I looked upon the girl they called Sandra, and she didn't look none too familiar. Her maw didn't look familiar either. I sat down and looked at the dancin' dogs. I hoped those people wouldn't come our way. Maybe I didn't know'd them, but did they know me? *Please God... maybe I was feelin' a might too gay considerin' what I had done.* I was just as sorry as I could be.

"Sula Cantrell! How are you? My husband said you're renting out your twin house again. Is that so? Is this who you're renting to?"

My heart was so heavy. I couldn't move. I was so hot and sweaty. If'n I got up, I'd pass out for sure.

"How do, Mrs. Parsons."

"Call me Nellie. Everyone else does. Let's not be so formal."

"Nellie. Yes, I had plum forgotten your name. You and your husband are new to Chatfield, aren't you? I've been here all my life, and well, can't remember every new person. Yes, this is my niece, Cinda... Cinda Houghton all the way from Hixton. And this is her son, Jay Jr."

"We've been here for nearly five years! When will people of this town ...well, never mind. Where's your husband, Cinda? You do have a husband?"

Sula piped up.

"Yes, of course. He's in the service. He's one of our fightin' men. He's serving our Country. She's visitin' while he's trainin' for a mission. I can't talk about it, you know."

*God bless you, Sula.* I tried to stand up. Those ladies put forth their hands, and I guessed I better shake them. Their hands felt all cool and clammy. They had such skinny little fingers. Didn't they work none? They were so fancy lookin'. They had on dresses, hats and gloves. Why they even had on high heels, and it was the middle of the day!

"You look familiar. Where did you say you hail from?"

"Houghton...I'm Cinda Houghton from Hixton. Pleased to meet ya. Excuse us."

I glanced back to see Mrs. Parsons' sister just eye ballin' me and Jay. I pretended to be interested in the flowers and took Jay with me. Bless Sula for talkin' with those women. Mrs. Parsons' niece was thankfully not lookin' at me. If'n she was my age, she probably didn't care who I was. From the way they were dressed, we wouldn't know the same people anyhow.

It was gettin' on to dusk. Dusk was the prettiest time of day. It was almost holy. The wind came gently by, bringin' newness to the day. There were colors, yellows and reds 'gainst the dark blue sky. That meant night wasn't too far behind but not afore bringin' this last hope of day. Lord I didn't 'preciate nature enough. I didn't rightly remember enjoyin' nature as much since I was a kid. I could soak up the sun. I could breathe up all the fresh air. Just a lyin' in the grass and watchin' clouds go by. I remembered the smells. I didn't smell those smells anymore. They were gone. Maybe it was somethin' you got to enjoy when you were young and innocent? That a way you'd 'member those special times 'cause if one was given this gift every day, well, it just wouldn't be a gift. Of course, this pleasure was parceled out to me double. I could enjoy nature when Granny would come for a visit.

"Cinda, are you alright? You are the most thinkin' girl I know. What fills your head? I know what's fillin' mine. We bess scoot home before it gets time for the dance. I don't mind sayin' that it can get a little rowdy here at night. There would be girls dancin' and men just out lookin' for a good time. Last year, I heard tell that after nine o'clock, when most respectable people and their families were to home, a ruckus broke out! It was... well, you wouldn't know them so what's the point of tellin'? I'll tell ya anyhow, but let's just keep movin'. See, some folks came from out of town, somewhere near where Mrs. Parsons' sister is from. I think that's why Mrs. Parsons invited her sister to this year's celebration. 'Cause of what happened. Anyway, the poor principal's daughter was violated right near the square! Anyhow, the town was in an uproar for weeks! When it was told that the people who mighta been involved in the violatin' came from out Rondo way, why, the Parsons were in an uproar too! There was no investigation or nothin'. We draw people from all over, and it was hard for the young girl to be certain. Finally, it was dropped outta respect for the principal's family. The Mayor promised he would control the town square dance better this year, but I have my doubts. Let's go!"

I carried Jay all the way back to Sula's. There was somethin' botherin' me 'bout what Sula said. I kept thinkin' 'bout that poor girl who was violated. When did He go away with this kin? Wasn't it this time of year? I was sure of it... well, pretty sure. I remember all of those scratches on his face…

'What happened to you? You're all scratched up.'

'What ? Nothing happened. I don't know what you mean.'

'You got scratches all over your face. You said you were goin' with your kin...how'd they get there?'

'I don't know. Someone just came outta the bushes and scratched me.'

'Out from our bushes? You mean right here, by our house?'

I ran over to the window and peeked out.

'Why that ain't right. What should we do?'

'Look I don't know what happened. I got into a fight is all.'

He got into a fight? I musta been a fool to believe that story. Why, I 'member it looked like someone with long fingernails scratched him. I couldn't 'member exactly when that was now... The problem was He was always sneakin' off somewhere. I wasn't allowed to ask where or why lessin' I wanted a beatin'. I just learned not to ask.

There in the cover of darkness, I thought on the last dance I went to. His cousin kept followin' me 'round. I tried to stick close to Him, but His cousin just kept comin' 'round me. I didn't know what to do. I tried to talk to His cousin, but that just made things worse. His cousin kept tryin' to put his arm 'round me, and I was so scared for the both of us. Everyone 'cept me was drinkin'.

Later I got a beatin' because it was my fault His cousin took a shine to me. He said somethin' 'bout me not belongin' where there was men and women drinkin' and dancin'. That was one of the times I tried to stick up for m'self. It wasn't m'fault. I wasn't encouragin' anybody! I got down right mad. I sure got beat. A black eye for all to see. I got a lecture to boot. He told me somethin' 'bout He was always right and I could never challenge Him ever again. What He said was the final word. Why, he even tested me. He'd say somethin' that was nary a word a truth to it, and I would say what it was for real and *pow*! I got beat. That was the last dance I went to.

We were home at last! I slipped Jay into bed. I left his clothes on. My poor angel was so tired. I got m'self ready for bed. For the first time in a long while, I looked upon my flesh. There were my mother's marks. They were everywhere. They were on my legs, my body, and my arms. I remember He said I was so fat. I believed what He said. I even felt sorry for Him havin' to look at me. Sula said I was Rubenesque. I guess that meant that I look like someone named Ruben? Anyway, she said it was a compliment. It weren't a knock. Granny used to say she had stove pipe legs and snake hips. I don't rightly know what that means either. It seemed to me, puttin' all our eggs into our basket on account for our looks weren't the right thing to do. Granny said looks were skin deep. It was the heart that matters. I didn't rightly know what was in my heart. I'd been so busy thinkin' what everybody else wanted me to think and sayin' what everybody else wanted to me say that I just didn't know what was inside of me.

The warm bath felt relaxin'. I just couldn't let my mind rest. Nor did I want those dreams comin' back that night. I sat in the bathroom dryin' off so as not to wake my baby. This was my one place of peace at home. Down to home, we may not respect one 'nother the way we should, Lord willin'. But if you went in the bathroom, you were safe for a while. Lessin' you overstayed your time. Boy, the bangin' would start. Dressed for bed, I dug into my secret place and found my important papers. I laid them out, one by one. There was my map. It was a might wrinkled. There was my money. No cause to worry none yet. Sula chargin' $40 a month seemed fair enough to me. There was His watch and all of His papers. I couldn't believe He was fixin' to get rid of Granny and take over on the homestead.

I remember when I come upon this stuff. I knew He was spendin' a lot more time with Granny, night after night. I was just a cranin' my neck to hear as much as I could without bein' seen or heard. He was just a pourin' out pure butter cream. I wondered if Granny believed nary a word. What did He say? He said somethin' 'bout wantin' the best for me and Jay and her, too. Horse poop! There I went again. I didn't care any. It was horse poop! He couldn't hear me now anyway.

That night He come out of her room all mad like. I just steered clear of Him. He left the house and said He was goin' to see His cousin. I didn't even ask which one. I watched Him leave and walk past the old outhouse into the dark of night. Granny was gettin' ready for bed. She called me in and talked all seer-like. Like I imagined one of them prophets talkin' to their kin about some future doom that's gonna come down on them lessin' they repent.

She started talkin' 'bout Maw. How she never shoulda run away and took Orville with her. Lord only knew where they were now. She heard tell that Maw was in an accident, drinkin' with some married man from down Chesterville way. Maw left Orville with some lady who mighta give Orville to his daddy. Last she heard they were in Chesterville. She told me how Orv's daddy was different from mine. As I watched her put up her hair, one pin curl at a time, I would get lost in her words. Each pin curl was tightly wound like the story she would tell. That particular night she said that everything would be fine. Not to worry she said. My daddy was a married man too. He was a migrant worker, married with grown children. Maw met him at a dance. To Granny, all dances were just plain evil. I wasn't to worry none about the house or money. What money?

We had money? Funny thing about pin curls, the next day Granny's hair would look beautiful. I can't say the same about our family stories none. She kissed me goodnight, and I left all fuzzy. Not sure what I was supposed to get from all those stories.

As I left Granny's room toward the back of the house, I spied a light shinin' through the floorboard of His bedroom. It was mine too, but it didn't feel like it was mine. The light was curious. It came from 'neath His side of bed toward the head. It was the light from the kitchen. Funny, I never noticed it afore. I was drawn to it, I guess you could say. Kinda like how Moses was drawn to the light just glowin' from Mount Sinai. Not sure what you would find there but knew you had to see it. I somehow knew if'n I went on further, there was no turnin' back. Just like Moses.

I dug around the floorboard and up came the board. I got a sick feelin' in the pit of m'stomach. I swallowed real hard. I ran to the window to see if He was a comin'. There was no sign of Him. There were papers, money, a watch, and a black book with numbers all over it. Some kinda figurin' I reckoned. I felt 'round for some more and come upon whole buncha matchbooks from the Kat Club, Sharky's and the Dew Drop Inn. I throw'd 'em back into the floor. I grabbed a hold of the papers first. I'd seen my name written over and over 'gain. Why? What was He doin'? I saw the deed to the homestead. It said DEED right on it. There were papers with more figurin'. Then I saw it. It gave me the shivers. It was an application to Pine Oaks Convalescent Home. I took in so much air I started a chokin'. Who was this for, Granny?

At first I started a shovin' everything back in the floor. No! He'd know I was messin' with His stuff. I'd get a beatin' for sure. I placed things back the way I'd 'membered it. I ran out of the room. Jay was sleepin' sound. I didn't know what to do. I should tell Granny. No! He might try to hurt her. I was runnin' around the house because I didn't know what to do. Thank the Lord I heard the car pullin' up toward the house. I ducked down to the floor and snuck into Jay's room. I pretended to be sleepin'. I started breathin' real hard. I heard Him come into the room. My heart was poundin' so loud. The Lord be praised, He cursed and went to bed. That was the night I started thinkin' on my big ol' plan to free me, Jay and Granny.

Granny wasn't here though. I felt down right bad 'bout that. Now there I sit like a big ol' barn owl that just ate the family cat! There wasn't any time to look on these papers since that night. It seemed like He was fixin' to write my name on some papers at the bank. I 'membered that day he took me for a drive. He told me to put on a nice dress and we'd go to town. I didn't even think anything. I was just so glad to go somewhere. Jay stayed to home with Granny. Granny wasn't smilin' any. We got to town and went straight on to the bank. He told me to come in with Him. I was surprised. He never asked me to go in afore. Off I went like some ol' fool. Thinkin' on it now sure felt bad. Some lady with a real tight polka dot dress greeted Him all nice like. She called Him by name. She grabbed Him by the arm and walked Him on back to the bank manager's office. I just stood there lookin' around. I didn't rightly know what to do. Pretty soon there He came, madder than a wet hen! He grabbed me and pulled me along toward the door, right back to His mother's car.

The DEED was in my name and Granny's. Sure shootin' Granny would never sign the home away to the likes a Him. He was fixin' to get Granny into Pine Oaks. As I looked on the application and all, I felt angry all over 'gain. I didn't get mad too often but when I did, look out! Just thinkin' that He was gonna try and take Granny's home made me all tense. My fists were all clinched up and red. His signin' my name over and over 'gain meant He was fixin' to pretend I signed on my own behalf, just like I was nothin'. Maw always said I was nothin' and wouldn't 'mount to nothin' either. Maybe He was right. Maw too. But there I sat. It was true 'nough couldn't go home. I was cut off from my only kin besides Jay. But there I sat.

Backed into a corner was no place to be. But somehow one got to see all 'round 'em. I knew darn well what was behind me. Reckoned I needed to get out of the corner and look on to the future with just me and Jay. *I'm sorry Granny.* I was sorry as I could be. I didn't rightly know how to get out of a corner like this. First thing might be to talk to Sula or maybe...I held the phone number of the bank. The bank manager gave it to me the day I left Rondo. Maybe he sensed I was in trouble. My eyes were burnin' not cause a cryin'. It was late on near to mornin'.

I woke to Sula bangin' on the back door. She sounded fired up. I drug m'self outta bed and checked on Jay. My, that boy could sleep through anything. It was good and bad I guess. The thought a him with those fool cousins of His just made me wanna hurl. They were just playin' 'round. They said They were just teasin'. I ain't ever seen teasin' like that. I hollered and went just plain crazy. I got yelled at pretty bad by Him. He said for me not to get involved in kids play. We went home soon after that. His Maw was just laughin' sayin' boys will be boys. What did she mean? When I asked Him I didn't get any better answer. I just know'd that I feared for Jay. I didn't want my baby 'round those fool cousins no more.

"Cinda, you wake, girl? How about we go to church? The new preacher is in town today only and won't be comin' 'round this way until two weeks from now."

I hadn't been to church in a while. The Salvation Army Church ladies came 'round from time to time and some people my Granny called Holy Rollers. If'n I was gonna get out of this here corner, I better talk to God 'bout it.

"Sure, Sula, church sounds fine. I'll get dressed. I won't be but a minute."

Walkin' to church felt good. I took in a good breath and told Jay to do likewise. Sula was all dressed up, hat and all. She looked all refined. That yellow dress sure brought out the red in her hair. Why, she found me a nice dress too. It was kinda tight through the middle though. I couldn't let all my air out at once. It felt like we was family walkin' to church. I ain't ever done it much with my own kin.

My own weddin' was pitiful. It was not what a girl thinks 'bout for sure. I was already with child. Maw was plain mad when she found out. Granny had to hold her back. She yelled for me to run. Maw was tryin' to hit me. She did get me and sat on my stomach. I was more scared than hurt. Somehow I knew the baby would be fine. Granny pulled her off and I ran. The weddin' was poorly attended. There was a few kin from His side. My best friend, sorta, from school was my maid o' honor. Granny came. Maw was in the back just a scowlin'. I 'member the preacher asked if we really wanted to get married. Maybe he heard 'bout how bad His kin was. We were married under God, but it felt more like a cursin' rather than a blessin'. 'Course me being with child didn't help me none. I pulled Jay near me. I didn't care how he came, he was my truest blessin'. He was my hope.

The new preacher was a young man. He seemed almost frail. He was a small man with tiny spectacles. He looked like he'd been fastin' too much to hear God's word for us. He talked 'bout Moses and the people of Israel. I lit right up. I was just thinkin' 'bout Moses. Moses was born to be a leader, he said. The people of Israel were a chosen people. Here Moses was asked to lead the people, and the Lord would be with him. The people didn't listen none, 'ceptin when it was good news or the way was easy. He talked bout the bricks and straw and the plagues. When he got to the part 'bout the death of the first born sons, I started bawlin' right there. Sula looked my way but didn't say anything. I was thinkin' on Jay and me. I weren't much of a leader. I weren't chosen, neither. I knew some 'bout trials. I sure wasn't 'bout to let Jay be taken by Him or His kin. The preacher said Israel went through those there trials to help them learn to look to their God. He was preparin' them for somethin' greater.

I was feelin' almost happy after goin' to Sula's church. The preacher called us to repent and in the end gave us hope. Maybe that was like heaven? I was walkin' kinda lightly, feelin' gay.

"I know where I met you before!"

I turned around to see Mrs. Parson's kin. She was all dressed up with a hat and gloves and all. Mrs. Parson and her niece were still up with the preacher. I know'd she was from Rondo, but I didn't know her none.

"I've seen you in Rondo! You walking with your child just now reminded me of where I've seen you before. You can't lie to me, girl. I've seen you walk to town from the country. Why are you lying about where you're from? Aren't you Sylvie's daughter? You live with..."

Just hearin' Maw's given name gave me the shivers. I stood there not knowin' what to say. All I wanted to do was run. Sula grabbed me.

"There's a double for everybody, you know. I think you are mistaken!"

We walked home the rest of the way real quiet like. Sula looked mad. I can't say that I blamed her. There it was the Sabbath Day, and I caused her to lie. Well, kinda since she really didn't know the truth.

"Thank you, Sula. Thank you for everything you done for me and for Jay. You been real kind to us, and I can't ever repay you."

Before I could say another word she butted right in.

"Don't say on. If you really want to thank me, you'll stop runnin' from your past. I don't know what's caused you to be so scared, Cinda. I do know that if you don't face it, you ain't goin' to have much of a future and neither will Jay. Think on that!"

With that she went into the backyard, through the gate and on up to her house. We were supposed to have supper together, but I 'spected that wasn't gonna happen. I felt so bad about what I done to Sula. So much so that I wasn't even thinkin' 'bout bein' recognized. I kept thinkin' 'bout what she said. No future, not even for Jay. She was right. She was right as spring rain. Tomorrow I would tell Sula the truth. Tomorrow I would call the bank manager. Tomorrow I would call Granny.

# CHAPTER 4

*Hurry baby. We gotta go now. We're playing for real now. I got my bags. Where's my money? Why doesn't this phone work? Why didn't I get ready sooner? Why did I wait 'til it was too late? He's home!*

*What are you doing? What's this? We're just playin' is all. We're just playin'. Slap. Slap. Punch. I'm gettin' hit, but I don't feel anything. What's wrong? Help! I can't breathe. I'm not breathin'. If I can just turn my head I'll breathe. I can't move. Help! Please help!*

Someone was poundin' at the door real loud. Was that my door or Sula's? Jay come a runnin' from his little bed. Makin' m'self a promise to come clean eased me a bit, and I let Jay sleep alone. I whispered that it would be okay. It was probably just somebody wantin' to talk to Sula. I slipped into my jeans, threw on my blouse and went into the main room. The knockin' stopped but I could hear loud voices. Then Sula knocked on my back door. She seemed really shook up.

"There's some police here and a lady from the county. They're askin' for a LuCinda Dixon. Is that you? I told them I had to get dressed. They're waitin' up front."

My heart sank.

"Yes, Sula, that's me. LuCinda Dixon. I'm from down Rondo way, Frog Creek. I ran away from my home and my Husband. He ain't dead."

When the bangin' started 'gain, I grabbed Jay and gave him to Sula. I went to my front door and told 'em it was me they was lookin' for. The policeman told me that I had to come down to the police station and answer some questions. The lady introduced herself as Mrs. Batawldin. She was there to see to Jay and see that I was treated fairly. I pleaded with them to let Jay stay with Sula. The policeman and Mrs. Batawldin looked at one 'nother. They asked Sula if she was any kind of kin, and she told them that she was.

"We are as close as kin could be."

Those were her 'xact words. The policeman grabbed my arm and just held onto it.

"No need for handcuffs, right?"

"No sir, I'm done runnin'. Can I tell Jay goodbye for now?"

I left Jay in Sula's arms and told him to play with Sula for a spell and listen real good. I told him to make me proud. I told him I would be back just as soon as I could. Just as soon as those good people brought me home. Jay was whimperin' like a scared little pup. He held on to his blankie and bear and Sula. I made sure I left smilin' cause that's how I wanted him to 'member me, smilin'. He had seen me cry enough.

A crowd already started gatherin' in front of Sula's. Mrs. Parsons and her sister were there. Her sister was actually smilin'. She was smilin' 'cause I ran away? The flower house lady came out too. I ain't ever seen her afore. A few old fellas and their wives, I reckon. They were all just standin' there to see me with the law. I sat in the back seat of the police car with Mrs. Batawldin. She smiled at me and said things would be okay. The policeman didn't seem kindly at all. He just glared at me through the rear view mirror. He even took off his sunglasses to show me his mad eyes. It was a bright sunny day and took off his glasses to be mean. I didn't look back on Sula's house. Seein' her and Jay would have set me to bawlin' right then. I made m'self a promise that I was gonna be brave and tell the truth 'bout me runnin' away.

Mrs. Batawldin started talkin' to me real soft like.

"LuCinda. I'll be with you the entire time. You must answer the questions as honestly as you can. You don't need to be afraid. You have rights. Do you know that? Do you know what I mean?"

Her soft voice didn't match her words. She made it sound like I was in some kinda big trouble.

"I plan on bein' honest, Ma'am. I plan on tellin' the truth. What do you mean about rights?"

She smiled.

"LuCinda. You are still under-aged. You are a minor. You have rights. If you want a lawyer, you need to tell me. I'll do what I can, but..."

"But what? Why do I need a lawyer 'cause I ran away? The money I took was mine! You make it sound like I'm in serious trouble!"

"But you need to think about Jay."

Now she hit me in my soft spot.

"What about Jay?"

"If you don't cooperate, I can't keep you and Jay together."

My eyes started wellin' up with tears. I turned away from her and stared out the window. My mind was racin' just like in my dreams, only I wasn't movin'. I closed my eyes and prayed for God to help me think and speak clearly. Just like Aaron did for Moses. Maybe Mrs. Batawldin was my Aaron, sent from God himself. I tried to calm m'self and not get so mad. My fists were already clinched tighter than ever. I opened my eyes and saw that the policeman was smilin'. Isn't it strange what makes people smile, other people's misfortunes. It was true enough I was in a spot. It was true enough I ran away. But since when was runnin' away a crime? 'Specially when all a body wanted to do was save her baby?

We arrived at the police station. I was "checked in" for procedure's sake. Least ways that's what Mrs. Batawldin said. I was checked for any weapons by another policeman. I was placed in a room with mirrors all 'round me. I ain't ever seen so many mirrors in one place afore 'ceptin at the Emporium in Rondo. Another policeman came in who wasn't in any uniform. He was red faced and real heavy. He was nearly bald 'ceptin a sweep o' hair atop his round head. He was smokin' a cigarette. It made me cough, and he put it out.

"I'm detective Frye. We're working with the Rondo Police Department on a case that involves a Mr. Wilford Dixon. Do you know him?"

Just hearin' His name gave me the shakes.

"Yes sir, I do know Him. I'm His wife."

"So he's your husband, right?"

I never thought of Him as anything of mine.

"Yes sir. We're married."

"You were brought in to answer a few questions. Can you do that? Answer some questions?"

"Yes, sir. I can answer some questions... 'bout what?"

"Are you trying to be funny, girl? This here is a serious matter. A man's been missing for nearly two weeks. Friday, first a May to be exact! Isn't that the time you arrived in Chatfield?"

"He's missin'? Will is missin'? Did you call on His Maw?"

"Who do you think reported him missing? His mother did. Just think some poor mother doesn't know the whereabouts of her son. Her daughter-in-law runs off with her grandchild and ..."

"Did He take off with Her car?"

"What?"

"Is that why She reported Him missin'?"

What I said musta got him all riled up 'cause he was madder than a wet hen. His face turned redder than a beet for sure. I started cryin'. I got scared seein' him angry at me like that. I knew what came next, and I just covered up and bawled. He got up and called for Mrs. Batawldin. Mrs. Batawldin came right on in. She put her arm on my shoulder and talked all soft like. Soft talk doesn't mean soft words.

"LuCinda, try to calm down. This is a serious matter. No one is saying that you did anything to Wilford. You must try to answer the questions."

I just kept on cryin' though 'cause I could feel that these here law people figured that I done somethin' wrong to Will.

"Can you stay on with me? That detective scares me and maybe if'n you were here he wouldn't hurt me? Please don't tell him I said that."

"LuCinda. See these mirrors? I am standing on the other side of these mirrors. There are other policemen watching and listening too. You are safe, child."

I looked 'round me. All 'round me. I wasn't in a corner no more. I was bein' hung out to dry like an old rug and now would come the beatin'. Tryin' to shake out the filth and make it all clean 'gain. I thought 'bout Moses and the whole of Israel. I guess this was one of the plagues I needed to get through. I wasn't sure I wanted to see the faces behind the mirror. I was just goin' to imagine that it was God tryin' to help me be free and not some people I didn't get the pleasure a meetin' face to face, waitin' for me to misstep.

"Okay. I'll answer their questions. I'll try not to cry any."

Mrs. Batawldin left the room. I could hear yellin'.

"She's pretending to be dumb. Isn't she? She's making a mockery of justice with her simple ways. Does anyone really talk and think like that?"

"They do if they've been abused, which I suspect she has. You don't know that she did anything wrong. You don't even have Wilford Dixon, right?"

"Let's look at what we do have. Her husband is missing. He goes missing on the very day she left town but not before stopping at the local bank and getting a substantial amount of money. She jumps on the bus, lands in Chatfield, and cons an old lady into staying at her house. Thankfully, someone recognized her and called the police station in Rondo to see if there was any trouble. I don't care if she's a minor. She's hiding something, and perhaps it's the whereabouts of Wilford Dixon."

Hearin' His name again just sent shivers up and down my spine. I put my head down and thought on Jay, Sula and Granny. Why, they didn't even know what was happenin'. I wondered if'n His kin know'd somethin'? What about that night I seen the old station wagon? Was that Will in the car? They think I'm playin' dumb. Do I sound dumb? Maw sure said I was dumb. Until Mrs. Dawling said I was a "quick thinker." I could do math beyond my grade. Readin' was easy for me too. I guess all my pretendin' caught up with me. I been so used to playin' dumb so as not to get beat that I done lost myself. Whoever that was? Now, if'n I was gonna be with Jay and be free, I needed to come clean. What about Granny? Didn't they talk to my Granny? I started to get up from the table and Mrs. Batawldin came in real fast like.

"LuCinda! We need to..."

"I need to know if you talked to my Granny. Have you seen her?"

"LuCinda, please sit down. I'm sorry to have to be the one to tell you this but... your Granny became ill while visiting her sister in Bowler. She's in the hospital and is not doing well. Her prognosis...her state of health is not known at this time. She's alive but doing poorly."

I didn't want to believe my ears. I kept shakin' my head.

"No! No, it just can't be! Can I talk to her? Can I talk to Mercy?"

I started cryin' awful hard. I buried my face in my hands and felt so alone right then. How could it get any worse? Why was God takin' it out on my Granny? I was the one who shoulda been sufferin', not Granny. Here I was sittin' in a jail and thinkin' that I should be sufferin' more. Granny would be right shamed if she knew I was seein' the insides of a jail.

"Does she know about me? Does she know I'm here?"

"No. What I can say is that she was asked if she knew of your whereabouts to which she replied that she did not. What she did say... and I think I have it correctly... is that she hoped you were finding your way out of Egypt. Does that mean anything to you?"

Granny was a seer! I knew it! I just knew she was givin' me ideas on how I could be free. I just didn't know what she meant exactly.

"No Ma'am, not exactly. I mean, I have some notion, but not."

She's alive but doin' poorly. I kept thinkin' this in my head. She was alive!

"LuCinda. I want to try and help you. Can we start with some questions about you? I have a tape recorder here, and I would like you to speak clearly and loudly right into this microphone. Now, if you would like, I could try and find an attorney for you. You haven't been officially charged with anything, so if you would just answer some questions perhaps you could go back to Mrs. Cantrell's and be with Jay if you cooperate. Do you understand? You are a minor and whatever you say will be kept confidential. Okay? Detective Frye asked me to ask the questions, since you're afraid. Frankly, I don't blame you— he is rather frightening."

She said that whilst looking at the mirror behind her. I guess he was right behind the mirror just as red as ever. I thought on some of the movies I seen 'bout criminals were being brought in for questionin'. It was just like the movies but only I was in it.

"Yes Ma'am. I want to cooperate, and I hope I have your good word on seein' my son again."

"Tell me, LuCinda. Where were you born?"

"I was born in Frog Creek. It's just outside a Rondo."

"How old are you?"

"I'm seventeen years old."

"What's your mother's name?"

"Sylvia Jackson."

"What's your father's name?"

"Don't rightly know. He was a migrant worker. He worked the farms near Rondo."

I could hear laughin' from behind the mirrors. I pretended I didn't hear it. *Ignorant fools*!

"I'm just glad he wasn't a law man. Now that would have been just plain embarrassing!"

Mrs. Batawldin smiled.

"LuCinda, tell me why you ran away from your home."

"It's a long story. I hope you got enough tape for this here recorder. I left my home because I was afraid. Will was not a good man. I don't know what you heard from His kin, but He was a mean man. Especially to me. He didn't hurt Jay with His hand too much. He just didn't have much to do with my baby. I guess He left that up to me. Anyway, I found out that He was fixin' to get the homestead from Granny. I found some papers, under a floorboard, 'neath His bed. They had my name written all over the pages. It looked like to me that He was goin' to pretend to sign my name to the homestead. The DEED was in these papers. There was also a paper...an application to Pine Oaks. Granny would have never signed the homestead away to the likes a Him and neither would I. I figured He was goin' to put Granny away somehow. I wasn't sure how though. But there was the application as plain as day. From that day forward, I started to plan how I would get away— me and Jay.

"I knew Granny was goin' to visit her sister, Mercy, in Bowler for a spell... for a time. She would regularly visit Mercy, 'bout two times a year. She was fixin' to ... plannin' to visit Mercy toward the end of April. I knew she would be gone for a while and I just couldn't bear the thought of her gone with just me and Him home alone with Jay one more time. I...knew... I knew that I had to get away but not until Granny left. I didn't want her worryin' none. I planned to write or call her and let her know where I was at in about June. I figured it would be safe by then. I didn't want Granny to know anything 'cause that way if He pressed her, she wouldn't know anything'.

"I planned for the first of May, a Friday, to get away from Him. I wanted to leave on a Friday 'cause that's when the red eye came through Rondo. Besides, Will and His kin generally went out drinkin' and spyin' on people. They would go after work. They'd all pile in His Maw's station wagon and I never knew when He would come home.

"Guess I'm tellin' you more than you wanted to know?"

"No, LuCinda, you're doing just fine. Tell me why you're afraid of Wilford?"

Wasn't it enough to just say he was mean? What did she want me to say? Why would she want to know? It was probably that mean old detective and policeman that brought me in.

"LuCinda? You said you ran away from home because you were afraid of Wilford Dixon, your husband. Can you tell me why?"

"I don't rightly know how to begin, Ma'am. He was plannin' on takin' my home from Granny and me. Isn't that 'nuff... enough?"

"LuCinda. No one can force anyone to sign away their home. Nor can anyone forge an important document. It would be highly scrutinized. It would be examined by the proper authorities..."

"Excuse me, Ma'am. You don't know Will. He would..."

"That is exactly what I am saying. No, I don't know Wilford. Detective Frye and the other police officers don't know him. I, we, want to hear that from you."

I looked at the mirror where I figured they were standin' and said the first thing that came to my mouth.

"They don't know Him any, that's for sure, but they're men. They're cut outta the same mold. They don't know what it's like to be nothin'. To be treated like nothin', to be a feared for your own life and your baby's life."

I started bawlin' 'gain. Lord this was going to be hard. I couldn't see how he thought I could get through this. Makin' bricks without straw would be a might easier. There wasn't anyone here but me. Mrs. Batawldin seemed nice, but they got her doin' their dirty work. Still, she did yell at that detective some. I sure liked her for it. Where did she get the strength to stand up for herself like that? Or... maybe... she was really standin' up for me?

"LuCinda. Let me ask something else. How did you meet Wilford Dixon? How did you marry him?"

Now that was somethin' else all together. I ain't thought on that for a while.

"I could try to 'member. I met Him while I was in school, middle school. He weren't in school any; He just hung around His kin. I heard tell He was graduated an' attendin' a vocational school somewhere. He spent an awful lotta time at the middle school though. He had a fancy car, dark blue. He would spin it around the schoolyard and everyone would watch. The boys would actually cheer. Anyway, He would talk to me real nice. He said He felt sorry for me. I guess He knew my Maw. She drank a lot and went out with a few men from time to time. He seemed to know that I was sufferin' a lot to home."

"We're you suffering at home, LuCinda?"

"Oh yes'm, I was. My Maw wasn't much on keepin' house or takin' care of my brother Orville. She mostly liked to watch Granny's TV and get all gussied up and go out on Friday nights. She would come home all drunk and not makin' much sense. She would wake me up and yell at me. She would make me clean up the house 'gain even though I cleaned it while she was gone. If'n it was too clean or she was too angry 'bout somethin' ... I don't rightly know what...maybe somethin' I done, why, she'd throw food, grease, flour and coffee grounds all over the floor and make me clean it 'gain. I guess I'd have to say that the grease was the hardest thing of all to clean. I would get beat regular. With her hand or with whatever was lyin' 'round.

Sometimes, when she would get home from one of her nights out, I would have to cook for her and listen to her goings on. I'd rather clean grease than listen to her stories... one night I learned just how much she hated me. She never wanted me and wished she coulda got rid of me. She was plum crazy. She was yellin', and I thought she was gonna kill me. She started goin' toward my brother's room, and I thought she was gonna start in on him. I didn't know what I was gonna do, but I knew I wasn't gonna let her hurt him. Lord be praised, she just lay down on his bed and went to sleep."

I had hardly taken a breath since Mrs. Batawldin asked me 'bout home. I looked up at her and seen she was dabbin' her eyes. It looked like she was cryin'. I wondered why. I just kept on talkin' 'cause I was feelin' lighter or somethin'. It felt like a whole lot a weight was lifted from me. My stomach felt like it was in a big ol' knot. I felt all hot and like I could hurl right here. But if I just kept talkin' it would pass.

"After times like these, Maw would get all lazy like. I don't rightly know how to describe it. I shopped for food. I paid on the bills. I'd go to the school meetins for me and Orville. I talked to the welfare people. Maw would just lay on the davenport, watchin' Granny's TV. I brought her food and water. She wouldn't even talk on the party line. It was like we were all in mournin' or somethin'.

"One time Maw tried to work. The welfare said she had to work or go to school. She worked at Rondo Red Star Dry Cleaning for a spell but had to quit 'cause the chemicals they used to clean the clothes hurt her hands. She tried starchin' but that too hurt her hands. She even went to school. The vocational school had a program for people to work in the hospital. She didn't want to do it none, but the welfare people forced her. She didn't even do her homework. I done her homework, and she...

well, me really, got "A's" on it. She had to quit the program 'cause the chemicals they used there made her hands all red and they started to peel real badly. Sure didn't seem to bother her when she was hittin' on me though. Ain't that peculiar?

"Well, when Wilford said that He understood how hard it was for me at home...I never told no one 'bout anything... not even Granny...I guess I just felt He understood me.

"I never really knew how old He was. I knew He was older than me. I thought He was goin' to school and was gonna make somethin' outta himself. I heard 'bout His kin. How They was nothin' but trouble makers. I heard They drank and carried on 'til all hours of the night. But I guess I never figured Will picked up on these things too. At first He was real kind. He started pickin' me and Orville up after school. He'd take us to get ice cream, soda pop and well... pretty soon He was comin' over after Maw would go out. He would tell me how pretty I was and well... I knew what He was doin' was wrong. I knew what I was doin' was wrong too. I guess I thought it was love. I couldn't have been more wrong.

"Pretty soon I found out I was pregnant with Jay. I waited 'til Granny got back from one of her visits. See, Granny let Maw and us stay at the homestead while she went visitin'. It was her house, left to her by her husband— my grandpa— when he died. They only had one child, Maw, and so they felt obliged to care for us. Maw was never grateful for this nary one bit. When I told Granny 'bout me bein' a mother, she cried and cried. Well, she cried when she found out who the daddy was. She told me stuff 'bout His family that I never know'd afore. She asked me if I wanted to marry the likes of Him and His kin. This was probably the first time I ever took ought 'gainst my Granny. I said I was marryin' Wilford, not His entire family. He was different from Them. He wasn't like His kin. She looked at me, shook her head and just gave up. Just like that. I shoulda know'd that she was tryin' to help me and knew better than me right then. I sensed somethin'. Like she was tellin' the truth and knew the future, but I just ignored it, thinkin' I knew better.

"Does that answer your question, Ma'am?"

"Yes... yes it does. I want to thank you, LuCinda. You are cooperating and answering my questions. Will you excuse me for a minute?"

She turned off the tape recorder and left the room.

When she stepped outta the room, I felt like I had done a whole week's wash in one mornin'. I could hear voices. There was no yellin'. That was a good omen. I thought on Jay and Sula. I wondered how long they would keep me there. When would I see Jay? I couldn't let Sula bring Jay here. No sir! If'n he ever ended up in jail, it would be his doin', not mine! *Please God, I gotta get outta here and be with Jay. Help him to grow up better than me so he will never see the insides of a jail.*

Just then Detective Frye came in. Mrs. Batawldin was right behind him. Dective Frye seemed a might toned down and this time he did the talkin'.

"LuCinda, we're going to ask you to stay with us for a while. It's lunchtime, and you will be escorted to a waiting room where you will be served lunch. There are some more questions we have to ask you but... well, we've been talking it over with one another and the Rondo Police Department... and if you could see your way clear to answering a few more questions... maybe you could go home...back to Mrs. Cantrell's tonight... but you will not be allowed to leave the City of Chatfield. Of course, this all depends on some facts we're checking on and if your story holds water."

"Any word on Wilford? Is He still missin'?"

"Wilford Dixon is still missing."

"Have you talked to His kin? His Maw, Hank, Trey, Junior and Junior? He's got a lot of kin."

"All I can say is that Wilford's family is cooperating. They have looked for him as well. It was his mother, Mrs. Loma Dixon, who first reported him missing. He was last seen driving her car on Friday, the first of May. I can't say who the Rondo Police Department has interviewed."

I knew it! She got to worryin' 'bout Her car. Her Son was second. He just happened to be drivin' it is all.

Thankfully the room they brought me to didn't have bars. I was afraid of bein' behind bars. Like I was a criminal and all. I got served a hamburger and fries. There was milk and a fruit cup. Now that was a treat! Just thinkin' on that made me stop. There I was sittin' in jail and enjoyin' some time to m'self. Was that how the children of Israel felt? They made their bricks without straw and they praised God. They were still slaves, but I bet they were glad. I really didn't feel like praisin' none, but I was relieved to be done with their questions. I was glad to be served a meal for once. I didn't like that I had to think on some of those things 'gain, let alone say them out loud. It was a good thing I couldn't see their faces behind them mirrors.

After lunch, I felt pretty tired. I coulda just laid down right there and slept. All that thinkin' on the past left me plum drained. Like when I had to haul water and do our laundry by hand. My hands were blistered from wringin' out His jeans. He coulda helped some. After Granny seen my hands, she bought us a new wringer washer from Sears. It was the nicest thing I had seen. It was big and white with red trim. I had my problems with that darn old black hose though. No more hand washin' for me! *Please God, can you help Granny? If'n she's sick, I wanted to be the one to take care of her.* I wasn't askin' for her to be healed 'xactly...exactly. I would help her get well. I couldn't think of anything nobler than carin' for my Granny. Jay too.

The door opened, and there stood Mrs. Batawldin. She asked me if my dinner was okay. I nodded. She explained that it was time to answer more questions. This time she and Detective Frye would be in the room with me. I wondered who'd be watchin' me through the mirrors. They led me in the room, and I sat down in the same chair. I waited for them to rig up that recordin' machine. I wondered where that light feelin' was that I had early on. I just felt all dragged out. Mrs. Batawldin started off.

"LuCinda, could you tell us what happened or what changed in your marriage to Wilford Dixon?"

"I can't say for certain when things got bad. It seems like they was always bad after I got married. Take when I had Jay. I was just fourteen when I give birth. I was in labor all day. I cooked, washed and even gardened some. I finally went to the hospital right after supper. Jay was born soon after. It was a hard labor, but it was worth it. He was the most beautiful baby you'd ever seen! Later on the nurse came in to push down on my belly tryin' to get the blood out she said. She found Wilford on the floor. He was sleepin', but she thought He was dead or somethin'. She woke Him up, and He was down right crabby. After she left, I asked Him if He was still tired, and I was about to tell Him to go on home when He started yellin' at me. He was sayin' how He was up all day. He didn't have a decent chair to sit in. He said I was layin' down restin' while He was up. I thought, I just had a baby and He was more concerned 'bout Himself? I didn't say anything; I figured He was tired was all.

"After that, I couldn't do nothin' right. The food was bad. The gravy had lumps. The cream o' wheat had lumps. The bread was hard. If 'n He wasn't complainin' on my food or my cleanin', He was complainin' on how I let m'self go. One day, thinkin' He cared about me and could talk with me, when He said I let m'self go, I said, "go where?" I said it with a bit of attitude. I was mad. I was tired 'bout Him sayin' that I was ugly and fat. I didn't feel that way 'bout m'self. When I went in for... for my check-up I measured real nice at 145 pounds. Least ways that's what the nurse said. She said I was just bloomin'. My cheeks were still all rosy and well, I was just a might rounder than afore. I weren't any skinny Minnie if that's what He meant, but I sure wasn't ugly. Well, that's when I got hit. He slapped me real hard. Then He pushed me and said I was tryin' to be like a man, sassin' Him like that. After He punched me in the stomach, I just doubled over. I guess I wasn't healed yet.

"That was the first a many more beatins. I got hit for not movin' fast enough. For lookin' like I was thinkin' somethin' when I wasn't. I got hit for knowin' more than Him. We was playin' some game with His kin, and They didn't know 'bout this particular thing. Will said it was somethin' that it wasn't. I tried to clarify it up for Them, and He hauled me off in the other room and hit me. Right there in His Maw's house! I knew everybody could hear it, and no one said a thing. When we got home, I got it again. I was never supposed to challenge Him at anything. He would always be right no matter what. At disbelievin' this, I said that no one was always right. Well, that was a challenge right there, and I got sucker punched. Later on, the next day in fact, when His Maw saw me, she sauntered up to me real funny like and said I got what I deserved. She went on sayin' that she could tell I didn't know how to treat her Son.

"As time went on, I just gave up. At least I think so. I could hardly stand Him bein' near me. I pretended to agree with everything He said. I wanted the same thing He wanted. I tried my hardest to think on whatever He might want ahead a time, so I wouldn't get beat. I tried not to even think on my own. It got to be just like livin' with Maw all over 'gain. Now and then He could be kind. Now that I think on it, whatever He did that didn't lead to me gettin' beat seemed kind. I even reasoned that I must be the cause of so much pain and sufferin' in my life. I turned to workin' hard. I worked on the house, the garden, sewin', cookin' and spendin' time with Jay. I wasn't allowed to see Maw, Orv or my Granny. I felt like a prisoner in my own home. The truth was it wasn't my home. It was His Maw's trailer. It was set out back behind Her house. He had to see Her, though I think He wanted to, every day. He was always workin' on that car a Hers.

"I could only get together with His female kin. At first I didn't want to get together at all. I finally got lonely enough, and I started to spend time with Them. I picked His favorite sister to be with, but even that was hard. One time I made a remark 'bout a young couple we seen down by the creek. We were all tryin' to beat the heat. This couple, they looked like they was courtin'. They lagged behind their family and snuck behind a tree, just holdin' hands. I don't even know what I said, but His sister, Shiloh, told Him what I said and boy did I get it. He said I was supposed to be pure. I wasn't supposed to talk like a tramp. I thought that couple looked sweet, and I wished for those days 'gain. I still don't get what was all fired wrong 'bout what I said.

"Funny how He wanted me to be all pure, though. He was always tryin' to get me to wear tight clothes and make-up. He bought all my clothes, and they weren't fit to wear. The blouses was always too low cut and tight. I hated it! I had to go to the Salvation Army to get the clothes I wanted to wear. Once He said that I didn't know how to treat a man. I wasn't enough of a woman or somethin' like that. I guess He meant like some of those ladies I'd seen Him gawkin' at. Maybe you know the kind? They are always wearin' tight clothes. The kinda clothes that shows off their whole body. Their hair is all up and ratty lookin'. They wear make-up piled on so much they look like they made outta wax. Not to mention earrings and rings everywhere, with nails so long and painted. Why, even their words are fake. I'm ashamed to say that I tried to dress like that. He seemed even nicer to me when I did. I think He was even proud of me, but I felt so shallow...I give it up.

"So, a long answer to your question, huh? I guess you can say we both done changed."

I noticed while I was a talkin' on so, the detective was wigglin' in his seat some. Especially when I talked about the kind of women Will liked. I wondered if he liked those kinda women too. I pretty much figured all men were like Wilford Dixon. Or maybe just Him and His kin were that way? I don't know. Maybe except that new preacher man, though he seemed to just have God on his mind. Not that that was bad, it's just that we live in this here world. We all... well, mostly women, gotta work, birth babies and care for our kin. We can't be thinkin' 'bout God all the time. Maybe that preacher man thought on our souls too. Maybe Detective Frye thought on more than bein' mean to me. After all, he seemed to care 'bout Wilford Dixon. I guess somebody had to.

"Mrs. Dixon, it's getting on to the afternoon, and I want to get to more serious questions. What happened on May the first?"

That detective made me jump when he said "Mrs. Dixon."

I hadn't ever been called that afore! I could feel my heart poundin'. I hoped this was as serious as his questions got.

"That was a big day. I didn't sleep much the night afore. I was tossin' and turnin', and Will kicked me outta bed 'cause I was disturbin' His sleep and that was okay with me. I crawled in bed with Jay. I fell asleep thinkin' on my big ol' plan. I woke up to Him hollerin' for me to get up and get Him some breakfast. I got Him His usual, eggs, bacon, and skillet toast. He told me He wouldn't need any lunch that day 'cause He had big plans. I know'd better than to ask what those big plans were. He liked to do that to me. He would tell me somethin' only half of it and leave me to wonderin'. I learned, after a while, to just let it go, like sand though my hands. Just like when I'm gardenin'... Besides, I had big plans m'self. He was dressed in His usual clothes, dress pants, shirt... nothin' out of the ordinary. I did see Him grab a gym bag when He went out the door. That weren't unusual 'cause it was Friday. Sometimes on a Friday after work He would go to the bars or bowlin' alley or just go drivin' round drinkin' with His kin. I watched Him go down the path, past the outhouse and I stood there a might longer just to make sure He was gone.

"As soon as I figured it was clear, I got movin'. I had to pace m'self just right. The red eye didn't come until five o'clock in the evenin'. I had to go to the Bank of Rondo just afore then, so I wouldn't be seen by anyone. I wanted to go to the bank and right to the bus station. Well, it wasn't really a bus station; it was a gas station that served as the bus station, too. I had to get to town from Frog Creek. Now that was my biggest problem. It took me and Jay 'bout thirty minutes a walkin' to get to the edge a Rondo. We practiced it only a few times. That was our slowest time. Maybe you don't care much about these here details, but they were mighty important to me.

"I cleaned the house as usual. Now, I don't think I told you all 'bout how we got to live with Granny? Do you want to know? We weren't livin' in a trailer no more. I was such a fool thinkin' that movin' in with Granny would help some..."

Mrs. Batawldin spoke right up.

"LuCinda. Let's save that for later. We need to know what happened on that day, please."

"Oh, sure I'll tell ya. When Jay and me left, I didn't leave any lights on. I figured that would give me more time if'n He should happen to come home earlier than usual. Me and Jay stuck to the road at first and would go off into the woods and fields if'n we saw a car comin'. It took us nearly forty-five minutes to walk to Rondo. I don't know why. I went on to the bank. I tried to see the bank manager, but this lady got to me first. I didn't recognize her. She seemed to know Wilford..."

"LuCinda? You need to be more specific now. Ya hear?"

"Yes sir, now this is what happened as I recall. I walked into the bank...

She said, 'The manager is busy with a customer. He can't be disturbed.'

I said, 'I'm a customer too, and I'll wait.

"I took Jay by the arm and sat down on one of the chairs in the lobby. This lady, she was all gussied up and smackin' on some gum. She started walkin' toward me. Her hands were on her hips. Her nails were all painted red, and her hair was so big."

'LuCinda isn't it?' she said. 'What are you doin' here at the bank? Is Willie with you?'
'Willie? Oh, you mean Will. No Ma'am, He ain't. He's at work.'
'So why are you here?'
'I got to see the manager for my Granny.'

"I flat out lied, but I didn't care any. This lady gave me the shivers. I just kept on lookin' at the big 'ol wall clock they got down there. It was four-thirty in the afternoon. That red eye was comin' soon. I was glad I checked in my bag already."

'You know, LuCinda...' the woman said. 'You're one lucky girl. Did you know that?'
'No Ma'am, I didn't know that.'

"I wondered if she had some work to do. What was she hired to do? Was she supposed to stand around and pester poor customers? She probably couldn't do much work with those big ol' long red nails and that hair, too."

She said, 'So, do you ever wonder where Willie goes on Friday nights?'
'Not so much anymore, Ma'am.'
'Call me Priscilla. No call to be all formal after all...'
'Oh, I wouldn't dream of it. Ma'am is what I call all women much older than me. It's outta respect.'

"I guess I got her good cause she stopped smilin' so big at me.

> Then she said, 'Like I was sayin'. I have seen your man out on Friday nights before. Did you know that?'

"Thinkin' that she was gonna start tellin' me stuff I didn't want to hear, I just had to get her away from me. Then I remembered the matchbooks I'd seen under His bed."

> I told her, 'Oh, I'm sure you seen Him out afore with His kin. They like to go to places like the Kat Club, Sharky's, and what's the name of that other place? It seems like He brung home a souvenir... Oh, I 'member… the Dew Drop Inn. I won't go to those places. It's not fit for respectable people such as m'self!'

"My plan worked 'cause she stopped dead in her tracks. She wasn't smilin' any more! I caught m'self smilin' instead. It was then that the bank manager asked me if I was there to see him. I looked up at the clock, and it was four-forty. I went into his office with Jay and told him that I wanted to draw upon some money that I had there. The money that my Granny said I could draw upon. It was like he knew I was comin' or somethin'."

> 'I have a check for you right here,' he said. 'Would you like to cash it?'
>
> 'Yes, please. Is it from my Granny?'
>
> 'Yes, she had me draw it up before she left. How is she doing? I hope she found her sister well? Could you sign these papers?'

"I was shocked. I grabbed the papers and signed 'em right away. It was four-forty-seven."

> He told me, 'I'll just have my secretary cash it for you. It's a lot of money. If you're traveling, I would suggest putting it in a safe place. If you have any trouble at all, please call me. Here's my number. I promised your Grandmother that I would help you. Is there anything I can do?'
>
> 'Yes, please don't let the lady named Priscilla know what I'm doin' here.'

"He didn't even bat an eye. He smiled and shook my hand. He held my hand with both of his. It was the warmest handshake I ever got. I do think I was blushin'. I went out of his office back to the chairs in the lobby. I tried not to make eye contact with Priscilla. She was watchin' me to be sure. She was watchin' the bank manager's secretary go to the teller. My heart was poundin' so hard. I thought everyone could hear me. I started to get all scared that everyone could tell I was runnin' away. It was four-fifty by then. I stood up. My knees were all shaky and wobbly. I held on to Jay."

> 'Here you go, LuCinda,' the bank manager said. 'Tell you're Grandmother Hello from me.'

"I felt somethin' hard in my hand. It was a clock! Underneath it was an envelope with my money in it, one thousand dollars. Thankfully, I didn't count it until Jay and me was safe on the bus; otherwise I woulda passed out right there. I didn't know Granny had that kinda money. I didn't know when she said if I ever wanted to get outta Egypt I better stop by the bank first.

I didn't know that she meant she'd give me so much money. I plum forgot 'bout it until I realized that I needed money when I got to plannin' my escape. Anyway, I ran outta the bank and headed straight for the bus. It was waitin' for us. I didn't care if anyone saw me. All I could see was that big ol' bus ahead of me. My time had come. Jay and me were finally gonna be free. It wasn't until I got on the bus that I saw Priscilla standin' outside of the bank. Cranin' her neck to see where I had gone. Least ways that's what I thought.

"I took the bus all the way cross state lines to Chatfield. I had planned to get off there 'cause that's what .... That's what me and Jay planned on. After I got off the bus I went into a café. Jay and me hadn't eaten anything for a long time, except those apples I bought at a stop earlier on. While we was eatin'... were eating, a woman came over to us and started chattin'. She was friendly enough, so we started visiting with her. I had thought about takin' the bus northbound, but when the bus driver come in and announced he was leavin' after he had his dinner... well, I just stayed put. I was talkin' real nice with Sula. She reminded me of my Granny. She was dressed nicely, like a lady. She looked strong and had some deep, penetratin' eyes. Afore I knew it, Jay fell asleep while we was talkin' about... well I don't 'member exactly."

> 'You got kin waitin' on you?' Sula asked me. 'I mean, wherever it is you're goin'? You don't have much baggage for the two of you...'
>
> 'No Ma'am, I don't have kin waitin' on me. We're just travelin' and I... I mean we don't have kin waitin' for us. I...'
>
> 'Look here, I gotta place just down the road. I got a twin home. Ever hear of them? Well, it's a house side

> by side. My late husband built it for our retirement. He thought it would be nice to rent out to people passin' through or new to the area. I ain't rented it out in a while. It got just plain monotonous! Anyhow, it's empty. Your little one is sound asleep. There's a hotel in town a ways if you want. Otherwise, you would be welcome to stay with me until you decide to move on.'

"Sula went up to pay her check. Everyone nodded at her as she walked by. The waitress greeted her real kindly. I felt like it would be okay to stay with her 'til I could find out when the next bus came to Chatfield. I didn't con her, she offered."

At this the detective cleared his throat and reached for some water.

"That's all that happened that day, May the first. I went to Sula's and I been there ever since. You can ask her for yourself."

"One last question before we break here and decide what to do after this. You mentioned something about Wilford Dixon's family. What were they like?"

The afternoon was hastenin' on. I wondered what he meant by "decide what to do after this?" Were they gonna keep me? Did they still think I done somethin' to Him? I didn't know where He was.

"Yes sir, I'll answer your question. I just wanna say that I don't know where Wilford is. I ain't seen Him since I left that Friday."

*Should I tell him about the night I seen His Maw's car?* I didn't rightly know if He was in there or not. I guess I really didn't know if that was the wagon at all. Maybe I was just scared silly enough that I thought it was Him.

"You wanna know 'bout His family? Could you be more specific?"

The detective was wigglin' in his seat again and seemed a might miffed at me. Mrs. Batawldin spoke up.

"You mentioned that Wilford Dixon's family was... well, at least you seemed to indicate that they were 'different.' Wilford undoubtedly spent a lot of time with them and they engaged in 'different' activities?"

"His Maw was the main family member. You could say She was the head of the household. She had lots of kids. All the kids lived nearby. His Maw had lots of siblins too. Why, the whole of Frog Creek was filled with His kin. They mainly did things with one 'nother. They weren't into socializin' with too many other people. They were a mean bunch. Granny told me stories 'bout them. At first I thought she told those stories to scare me off of Him, but in time I realized they were all true.

"Take like when we moved from the trailer. Boy, His Maw was mad. He spent all night talkin' to Her. He said He was tryin' to smooth things over. He said She felt bad 'cause we weren't grateful enough for what She done for us like givin' us the trailer to live in and all. It was a dump! Here my Granny was offerin' us a place to live, for a small price a rent. After Maw run off with some married man— again—Granny wanted someone to be in the homestead. I talked this up 'cause I thought I could get some peace in my life. The only drawback for Him was that Granny would occupy the back room. It was her condition.

"His sisters, especially Shiloh, said He was less than a man, movin' into his in-law's place. His brothers Junior and Trey, they said some vile things 'bout Him not bein' a man and other things I don't want to say out loud. His cousin Hank was just a cryin' thinkin' that He would never see Him again. Granny's homestead was less than a mile away from their valley.

"Not long after I moved back with my Granny, Hank come to the house one night all drunk and beat up. I took pity on Hank and I tried to clean up his head and face. He was all beat up. I just kept cleanin', and Will was talkin'.

> 'What happened to you? Who did this to you?'
> 'I don't know some guys at Sharky's. First we were shootin' pool and the next thing you now they started pushin' me. It was three against one. Let's go! Come on; let's go get 'em."

"Will had gotten His baseball bat, put on His boots and headed toward the door."

> 'Why do you have to go?' I asked him.
> 'I have to go. Hank told them that he was going to get me. Whoever these guys are they'll be expecting me. I'm not afraid.'

"Out the door they went, and I fell asleep waitin' for them. Granny never did wake up, thank goodness.

"This was not the only time this happened. Why, one time the whole family was at the local schoolyard waitin' for a fight. His Maw, sisters, brothers, cousins, the whole lot of Them. I begged to go along 'cause I wanted to see what They did when this sorta thing happened.

"This ain't all. One time His Maw heard that one of His sisters was off seein' some man. I didn't know who it was. The man, I mean. We all piled in the car. His sisters put blankets in the back of the station wagon— that's where the kids went— and off we went. We followed His sister from some bar to some back alley in Rondo. There we saw His sister kissin' away on this man. They were all laughin' in the car.

"I didn't quite get it. Wasn't this Her business? Why did we need to be seein' that? They acted like we were at the movies or somethin'. Then I found out that the man was Her kin. It seems that they were related on His Maw's side of the family. He came lookin' for his own Maw and met up with Shiloh. At first I thought that His sister didn't know it but turns out that wasn't the half of it. When Her kin had come to Frog Creek Shiloh was plannin' on settin' up a meetin' with all his kin, but instead the two of Them ended up drinkin' at Sharky's and went on to the Dew Drop Inn. It was a scandal. The whole of Frog Creek knew. I heard tell that His Maw and Him went to a little trailer at the edge of town and drug Her out of the trailer, just a kickin' and screamin'.

"Durin' the whole of our time together, it seemed that His family was more important. Why, He even had Jay sayin' that His Maw was the "good Grandmammy" and mine was the "bad Gramma." Jay couldn't even talk much, but there he was sayin' what his daddy wanted him to say. His family was more important, more hurt, more in need, more of everything. Every holiday, birthday, and whatnot was celebrated with His family. Lot of this time They spent arguin' with one 'nother. Who was stronger, who was smarter, who was more of a man...when it got down to whose kid was the best... why, I just shuddered and wanted to get home. The worst thing was the drinkin'. It just never seemed to stop. It seemed like after all the smartin' and showin' off was done, there was nothin' left to do.

"One particular time I 'member is when His favorite sister and Him was drinkin'. She had Her husband there and I was there. Pretty soon They started arguin' 'bout what I can't rightly say. It seemed like whatever the other said was not quite right with the other. Awful words were said. He dragged me home and for the fist time in my life, I saw Him cry. Pretty soon there was a knock at the door and there She was! I went to open the door, but He pulled me back. He was laughin' now, and I was confused. He wanted to hurt Her, just like how She hurt Him. I tried to say how maybe it was time to make-up and forget the whole thing. The next thing you know, He was hittin' me. Sayin' how I had abandoned Him in His time of need. It was a mystery to me how He thought on Them so. They done a lot of mean things to Him at times.

"When was the last time you saw Wilford Dixon's family?"

"I saw His Maw 'bout two days before I left Frog Creek. She came by the house and wanted to see Wilford. She didn't come in the house at all. She just stood out there smokin' Her cigarette. He went outside and took Jay with Him. I watched from the front room window. I couldn't make out what They was sayin'. Pretty soon I heard Him call for me to come and take Jay. I went out there real quick like and took my baby. I went 'round back to check my wash. Since I was fixin' to leave, I tried real hard to keep up with the wash. I set Jay down beside me. Jay was a good boy. I didn't have to remind him to stay near me. He'd stray away a bit, but he knew where he was safe. I was checkin' on my wash when I heard yellin'. What I did hear was kinda' peculiar... it didn't make much sense to me.

> 'My car is actin' funny— it's idlin' too fast. Must be all the drivin' you've been doin. Maybe it's all the funny little things I found inside?'

> 'Don't start any trouble. If your car is idlin' funny, I can fix it. Won't take but a minute.'
>
> 'You sure think you got it nice here, don't you? You really think you're gonna' get this place?'
>
> 'Quiet now... there, I think it's fixed. Let's take it for a test drive.'

"As I was foldin' my wash, He came out the side door and told me He was goin' for a ride with His Maw. Her car was actin' funny, and He wanted to see if He fixed it. I gathered my wash and Jay and went on it the house. I felt brave just then and asked what she wanted to talk about.

> 'Oh, you know Maw. Something is ailing her about her car. If it ain't her car, it's her house.'
>
> 'Is that what she meant by you gettin' this place?'
>
> 'What are you doing, eavesdropping on me? What's the matter with you?'
>
> 'I was out back takin' down the wash. I'm standin' outside. That's all there's to it.'

"Truth is He was comin' at me, and I was backin' away. I guess seein' that I was scared was enough for Him. He left without sayin' another word. He got inside His Maw's car. She let Him drive and off They went. I didn't see any of His kin, except for Her."

It was gettin' on to evenin', my favorite time of day. I wondered if they were gonna let me go. A man came in all winded and wanted to speak to Detective Frye. Detective Frye excused himself and left.

"Mrs. Batawldin, you said if I cooperated, I could go on home. Can I go back to Sula's and be with Jay?"

"If it were up to me, LuCinda, I would say yes. We have to see what Detective Frye has to say. He'll need to check with the Rondo Police Department for any updates. LuCinda, I want to say that I know how very hard it has been to talk about these things that have occurred in your life. It's not easy facing one's past. I also want you to know that ... well, that I believe that what you have shared today is the truth."

I felt right happy just then. I wanted to say somethin' kind to her too, but we were interrupted.

"LuCinda Dixon the Rondo Police Department just called me. Well now, they want us to hold you on suspicion of murder. See, they've been looking for you for a while now and seeing how you run off... why, we got to hold you on account of Wilford Dixon is dead."

I put my hands to my mouth. My head was spinnin'. Wilford was dead! He was dead? Detective Frye was goin' on 'bout some kinda rights I had, but I couldn't focus any. He was dead? He was really dead?

"Are you sure He's dead? I mean, it's really Him?"

"Yes. He was found around the tenth of May. I can't tell you any more than that. The Rondo Police Department wants us to hold you until they can free up their jail. It seems they're full. They caught some moonshiners, and they're plum full."

"Oh... they musta caught up with them Slatter Brothers."

Detective Frye looked surprised at my knowin' it was them that they caught. He was actually addressin' Mrs. Batawldin and I just cut in. I felt so numb and strangely relieved that I couldn't rightly explain. Detective Frye looked right at me this time.

"It was the Slatter Brothers who found Wilford."

For the first time in my life, talkin' felt safe.

"Oh, they're good folks. They were probably runnin'

shine somewhere and had to make a choice between shine and Wilford. Too bad they got arrested for tryin' to help. Where'd they find Wilford? Was it near Thirsty Creek? You see, that's where the Slatter Brothers cool their shine. The creek is just as cool as can be. They store it down there. They tie it onto dead trees that fall in the creek. Everybody in Frog Creek knows that."

I didn't even take a breath. I couldn't stop talkin'.

"I can't rightly believe you're keepin' me here. I told you everything I know. I ain't seen Him since Friday, May the first. I have been here in Chatfield ever since that day... I...."

"Wilford Dixon's been missin' since Friday. He was last seen by His Maw on Friday, May the first. That's what the Rondo Police Department said."

"When? What time? I sure hope somebody's askin' Them questions too. You are thinkin' that I done it, right? Otherwise you wouldn't be keepin' me. Even after all I done told you, you still think I done it?"

"Now see here, girl, they'll be sending someone over tomorrow from Rondo. All this here will be sorted out then."

I was breathin' real hard. My fists were all clinched up. I wanted to get away right then. They tricked me! They knew He was dead all along. They were just seein' if I was tellin' the truth. I plum collapsed in the chair. I closed my eyes and tried to breathe real slowly like. I don't know how I got the strength to calm down, but I did.

"Mrs. Batawldin, I'd like a lawyer now. I guess you're gonna keep me here tonight. Do I get a phone call? I'd like to call Sula."

## CHAPTER 5
## Send Me a Deliverer

Hello, Sula?"

"Girl, how you doin'? I'm just as sorry as I can be. You know they found your man? Everybody in town's just a talkin' away. Don't you worry none. I know you didn't kill anybody. You're just a scared child runnin' from something you feared. Don't you worry 'bout Jay none. He's playin' with me and the preacher. Yes, the preacher is here seein' to my well being. Don't you worry none. I'll find you a lawyer. I got friends in this here town. Cinda, you there girl?"

"Yes Ma'am. It's just that I'm all choked up about you believin' me when I never even told you the whole truth. I never even thanked you properly... I never even..."

"Stop right there! You don't have to say nothin' about that. There will be plenty a time for that when we get you outta there. You hear? Now listen to me. You don't have to say nothin' to the police. You hear?"

"It's a little too late for that, Sula. I done told them everything I knew 'bout what they asked me 'bout. Sula, where did they find Wilford? What do you know?"

"Well, I heard from Mrs. Fortney 'cross the street. You know lady who lives in the house with all the flowers you admire so much? She said... just so you know, she believes you're innocent too. She said anyone who admires flowers so much is good people to her. Anyhow, child, she said Mrs. Parsons was heard tell that your man was found by some moonshiners. They come upon him at Thirsty Creek. Does that sound familiar? Anyhow, they found him. He was just lyin' there. A car was found down the road. His kin, so I'm told, is just as angry as can be. Cinda, they think you're involved somehow... since you ran off with Jay. Did you know that?"

"Yes, Sula, I know that now. They're keepin' me here 'cause Wilford's dead. They think I done it...I don't know how this coulda happened. They say I'm bein' held for suspicion of His death. What did I do to deserve this? Oh Sula, you gotta see if my Granny is all right. You just gotta see if she knows 'bout this. It's gonna break her heart. Now listen, they're wavin' their hands at me, I only got one more minute. In the bathroom I got some papers with some numbers and..."

"Found it!"

"What?"

"When the police took you, I went to work. I started goin' through your house with a fine-tooth comb. Shoot, Cinda, I knew you were hidin' from something, but I didn't know what. I started searchin' for something to help you. I found all your papers and other stuff. Don't worry about the you-know-what. It's all there."

"You found my hidin' place?"

"Now, it wasn't that I didn't trust you. I didn't trust the law. And if they're listenin' in... I said I didn't trust them. I was afraid they would come through here and take whatever they wanted to. Who knows what they woulda done with it? Anyhow, it's all safe. It'll be safe with me! No one's gettin' it from me!"

"Sula, you are a Godsend. Maybe God is lookin' after me after all. Kiss Jay for me. Hug him for me, too."

I could feel the tears comin' on somethin' fierce. I just hung up. Sula would understand.

The same policeman that brought me in was bringin' me to my room. It wasn't at all what I expected. It was a room with a bed, a desk and the tiniest water closet I ever did see.

"This is my room? I'm not gonna be in no cell?"

"Detective Frye wanted you to wait it out in here. Supper will be served at six."

That mean old policeman looked like he wanted to say somethin' just then, but he left. I heard some clangin' at the door. I was locked in. It wasn't quite a cell, but I was a prisoner for sure.

All I could do was cry. I sat down on the tiny little bed and cried. I wasn't gonna wail none. I wouldn't give those law men the satisfaction. I forgot to see what happened to Mrs. Batawldin. I plum forgot 'bout her. I wondered if she was gonna help me or not? How was Sula gonna help me? I heard tell lawyers cost a lot. Maybe I ought to call that bank manager at Rondo. He'd probably heard by now. Maybe he wouldn't help me after all. I'm being held for suspicion of murder of Wilford. He was actually dead? I never really wanted to look upon Him ever again, but I kinda wanted to see if He were really dead. You know, just to make sure.

"Supper time!"

I didn't even hear the door get unlocked. There was a lady, all pretty with her hair in a net. She was just a smilin'. She looked right friendly.

"Tonight is roast beef with all the trimmings. No coffee, milk. You know, since you're young and all. I'll set it here on the desk. I'll give you just twenty minutes to eat. I gotta get home. There's a program on I wanna hear. Don't know when we're gonna get us a TV. Here's your silverware. Be sure to eat it all."

My, they sure fed a person well in that there jail. No wonder the jail got full. As she was talkin' 'bout eatin' all the food up, she pointed to the plate...made some kinda motion with her hands. It seemed kinda odd to me. I walked on over to the tray a food but didn't see nothin' out of ord'nary.

"Thank you, Ma'am."

She was already gone. The door clanked a bit.

I tried to eat. I sat at the desk. With my head bowed, I really didn't feel like sayin' a blessin' for me or the food. I'd offer a prayer for Sula, Granny and Jay. *"Please God, if'n I can call upon ya now. You know, since I'm in jail and all. Please watch over Granny, Jay and Sula. They don't deserve the trouble I'm a givin' them at all. No Sir, they don't! Maybe I don't have a right to call upon divine help but since the children of Israel did, I guess I can too. They were a might hardheaded too. I know I done let you down. I tried to make it right by stickin' with Wilford. You know better'n all how He treated me. Maybe I shoulda stood up to Him more, got some help...Granny's just too old to be dealin' with this here. He mighta hurt her. I just couldn't take that chance. Maw's nowhere to be found. Well, runnin' away seemed like the thing to do. Maybe you could see your way clear to send me a Deliverer, like a Moses or a speaker like Aaron. Amen."*

The roast beef tasted fine. I knew I'd better drink all the milk after all the trouble that nice lady went to give this. I wondered why she was pointin' to the tray. I lifted the plate up and there was a note. A note! How...who'd be sendin' me a note? I felt like there were a buncha eyes on me. I looked all round... no mirrors. My hands were just a shakin' as I read it:

Cinda,

It's me, Sula. Don't worry any. Mrs. Spinler and I been friends for a long old while. She owed me a favor. Now listen. I got us a lawyer. His name is Mr. Pervis. He's helped me out once before. Since this here is Chatfield, well, no one would be knowing him in Rondo, and he agreed to take the case. Especially since I showed him all your papers and could swear that you have been here ever since you came. Don't worry any, I trust him. We're gonna try and get you out just as soon as we can. I'm gonna try and come see you tomorrow.

Love,

Sula

P.S. Don't worry about Jay. I told him you were out getting him a surprise. We'll worry about that later.

I held the note to my heart. This was my deliverer and my voice.

*Where'd I put that number? It's here somewhere. It's ringing. There's no answer? How can that be? Please answer. He's gonna be home soon! I need help with all my bags. How can I leave all these here bags? I'll try again. No answer. He's home.*

*What are you doing? What have you got in your hands? Nothin'. Me and Jay's just playin' is all. You going somewhere? No sir! Slap. Slap. I can't feel nothin'. Why don't I feel nothin'? I can't breathe. I can't move. If I could just turn my head, I could breathe...*

"No! Help! Help me... please!"

I woke myself up. I didn't know where I was. I heard keys clangin' and a door opened up.

"You alright in here?"

"I need help...They hurt me...I..."

"You're just having a bad dream. Wake up, now. Come on, wake up."

"I'm all sweaty. Where am I..."

"You're in the Chatfield Jail. You alright? You just had a dream. A bad dream from the sounds of it."

"I remember now. Yes... it was a dream. I'm all right. Thank you."

"There's some water on the desk, better take some. Better try to sleep some."

I had another dream. I guess there was no gettin' away from 'em. The water felt good. I didn't know that anyone could hear me in here. Land sakes! Was I ever gonna stop havin' these dreams? I guessed I didn't need to check the doors and windows that night. I couldn't sleep. I wondered what was gonna happen tomorrow. There I was, lyin' in a jail, and I couldn't wait for tomorrow. I didn't know what it'd bring, but I just had to have hope. What would they ask me to do? Would they have more questions? *Lord, please don't let them ask me to look at Wilford's dead body.* I didn't want to look at it none when He was alive, let alone dead. I wondered who identified Him. I hoped it was His Maw. Maybe She'd know that She didn't know how to treat Him, either.

"Rise and shine! It's seven in the morning. I got breakfast for ya."

My head hurt. The last thing I know'd I was cryin'.

"Yes'm, I'm awake."

"There's a nice warm breakfast for ya."

The nice lady started talkin' all quiet like.

"See here, Sula give me these clothes for you last night. There are fresh linens in the bathroom. 'Fraid you're just gonna have to spit shine, know what I mean?"

"Yes'm, thank you kindly."

Mrs. Spinler was talkin' regular now.

"You all got 'til seven-thirty to eat this mornin.' Enjoy!"

I looked at the clothes she gave me. Sula! It was a real nice dress. A summer jumper with a little cotton blouse, with a hair ribbon to match! She gave me fresh socks and new saddle shoes. It was like she really knew me.

I ate my breakfast fast, just so's I could put on my new clothes. I 'member one time Granny bought me some new clothes. She came for a visit bearin' gifts. She was tryin' to soften Maw, I guess. I ran into my room and put on those clothes faster than anything. I came out and show'd them off to my Granny. She smiled and told me to go on outside and play. I met up with some kids, and we all run off to play.

'Are those new clothes, Cinda?'

'Sure enough. My Granny came for a visit, and she brought me these.'

Those girls whispered to one another and the next thing I knew we was headed toward old man Gange's house. All us kids climbed up on his garage to reach his apples. They were just crab apples, but they were sure good! After we had our fill, we just started playin' on the old man's garage. Pretty soon those girls were just a laughin'.

'What's so funny?'
'You are, Cinda. You have a buncha holes in your shorts!'
'I do?'"

I turned around and tried to look at my behind and sure enough, there were a bunch of holes on my brand new shorts.

'Ha-ha! Those clothes don't look so new now. Ha-ha!'

Off they run, leavin' me there to stand. I felt so bad. I just knew I was gonna get in trouble for what I done. Pretty soon I was mad. Those girls knew that climbin' on old man Gange's garage would ruin my clothes. Soon as I started to feel mad, I started feelin' bad again. I guess I was braggin' a little too much on my new clothes. I guess I got what I deserved.

I walked toward home all slow like, fearin' the worst. I walked into the kitchen to see Granny and Maw sittin' there actually talkin' nice to one 'nother. I started bawlin'. I told them everything that happened. Granny looked sad but said it was okay. Maw looked at me with those evil eyes a hers. Later on, Maw said somethin' to me which stuck to me to this day.

'Cinda, you were just a fool! Those girls wanted to ruin your new clothes. Rather than them doin' it, they got you to do instead. You gotta watch out for people like that. They'll pretend to be your friend, get you to try somethin' that ain't good and drag you down with 'em. After you're all hurt and scared, they'll leave you and move on to the next trustin' fool.'

It was too bad I didn't learn from that experience.

After I got my clothes on, I was wishin' for a mirror. My wishin' was answered soon enough. A policeman came to get me to answer more questions.

"Come with me. You'll be going up before a judge today. First you gotta be seen by your lawyer. Didn't know you knew Mr. Pervis. He's here, along with Sula Cantrell. Mrs. Batawldin's here too."

"Thank you."

I didn't know what else to say. I followed 'long side of him, promisin' myself I wasn't gonna talk on so much anymore. I looked on my surroundins. There were a lot of little rooms with desks in them. We walked by a room with lots of guns in it. I wondered if Wilford was shot. For the first time, I thought on how He actually mighta died. Did He get into a fight with one of His kin? Maybe it was some guys, the same guys that beat up Hank one night. Maybe He finally drank Himself dead. I couldn't believe with all the possibilities out there that I was the one shut up there in jail.

We walked on to a different room than yesterday but there weren't any mirrors.

"Cinda! Oh, you look good! Well, considerin', I mean. Those clothes fit you just perfect!"

"Sula!"

I just hung on to her so tight. I didn't want to let go, until I remembered Jay.

"Jay! Where's Jay?"

"Don't you worry any. Mrs. Fortney's got him. They're playin' in her garden. He's helpin' her water her plants. He's okay. Try to think on yourself, girl. Now look here, this is Mr. Pervis."

"How do you do. I'm Cinda. Can you really help me?"

"I've given Mr. Pervis a written copy of your interview yesterday."

I looked around, and it was Mrs. Batawldin. She was standin' there smilin'.

"Thank you. I guess. Not sure if that'd help me none. After all I said they still suspect I done somethin' anyway."

"LuCinda. We really don't have a lot of time. Now, I need to ask a lot of questions, and we go before the County Judge at eleven o'clock this morning. Now, Sula can be here if you want her to be here. She somehow managed to get Detective Frye to agree to this. Not sure how, but I'm not going to ask."

Sula just winked at me.

"Of course I want her here."

"Mrs. Batawldin's here because you're still a minor under the law, in our state. She's here to see that you're treated fairly."

"Now with that— what you say in here is confidential ... between us. I read what you said yesterday. Are you sure the last time you saw Wilford Dixon, your husband, was Friday, May the first?"

"Yes sir...well, I didn't exactly see Him after that, I don't think, but I did see His Maw's wagon. I didn't tell no one 'cause I'm not really sure."

"Can you explain to me what you mean? Please, speak up and be specific."

"One night, after one of my bad dreams, I got up and tried to cool myself some. I was sittin' on the davenport in my house... well, Sula's twin home, and I heard somethin' outside. I got scared, thinkin' that somehow They found me. I went over to the window and I saw a car. It was His Maw's station wagon. I'm pretty sure it was. Anyway, I saw someone droppin' somethin' out of the window, right passenger side. I was really scared. I felt sick. After I felt better I went to the back window and saw the wagon drive on. That was all."

"Could you make out whom it was that dropped something out of the window?"

"No, sir, it looked like a man, though. He had on a black and white checked coat. Wilford didn't own a coat like that."

"Phone books! You asked me about how the phone books got there. I remember that day."

"Sorry I lied to you, Sula. You asked me if I seen a ghost. Truth was I did. I really did want to know how the phone books got there, though."

"Can you remember what day that was, exactly?"

"I can. It was Thursday the seventh a May or was it the eighth? We got our phone books sometime that night."

"Curious.... Mrs. Dixon said that the last time she saw her son was on Friday the first of May and he was driving her car? Are you sure of the date? Can you swear to it?"

"Yes, I think so. I mean, it was dark, but the wagon sure looked like His Maw's wagon. Can't you see who delivered phone books out this way?"

"Yes, of course. I'll write myself a note. Now Cinda, was it customary for Wilford to take his mother's car... station wagon... for such an extended period of time?"

"I can't say that it was regular. He would sometimes get to use it for a while but not for that long. His Maw would go plum crazy. Wilford had a car. He just didn't get it runnin' long enough. He parked it over to His Maw's house. I thought He parked it over there for an excuse to go over there and work on it. I can't remember the last time His car was runnin'."

"This is certainly curious, indeed. LuCinda, how long was your husband working at the meat packing plant?"

"That's a right funny question. He didn't work at any meat packin' plant. He worked at Data Systems in Coleville. He got that job after He finished at the vocational school. He was workin' at the entry level, He said. He was deliverin' mail and orderin' parts. Why, He said He was even workin' on developin' new machines."

"I'm sorry to tell you that he was not working at Data Systems. Let me look at my notes... yes, he held that job while he was going to school. Since he didn't complete his training, he was let go. The next place of employment listed was at Johnson's Meat Packing Plant in Coleville. Oddly enough, Wilford was laid off on May first. "

I couldn't believe my ears. How could I be so dumb? How could I just believe everything He told me? Why didn't I know? Why didn't I hear anything from His kin? You'd think I woulda heard somethin' like that.

"LuCinda? I'm sorry. This is obviously a shock to you. You didn't know?"

"Know? I didn't know anything about that. I can't believe it. I never questioned Him. I just believed whatever He said. Well, that explains the gym bag He grabbed when He went to work. That explains why we were so poor for a while and forced to eat at His Maw's all that time. That explains why He was willin' to move to my Granny's house."

"We have to move on. We don't have much time. Wilford was found near a place called Thirsty Creek. What do you know about this place? Did He frequent it often?"

"Thirsty Creek is just about six miles from Frog Creek, due south. It's best known for the Slatter Brothers and their shine business. The Slatter's hold their shine there to keep it hidden and to keep it cool. I don't know if they ever done their sellin' there, but I know that's where they would hide it from time to time. It's also a place where... well, a place where Will took me when we was sneakin' 'round courtin'."

There was a knock at the door.

"Excuse me, there's a telephone call for Mr. Pervis."

I was glad he left. I couldn't go on no more. I buried my face in my hands, and the tears started flowin'.

"There, there, Cinda, you just go and have yourself a good cry. Lord Almighty, what you been through. It just makes me so mad, yet sad for you. Girl, you gotta be strong. You gotta face up to this here day, so you can put all those sad days behind you where they belong. Sula's got faith in you. Do you hear? I got faith in you."

I held on to her and hugged her back. It felt just like we were kin. Kindred spirits, even. It's like I always had known her.

"LuCinda?"

Mrs. Batawldin. I had plum forgotten about her again!

"I have to agree with Mrs. Cantrell. You do need to be strong. You're going before a judge in a little while. I'll be there with you. Mrs. Cantrell can't be with you, and I'm not really supposed to pass any judgment on any of these proceedings I'm involved with...and ... I said it yesterday and I want you to know that I still believe that you are telling the truth. I've got to prepare for another case I need to be in court for, so I will see you in the judge's chambers."

I woulda hugged her too, but Mrs. Batawldin was doin' her best to be all business-like.

"Thank you. Thank you very much."

"Now don't you worry any. Mr. Pervis is right clever. He'll figure this mystery out."

"Sula, I almost forgot, what about my Granny? Did you ever get a hold of her?"

"No, child, I got a hold of her sister, who gave me the number of the hospital. Her sister just came back from visitin' your Granny when I called. I called over to the Bowler Memorial Hospital, and I didn't get much outta that nurse. She just said that your Granny was restin'. She's still doin' poorly. She's callin' out for you. She told me that they were keepin' her as comfortable as possible."

*Please Lord don't let my Granny die afore I can see her again.* I just had to see her. I sure felt lonely standin' there next to Sula. She done said she loves me and cares 'bout me, and still I felt alone. Mr. Pervis came in just then.

"LuCinda, what do you know about Sharky's, Kat Club and the..."

"Dew Drop Inn?"

"Yes, the Dew Drop Inn. That call I received was from my assistant. I sent him over to Rondo to do a little checking soon after Sula rousted me out of my bed to tell me about your case. You'll be pleased to know that the Rondo police found the secret hiding spot your husband had underneath your bed. Now what can you tell me?"

"Will and His kin liked to go to Sharky's a lot. Now and then Him and Trey, Hank and the Juniors went to the Kat Club. They're bars, places where He would go and shoot pool. I've seen 'em. I've never been in 'em, though. I 'member His Maw followed one of His kin outta there late one night. We were all in the wagon just ridin' around when His Maw spied His cousin's car. Anyway, when His cousin come out with a girl, I didn't recognize her none. It sure wasn't His cousin's wife. We followed them for a spell until they stopped. Will,

His Maw and well, everyone but me piled outta the car and started hootin' and hollerin'. Pretty soon they come runnin' back, just a laughin' and off we went like nothin' happened at all."

"I don't know much about the Dew Drop Inn. Is that another bar?"

"LuCinda, I'm sorry to have to ask you this but was Wilford a ladies' man? Was he seeing other women?"

"I don't know. I had my doubts when we were first married. Well, let me say that I knew He was used to seein' other girls when we were courtin'. I just kinda figured that once we were married, He'd settle down. I never worried any until one night He came home all drunk. He knocked on the door, I opened it, and He wouldn't come in.

> 'I'm home,' he said. 'Before I come in, I want you to know that I was dancing with another woman tonight.'
> 'And?'
> 'Nothing happened.'
> 'Who was she?'
> 'Daisy Lawton! Yup, it was her.'

"I knew the Lawton girls. There was Betty, June and Daisy. They were girls just out for a good time. Daisy was 'bout my age."

> 'Daisy's underage,' I said to him. 'How was she in a bar?'
> 'I can see that I'm not wanted here, so I'm going. It's your fault I'm going too.'

"He was so drunk that He fell right down the steps. At first I thought He hurt Himself, but He just laid there laughin'. I didn't care any. I started cryin' and couldn't stop. Daisy Lawton? I went to school with her. I figured that when the preacher said we were supposed to forsake all others, I guess Wilford meant that *I* was supposed to forsake all others. Later on His sister Shiloh called and yelled at me. Said I pushed Will down the stairs. He showed up on her doorstep all bruised and bleedin'.

> 'I didn't push Him,' I told her. 'He fell down all on His own!'
> 'You think you're so smart. How can you beat on a man when He's drunk?'
> 'I didn't even touch Him.'
> 'You're just stupid! You don't know anything.'

"She hung up, and I got scared. I thought maybe She and Him would come over there and I would get a beatin'. I grabbed Jay outta bed and went over to His Maw's house. It was quite a walk, holdin' Jay and all. It was the first and last time I went there seekin' refuge.

> 'What are you doin' here so late?' She asked me. 'Where's Wilford?'
> 'He's with Shiloh. He's drunk and I'm afraid that He'll start trouble. Can I stay here for the night?'
> 'Suit yourself.'

"Pretty soon the phone rang. It was Shiloh. I could tell the way His Maw was talkin' that it was Her.

'No, she doesn't look beat up. No, she is sittin' in the other room. What happened?'

"His Maw went up the stairs to bed after she talked on the phone with Shiloh. I tucked Jay into the room off the kitchen and closed the door. The next day I was sittin' in the same spot when Will came in the house. He started right in on me. He started slappin' me and yellin'. His Maw and His sister Cassidy came down the stairs. They just stood there and watched me get beat up. After He was done, He left with His kin for a ball game.

"We never talked 'bout that night again. I tried my darndest to find out if He was seein' other women, but since I was too young to drive, I couldn't go anywhere. I just kept my ears open and checked His clothes when I cared to. Why do you ask?"

"The Dew Drop Inn is a motel. It's outside of Coleville. My assistant told me that the clerk at the motel can swear that Wilford Dixon was there on Friday, May first... at one-thirty in the morning. He was driving a station wagon."

I started cryin'. I was so happy! I think Mr. Pervis thought I was cryin' 'cause a Will. 'Cause He was there with another woman.

"Sula! Did you hear?"

"I sure did. Somebody saw him long after you arrived in Chatfield. And I can swear to the fact that's been here ever since. I seen her everyday since that day she and Jay first arrived. That should be enough to get you on outta here!"

Sula and I stood there huggin' one another.

"I agree with Mrs. Cantrell. But LuCinda, all the facts aren't known yet."

"Another thing that my assistant has told me that is rather interesting.... The car that was found near Wilford's body was a dark blue Chevy, not his mother's station wagon."

"What?"

Now I was gettin' down right tired of this—every time I was feelin' happy somethin' would come along and take me down again.

"His old blue Chevy. You mean that thing runs? Since when? I thought Detective Frye said they found His Maw's station wagon by Him."

"No, a car was found about fifty feet from the creek itself."

"I guess I just assumed it was the wagon.... but His Maw said she last seen Him on Friday the first of May, drivin' Her wagon. I don't get it."

"Yes, that's what the Rondo Police Department reported. Wilford Dixon was last seen by his mother on Friday, May first all right, but the time was never reported. It seems Wilford used her car to get to work at the meat packing plant. He did report for work, and received his pay at the end of the day, at five-thirty in the afternoon to be exact. The next report that we have of anyone seeing Wilford was at the Dew Drop Inn Motel at one-thirty in the morning. He left sometime during the early morning before the day clerk came on duty."

"LuCinda, there's something else. Do you remember what you saw under the floor board in your bedroom?"

"Yes sir, I do. There were papers, His watch, and some match books, but I threw those back."

"I see from your statement to Detective Frye that you put these items back but when did you take them out again?"

"The day me and Jay left Frog Creek."

"Did you notice anything else in there? Please think carefully."

"No... I really don't think I saw anything else. I just wanted the papers that He wrote my name on over and over, and the application to Pine Oaks. I just grabbed His watch to be mean. Why do you ask?"

"Do you think you could have seen a picture?"

"No, I didn't. Like I said, I just wanted the papers mostly. I didn't take them out until just before me and Jay left. You know, in case He came home all of a sudden like."

"For Pete's sake, Paul, just spit it out. What you tryin' to say?"

Sula was right angry.

"My assistant tells me that something is being held under wraps. The Rondo Police Department isn't talking about it. My man tells me that there is something to suggest that there may have been a picture or pictures in there. No one knows about this except the Rondo Police Department and us. My man made sure of this."

"Pictures? I didn't see any pictures in His secret spot."

"Let me tell you, the only people that know that Wilford's mother's station wagon was seen here in Chatfield on May seventh or eighth is us. We've got to go. It's nearly eleven A.M. I'm surprised that they haven't come for us. I'll go check and see if there is a reason for this delay."

I felt all tired out again. I didn't know where this was all goin'. I wasn't sure I'd be free. It seemed like He was a person I never really knew.

"You all right, Cinda? I'm just as sorry as I can be for all this here that's happenin'. Lordy, this is big. It's bigger than both of us, I'm afraid. When things like this happen, I mean, when our problems get bigger than us, why that's when we need to rely on God. There's just no other way."

"Yes, I know, Sula. It's like when the children of Israel was tryin' all they could to get outta Egypt, why they just kept doin' their best. One obstacle after 'nother was put before them. Ol' Pharaoh worked mighty hard on 'em. I'm tryin' not to lose faith. No... no, that's not quite right. I done lost what faith I had after livin' with Wilford for so long. It was down right hard. First Maw and then Him. I guess I'm tryin' to muster up some more faith so's I can keep on for Jay. I think in my case, God's gonna need some help from me. He can't do it alone. Moses didn't do it alone, he had God's help. God didn't do it alone, he had Moses."

"Ladies, they're ready for us. LuCinda, I'll do the talking. Sula, unless you got another card up your sleeve, we'll see you in the lobby of the courthouse."

"No cards up my sleeve. Take good care of her, Paul. I'm countin' on you."

That mean old policeman was back again. He escorted us from the jail right up to the courthouse, sayin' that since I was still in police custody, he would need to walk with us. Lucky for me the police station and the courthouse were close. I tried not to look around me at all. I didn't need to see anyone wishin' me ill.

The judge's chambers, as they said, were down right dark. It turned out Chatfield had the only courthouse with a sittin' judge in it for miles 'round. It also turned out that the judge was just back from a vacation. Mr. Pervis said that would be helpful to us. There was a man from Rondo there, some kind of prosecutor.

"I have before me the case of the City of Rondo vs. LuCinda Dixon. Now, what's this all about? This here young lady is from Rondo. She's here in my court instead of in her own home state? What's the meaning of this? Why are we holding her? I'll hear first form the lawyer from Rondo."

"Judge, Mrs. Dixon is being held here per our request. Initially, Mrs. Dixon was brought in for questioning regarding the disappearance of one Mr. Wilford Dixon, her husband, on May eleventh. He was reported missing by his mother, Mrs. Loma Dixon, sometime on Friday, May first. He was found dead on May the tenth. His wife, LuCinda Dixon, was then held for suspicion of murder."

"Goodness man! It's now the twelfth of May? A man's reported missing on the first of May and now all I want to know is are you charging her with murder or not?"

"Please, Your Honor, His wife LuCinda Dixon was brought in for questioning regarding the disappearance and death of Mr. Dixon. There have been inconsistent pieces of information as to the last reported sighting of Mr. Dixon; however, we'd like to have Mrs. LuCinda Dixon held in the Chatfield Jail until at such ..."

"So, we got us a missing man who's now dead. We got us inconsistent information about his missing and death. But you want us to hold this here young lady? No sir! What am I missing, Mr. Pervis?"

"Thank you, Your Honor. What the prosecutor is missing is the fact that there are inconsistent reports of Mr. Wilford Dixon's last reported sighting. Mr. Dixon's mother reported last seeing him on the morning of May first, which is consistent with the time that Mrs. LuCinda Dixon last saw the deceased. What the prosecutor is missing is the fact that Mr. Dixon went to his place of employment at Johnson's Meat Packing Plant in

Coleville and clocked out at five-thirty in the afternoon and received a lay-off notice in his paycheck. What the prosecutor is further missing is the fact that Mr. Wilford Dixon was also seen in the early morning hours, one-thirty in the morning to be precise, at the Dew Drop Inn, at which he secured a room for the night… I'm terribly sorry, Mrs. Dixon.

"Further, we have numerous eye witnesses that can attest to the fact that Mrs. LuCinda Dixon has been residing here in Chatfield since May first and has never left Chatfield. She arrived in Chatfield attempting to escape the maltreatment by her husband, Wilford Dixon. She was in the company of her young son, Jay. Further, upon arriving in Chatfield, she went to the home of Mrs. Sula Cantrell for temporary lodging. Again, there are numerous eyewitnesses who can attest to the fact that Mrs. LuCinda Dixon has never left the fair city of Chatfield, as they had contact with her on each day up until she was brought in for questioning in the disappearance of her husband. Mrs. Dixon does not drive. Her only source of transportation would be the red eye that comes through Chatfield every Friday evening. It would have been impossible for my client to leave Chatfield, leave her son Jay without the knowledge of Mrs. Sula Cantrell, to go to the City of Rondo, across state lines, mind you, and return the next day. Your Honor, please, we request that LuCinda Dixon be allowed to be released for lack of evidence in the death of Wilford Dixon."

"She's been with Sula, huh? I hope you can do better than that, Mr. Prosecutor."

"The City of Rondo would like Mrs. LuCinda Dixon to be held in jail until at which time further evidence can be gathered..."

"You charging this here young lady with the death of her husband or not?"

"Well, no... not exactly. We still consider her a person of interest, having possible knowledge of the events leading up to Mr. Wilford Dixon's death. Recent events are making it difficult to pinpoint the time of Mr. Dixon's disappearance and subsequent death."

"So let me see if I have this straight. You want us to hold Mrs. Dixon, deny her God given rights of freedom until you gather some more evidence in the death of Mr. Dixon?"

"Yes, Your Honor. Yes."

"Son, I don't know where you learned law, but in this here state, in my court, I can not order this young lady to stay locked up in my jail while you do your job. Land sakes! However, I can kindly request that she stay in our fair city, with Mrs. Sula Cantrell, so that she will be obliged to answer any further questions that you may have for her. That good enough?"

"Yes, Your Honor. Thank you very much."

"Mr. Prosecutor? Unless you provide me with the necessary paperwork to transfer her over to your city to face charges of murder or to be held in your jail, you might wanna thank me too."

"Your Honor, I'm not prepared to do that at this time. Thank you."

"There, that's done. Now you go on to Sula's. She is a nice woman. Don't forget to tell her I said so. Now you boys come here and just take a look at this picture of my sailfish..."

I walked out of the judge's office only to find Sula standin' right there.

"Well, what happened? Are you all right, Cinda?"

"Yes Ma'am, I am. I think I'm free to go to your house. I don't rightly know what happened in there."

I just held onto Sula and hoped she'd understand if'n I couldn't talk none.

"LuCinda. Sula. There you are. Did LuCinda tell you?"

"Why don't you just tell me, she's a might overcome."

"She's free to go to your home, Sula. She's got to stay right here in Chatfield in case she's needed for further questioning."

"What's that? She ain't free? What about all we know about? Did you tell them that she done seen..."

"Shh! Not here. Not now."

Mr. Pervis done scooted us off into a little room near the judge's office.

"We need time and that's what we got. Now, now, Sula, I know what you're going to say. The facts are that they can't charge her with Wilford's death. We know that, let them work this out for themselves. As far as I'm concerned, LuCinda, you're innocent and I'm going to see to it that you are cleared from this, but we need more time. Things don't add up, not yet anyhow. My man will contact me later today. After that we can plan our next move. I know this is hard for you to understand... you've got to be patient. Look, LuCinda, because of the judge's order, the Rondo police can't just come here and whisk you away. Neither can Detective Frye for that matter. Just promise me that you won't talk to anyone about the case unless I'm there. Understand?"

"Yes sir! I understand... it's just that the people in Rondo, the police and all, they still think I done somethin' wrong... like I'm hidin' somethin'. I don't know what it is."

"This has been a long ordeal for you, I know. But perhaps there is something you're not thinking of? You know something you've overlooked? Go with Sula for now, and we'll talk later."

Sula and I walked arm and arm out of the courthouse. I thought we was gonna walk to her home, but then I saw it. Sula had a powder blue truck.

"Sula, is this here yours?"

"Yes, it is. It's a pick-up. Land sakes, I had to get me something that was gonna last. That little old car I had afore wasn't gonna do. No, I felt I needed something bigger. Don't know why, but here it is. Jump in. I think there's a little boy waitin' to see you."

I jumped up and climbed right in. I hadn't been in such a nice fancy truck before. It smelled so new. For a little while, I felt special. Like people cared 'bout me. It was true, I was not entirely free, but at least I mattered to someone.

"Sula, any word on my Granny?"

"No, nary a word, but it sounds like people will call if there's a change. The last word I got is that she's doin' the same... poorly."

I opened the door to my house and found Mrs. Fortney watchin' Jay play. They were in the front room.

"Jay! Mama's home! Come here, baby. Mama's home and everythin's just gonna be fine."

I held him tighter than ever.

"I playin' cars, Mama."

The cars were another present from Sula, no doubt. She was gonna spoil that child.

"Thank you kindly for helpin' Sula and me with Jay, Mrs. Fortney. I don't know how I can ever repay your kindness."

"Don't say on. It's been my pleasure to be needed. Land sakes, if a body can't see their way clear to help someone, well, they just ain't livin'. Sorry as I can be 'bout all this here trouble. Sorry to hear 'bout your man bein' dead and all. Probably shouldn't talk like that in front of the youngin'. I'm just sorry he ain't alive to face up to what he done. Men. They can sure help start on a family, but darned if it ain't hard for them to see it through. He ought to pay! That's what I say. I bess' get home to my flowers. They'll be needin' me. See you all later."

I didn't rightly know what Sula all said to Mrs. Fortney 'bout this here mess, but I respected Sula's right to say on. After all that I put her through... when all she done was offer us a warm place to stay. Why, it just didn't seem fair. I watched Jay play. I couldn't take my eyes off of him. Sula came in all winded, her hair just all outta place.

"Now, you just rest here a spell. I got us a surprise. We're gonna have us a regular celebration. I'm gonna make some of my special fried chicken. I'll invite Mrs. Fortney... oh; I suppose the preacher man and Mr. Pervis. It'll be just a small supper. We'll have it in the back yard. Now won't that be nice? I'll see you all later."

I smiled at Sula. I didn't even offer to help. I grabbed Jay and held him. *Dear Lord, you just gotta help me raise this here son a mine. I did all this for him and me. Mostly for Jay, though. All the trouble I caused... maybe I can't ask you for much. It was just gettin' hard. Maybe I just needed to ask for one more day with Jay. And if'n it wasn't too much, one more visit with Granny. Amen.*

I smelled on Jay's head. It still smelled like a baby, even if he was three. I don't think there's a smell sweeter. Jay snuggled right in and fell asleep. I got to thinkin' 'bout my life. I just couldn't believe that I didn't know Will had 'nother job. That He got fired too. Maw always said I was too busy day dreamin' to pay attention to what was goin' on. It wasn't true! I was busy carin' for my brother... for Jay. I can't say why I didn't know 'bout what Will was up to.

When Jay was a baby and we were livin' in that trailer of His Maw's, He would come home all tired and angry sayin' how hard school was. I don't remember Him bein' happy much.

Later on He would talk 'bout gettin' His boss to consider usin' Him to develop new machines for businesses. Was that Will's way a tellin' me He was let go? Was that why He was so all fired anxious to move into Granny's homestead?

After Maw disappeared with Orville, why Granny said she felt right lonesome. I would see her in town now and then. Once I even snuck over there to visit. That's when she told me that I ought to consider livin' there. The fact was she wasn't leavin', though. The very back room had to be hers, even if she was away on one of her visits. That old Will! He wouldn't even let me see my own kin. He was just plain mean was all.

By the time Jay was nearly walkin', we were all moved into Granny's. I know He took a lot of ribbin' from His family at first. But all of a sudden it stopped. Was that when He got the idea that the place would be His? He was a lot meaner, slappin' on me for the least little thing I done. When He'd come home from work, or so I thought, He would eat up His supper real quick and head out to the garage and work on that precious car a His. Granny and I would do up the dishes, visit and watch Jay play.

It was during those times that Granny would get out her yellow bowl of bobby pins, put up her hair and tell stories. We'd all be in her room, feelin' all cozy. I would just shiver when He would come in. Granny told me a story once... somethin' 'bout a man's ego. Was that 'bout Will? Sayin' that if men can't provide for their families, why they start feelin' poorly on themselves and take it out on others. I guess Granny did know that I was gettin' beat up. Here I thought I was keepin' it all a secret. What a fool I'd been. Here I thought if'n we moved in with Granny, my life would ease up a bit. Oh, not the work, just the pain. I wasn't foolin' Granny none at all.

By the time Jay was runnin' and gettin' into everything Will was still mean. He was harpin' on me 'bout sittin' at home doin' nothin' but gettin' fat. He would go on and on 'bout me lookin so old. I had done let m'self go. I coulda been with other girls, He'd say. But I chose you and now look at ya. Those words just hurt. They cut me just like a knife. After He'd say all those things, He'd leave and I'd watch Him walk out past the old outhouse. I felt so bad. I'd start thinkin' on what He said. I was sixteen years old. That wasn't so old. I still looked like m'self. I was rounder since I had Jay. I didn't mind the way I looked. I remember feelin' sorry for Him 'cause He had to look at me. Now that I think on this, maybe that was His way of sayin' He had to settle for less by workin' at the meat packin' plant. Sure was a funny way of talkin'.

What about the phone books? How did they fit in? Who was deliverin' them? If it was His Maw's station wagon, coulda only been three people that old lady even let drive it: Will, Trey and Herself. My guess was Trey was drivin' when I saw that station wagon in town there. Maybe he had one of the Juniors with 'im? It seemed like Trey would disappear for a while, come home, tie one on, sober up, and it would start all over again. It sure was funny when They found out Sherm Gaye was deliverin' phone books for a livin' 'til he got himself a regular job. They just laughed him to scorn, 'specially Will. Now that I thought on it, Trey wasn't laughin'.

What 'bout His Maw reportin' her car stolen? I didn't get that at all. If Trey was deliverin' phone books, then His Maw woulda had the blue Chevy— right? Now why would His Maw go and report the wagon stolen when Trey was drivin' it? 'Cause Will had His own car. But Will was last seen by His Maw with the wagon. My head was hurtin'. There had to be somebody tellin' a whopper 'cause this didn't make no sense.

Just think, there was all that there livin' goin' on, and I didn't know nothin' 'bout it. It was my life... wasn't it? Why couldn't I make any sense of it?

"Cinda? You all right, girl? Sorry it's so late, it nearly five o'clock. Land sakes, I just go to cookin' and well, it's done. Where you at, girl?"

"We're in here, Sula. I guess I fell asleep on the davenport, holdin' Jay. I was so tired...I'm sorry; I didn't even offer to help none. Why, I..."

"Don't say on. You and Jay needed to get back in rhythm again is all. Now come on. You all better be hungry."

I didn't even now what I looked like. I took Jay in the bathroom and washed his face and combed his hair. I sent him outside to the yard whilst I got dressed. I put on the red pedal pushers Sula give me. What a color! I would never have picked those out for m'self. I put on a plain white blouse so people wouldn't think I thought too much of m'self.

The backyard was down right gay! There were flowers on every table. There were just four tables set up, but it sure looked like a banquet or somethin'. Why there was table linens made outta white eyelet lace. The linen felt so fine. They were starched up real nice, too. I could hardly bring m'self to touch it. And there it was Sula's fine china. If this here was a simple celebration, why I sure wouldn't even be able to go to one of Sula's fancy celebrations! I felt so overcome; I ran up to Sula and gave her a big old hug.

"Sula... this is so much! I ain't ever had such fuss made over me... I don't know what to say."

"Then don't. Eat! Look on at all the food I made. Try some of my special fried chicken."

"Cinda? How you feelin', girl? Sula said you slept some. You didn't happen to see her fry up her chicken did ya? No? Huh. I've been tryin' to get this here recipe since I don't know when. Don't tell her I asked ya 'bout it, here?"

Mrs. Fortney scooted on to the next person, askin' 'bout Sula's recipe.

"Sorry, Preacher, I done forgot. Say, we're gonna have a blessing on the food and this here day. Keep it short, huh? My chicken is best warm."

I couldn't believe Sula was tellin' a man a God how to pray. Why, even Mrs. Fortney had somethin' to say.

"Lord only knows when we'll be eatin' now."

Good thing she said it under her breath. I think I was the only one who heard her. It seemed the preacher developed a reputation for prayin' too long for some people.

Afore long, Mr. Pervis joined us. He looked rather sober.

"Well look who's here! Come help us celebrate, Mr. Pervis!"

Sula handed him a mess a food and directed him to a place next to me. I guess we all sensed he had some news.

"Mr. Pervis, it is gettin' on to my favorite time of day. I hope you got some good news to tell me?"

Just then a gust a wind came up all 'round me and held me for a while. I closed my eyes. I didn't care what Mr. Pervis thought on me just then. I figured it was time for me to 'preciate what God was givin' me. Then it sorta hit me! Sure, some of us got a whole lotta bad heaped on us, some more than others, but if God was good, then there was good in all the bad. It was just harder to see or feel.

"Are you thinking about something, LuCinda? You seem lost in thought."

"Yes sir. I've been thinkin' 'bout how my life was just goin' on without my really livin' it. I've been thinkin 'bout how I didn't know Wilford. How could I be livin' my life, not knowin' what was goin' on 'round me? He done lost a job. He found 'nother one at the meat packin' plant. He was still playin' 'round. I ... just..."

"LuCinda, please don't blame yourself. My entire profession as a lawyer has been spent helping people who have been quietly living their lives until the actions of another come swooping down on them like a storm cloud. It's hard to see amidst a storm, LuCinda. Try not to judge your life through this storm."

The preacher walked Mrs. Fortney home. Mr. Pervis, Sula, Jay and me sat there in the backyard drinkin' in the last of the day.

"So, Mr. Pervis, you come here just to enjoy my fried chicken or you got something to tell us?"

Sula got right to the point.

"My man in Rondo tells me that it's getting harder to get information. People are keeping to themselves. Even the Rondo Police Department isn't saying much. They are still waiting for the autopsy report to come in. There are too many unanswered questions and we need more answers."

I didn't know what possessed me, but I had a thought.

"You could tell your man to go to the Bank of Rondo and talk to a lady named Priscilla. I think she'd be only too happy to talk to him. He could pretend to have some interest in keepin' money there."

Sula piped in.

"Tell your man to go to the local diner, too. I never know'd of diner folks to keep quiet 'bout nothin'. Tell your man to sit there a spell and sure shootin' someone's gonna come up to him and give him an earful. Land sakes, if I know people, which *I do*, someone's gonna come up to him and tell him just what they think happened."

"Well now, I thought I was working for you, ladies. It seems that maybe you both could be my assistants. You ladies are much prettier than my man in Rondo."

"Oooh, land sakes, say on, Mr. Pervis. You sure know how to treat a lady!"

That was Sula, true as could be. I was grateful for the cover of darkness. I was blushin'. I think my face was as red as my pants!

The next mornin' I awoke to the sounds of nature. I couldn't recall that happenin' in a while. I lay there and watched Jay sleepin' in his little bed. My, he sure was growin'. He ate so much and slept so hard. He must have been goin' through one of them growin' spells. *Dear Lord, help me to raise this here boy for 'nother day. Help my Granny too. I ain't askin' for her to be healed, just let me and Jay see her 'gain. Amen.*

I slipped out of the bedroom to get dressed. I closed the door to the bathroom so I wouldn't bother Jay. I thought on my secret storage place. I opened it up. All I had there now was my money, my map and His watch. Sula give me everything back 'cept my papers. We give those to Mr. Pervis. He didn't see much call to keep anything else. I picked up His watch. The first real gift I ever give Him. Funny how I grabbed it. I just felt like He didn't deserve anything from me. I just took it to be mean and now I felt kinda sad 'bout it. I put everything back into my hidin' place. I thought on my deliverin'. I was turnin' eighteen years old next month. It sure would be nice to be free... out Egypt by then.

There was a knock on the door. It was Sula.

"You in here? How you doin'? Sleep well? I see Jay is plum tired out still."

"Yes Ma'am, I slept well and Jay still is. First time in a long time, I slept sound."

"How 'bout we go on down to the diner and see Maude? Let her do the cookin' for a change."

"Sounds good. I'll roust Jay and..."

There was a knock at my front door. I opened it up, and there stood Detective Frye and Mrs. Batawldin too.

"Come in, won't you. Jay's still sleepin', so if you could be quiet, please."

I was lookin' at Detective Frye. He sure did talk loud even though he was always so red-faced and winded.

"We wanted to come by and let you know that they're sending a man from Rondo this morning, a man assigned special to the case of Wilford Dixon. They called yesterday to see if we could bring you in for some questioning..."

"Now just a minute! Mr. Pervis, her lawyer, said she didn't have to talk to you or anyone else about this here case unless he was present. Did you call Mr. Pervis and tell him? I bet you didn't. I bet you wanted to just bring Cinda in without even consulting her lawyer. What you got against this here girl? Milton, you ought to know better! I gotta mind to call your mama!"

Milton? Detective Frye's proper name was Milton? Suited him.

"I'm just doing my job, Sula. Mrs. Dixon here is supposed to be available to answer questions 'bout the death of her husband... and that means she's got to come on in when questions need answering."

"Please, you all are bein' so loud... Jay doesn't know 'bout his Daddy and..."

"Daddy?"

"Jay, oh Jay. You woke up, son. It's okay. Everythin's just fine."

I didn't know that Sula slipped out and was already on the phone to Mr. Pervis.

"I would be happy to come down and answer any questions you have, Mr. Frye. It's just that Mr. Pervis told me not to talk to you all unless he was there and well, now I don't know what to do."

Sula come in the room and was still madder than a wet hen.

"I just talked to Mr. Pervis. I will bring Cinda down to the station and Mr. Pervis will meet you there."

Mrs. Batawldin took the lead and stepped out on the porch. Detective Frye looked mighty upset but went out just the same.

Jay, Sula and me rode down to the police station in Sula's truck. I couldn't bring m'self to speak.

"We'll go on down to the diner as we planned. Maude will just love to see Jay. Don't you worry none."

I nodded and smiled. I kissed Jay goodbye. He had on a big ol' cowboy hat that Sula found for him. He sure looked grown up in that hat. As they drove off, I felt all achy in my stomach. This is gettin' all too regular, me sayin' good-bye to Jay. I thought 'bout prayin' just then but figured God was tired a hearin' me say the same ol' prayer.

Right as rain, Mr. Pervis showed up. Detective Frye came out onto the courthouse steps, still just as winded like he ran all the way from Sula's. He didn't look so upset though.

"Come on back, y'all. We'll be meeting in the investigation room."

"We'll be right with you. LuCinda, I don't know what this man who has been assigned to Wilford's case will want. I don't know what new information he has either. This is all so irregular, at least for me. In either case, please limit your comments to his questions. Do you understand?"

"Oh, I sure do. I know I go on some 'bout things. But, you know, one thing leads to 'nother and I'm still tryin' to figure this here all out."

"I know... I mean, I think I understand, but you've got to trust me. That may not be easy either, but you're going to have to try. Okay?"

I nodded. It sure wasn't gonna be easy. Last time I trusted a man... well, I found out I was pregnant with Jay and it'd been downhill ever since. Sure wasn't gonna be easy.

We all sat in a might bigger room than before. There was a huge table that we all sat around that was just filled with coffee stains and cigarette burns. Detective Frye, Mrs. Batawldin and an empty chair were on one side. Mr. Pervis and me were on the other. There was an old blackboard on the wall that was sorely in need of cleanin'. There was a clock by the door that seemed a might tired. The second hand kept gettin' stuck on the number seven. Funny, I thought that number seven was supposed to be lucky. The one window in the room was covered by an old shade. At least the window was open. That seemed to soften the room just a bit. It was a nice day and if a body had to be inside, at least the window could be open so's the air could sneak in.

The mean police officer was back. He came in with a tall, pale, skinny man with such a full head a hair right behind him. The skinny man had a big old briefcase that looked too heavy for him to tote.

"This here is Mr. Clement from the Rondo Police Station. He's been waitin' out front. I brought him back here. There you go, sir."

"Mr. Clement, I'm Detective Frye. This here is Mrs. Batawldin from the county, Mr. Pervis, Mrs. Dixon's lawyer... and this here is Mrs. LuCinda Dixon, Wilford Dixon's wife. Have a seat right here beside me."

Sittin' next to each other, I could see how much Detective Frye and Mr. Clement were the opposite of one another. I kinda chuckled to m'self, forgettin' where I was. I cleared my throat, thinkin' that would cover it up some. Mr. Clement took the lead in our meetin'.

"I'm glad to be here. It's rather difficult to meet with all the parties concerned in this here delicate and serious matter involving the death of one Mr. Wilford Dixon. This here is an unusual situation in which we have a person of interest, one Mrs. LuCinda Dixon who's presently residing in Chatfield... why, clear in another state. Now, I do understand that the Chatfield County Judge conditionally released Mrs. Dixon here, because we aren't ready to proceed with any further charges. This is based on the information that we have gathered from our investigation and from the information that Mr. Pervis here so graciously sent us. Thank you, Mr. Pervis. I must say that we still consider Mrs. LuCinda Dixon someone who may have knowledge of how Mr. Dixon at first disappeared and about his subsequent death. Now we could pursue this matter in court... sort out all the details... but the way I see it there are several pieces of a gruesome puzzle missing."

"The fact is Mr. Clement, you and the Rondo Police Department are not capable of proving LuCinda Dixon had any involvement in the disappearance and death of Wilford Dixon."

Mr. Pervis seemed right unfriendly toward Mr. Clement. I sure wondered where this was all leadin'.

"True enough, Mr. Pervis. True enough. This being an election year, the powers that be, why, we want to halt the procedure, which went off half-cocked. I mean... we may have rushed a bit at first and based upon the information we were given at the time... man goes missing, his mother calls the police department, the missing man's wife runs off with his only child on the same day... then his wife knew where her husband's body was found even though no one told her where it was found...well, now you can see how this looked at first? No, no, some people didn't do their job as thoroughly as they could have and now I'm here to see this through. I want her to have her say. That's why I'm here."

This man was just plain gettin' on my last good nerve! He kept diggin' in his old briefcase, like we had all the time in the world. I was just wigglin' and squirmin' in my seat. Mr. Pervis musta sensed that I was gettin' a might riled up. He handed me a piece of paper and a pencil. I guess I was supposed to take out my frustration on that there paper. The truth was Mr. Clement was startin' to sound like Will Himself. All better knowin' than everybody else. Like we was all so stupid and he was doin' us a favor by just bein' here.

"There are several pieces missing in this here murder. Now, I did say murder, didn't I? It seems Mr. Wilford Dixon died of... now where did I put that report? Ah... here it is. Says here that he died of suffocation, he had a swollen uvula the size of an apricot. Says here he had a couple of fractured ribs too. There were bruises on his body that suggest someone hit him a might too hard. Oh, and he was as intoxicated as they come. Now, initially we thought that there was no sign of a struggle... but further investigation conducted by *myself* showed that Mr. Dixon was actually clawing at the dirt... mud, really, around him. There were heel marks, which showed that he was probably trying to get himself up but couldn't because someone was holding him down. Now, here's an odd thing. We thought robbery was not the motive because he had his wallet with fifty dollars in it. But Mr. Wilford Dixon got paid two-hundred and fifty dollars that day which included a little extra for being laid off. Also, it was reported that his watch was *on* him but it wasn't..."

*Gasp*! I took in too much air all of a sudden. I started chokin'.

"Easy, LuCinda, could we have some water in here? Mr. Wilford Dixon may have maliciously treated my client, but I am sure it's still hard to hear these details."

Mrs. Batawldin gave me some water and put her arm around me. She brought her chair closer to me too.

"Thank you. I'm fine. Just fine."

Why, Mr. Pervis knew I had Will's watch. What was goin' on? His watch? *Oh Lord, please help me not to hurl right here.* I was about to write somethin' down on paper, but I was afraid Mrs. Batawldin would see. Besides, I wasn't sure I could write my hand was shakin' so bad.

"Yes, now as I was saying. Mr. Dixon's watch wasn't on him as initially reported. It was found behind the car, which was even further away from the body."

His watch was there? Now I was a bit confused. When did He get Himself 'nother watch? Whose watch did I have? Didn't I even recognize His watch? I tried to calm m'self, but it wasn't workin'. Mr. Pervis put his hand on mine and asked me real quiet like if I wanted some air. I nodded yes.

"Mr. Clement, my client would like to take a bit of a rest. She could use some fresh air, if you please. How about we take a fifteen minute break? After that perhaps you could see your way clear to let us know what my client can do to help find the real guilty party in this murder? Excuse us."

Mr. Pervis guided me right on out the nearest door. I was sorely in need of refreshin'. After we got outside, I just started to have the dry heaves. Between heaves I apologized for my unladylike behavior.

"I'm sorry for this here. I don't know why I start to feel so sick when I'm so scared...it's like I can't help it."

"It's okay, LuCinda, try to calm yourself...take deeper breaths and ... try to hold onto something."

I grabbed the railing of the police station's back stairs and took in some air. I stayed like that for a while. Mr. Pervis was pacin' so fast. Soon he took to askin' me some questions.

"LuCinda, now I know you have Wilford's watch. Did he have another one?"

"No sir, not that I knew. I gave Him a watch when we were first married. I never saw another one."

"Are you sure the watch you have is the one you gave him?"

"I think so. I didn't study it none if that's what you mean. I just grabbed it and I've been carryin' it ever since the day I took it from His secret spot."

"Okay. When we're done here, we'll have to examine that watch. LuCinda, I'm going to have to ask you not to say anything about the watch. Also, say nothing about seeing your mother-in-law's wagon... oh, and nothing about the alleged picture. Okay? I can't have you reacting like this again. We have to see what this man Clement's intentions are. For some reason, I don't trust him."

"Sure enough. I'll try. I won't say anything. Oh, and I don't trust him neither."

Mr. Pervis smiled and helped me up the stairs. When we entered the room, Mr. Clement started right in again.

"I see I have upset your client. And I do apologize, Mrs. Dixon. Let's cut to the chase, shall we? It appears that Mr. Dixon has been murdered. There are several pieces of a puzzle that do not fit... in some ways we got too many pieces but not enough in other areas. Now, seeing how we would all want to avoid another mistake like, for example, charging Mrs. Dixon with the murder of her husband, well, now I'd like to ask a few questions... if that's all right with you, Mrs. Dixon, and you, Mr. Pervis."

"My client most certainly wishes to cooperate, Mr. Clement and ..."

"Now see, that's what I'm talking about. She could answer a few questions for me and well, why don't we just start with a few questions about her relationship with Trey Dixon. How about that?"

"Trey? What do you mean relationship? I declare! Why, I..."

"LuCinda? Wait just a minute, please. I'd like to ask Mr. Clement the nature of these questions first."

That Mr. Clement was goin' too far! How could he say such a thing? Why, he was just like Will, tryin' to put words in my mouth that were never there. I did what I could to not say 'nother word.

"Well, now. That question certainly got a rise out of your client. Now, you're the ones that wanted me to cut to the chase. I would have been only too happy to explain the nature of the questions beforehand. It seems that Mr. Trey Dixon had a phone book delivery route over this way... now, here... did I put the date, oh yes here it is... he was delivering phone books to the Chatfield area and surrounding communities during May seventh or eighth. Mrs. Dixon, were you aware of that?"

I looked at Mr. Pervis, and he nodded for me to talk.

"Yes, well, I mean not exactly. On the night of May seventh, early in the morning hours, I was up in my house, really Sula's house. I had a bad dream - nightmare really. I woke up and tried to calm down by walkin' 'round the house, thinkin'. While I was up I heard the sound of a car. I don't mind sayin' that I was scared. After all, I had done run away. I didn't know if Will would come lookin' for me and Jay. Anyhow, I looked out the window and saw a station wagon. I'd have to say that I knew that the wagon belonged to His Maw... Will's that is. At first I thought They was comin' to get me and bring me home. But after I calmed down some, I seen They was droppin' somethin'. I saw the wagon go slowly up the street and that was that. It weren't 'til the next mornin' that I found out 'bout people deliverin' phone books. I had one right in my door. I didn't know Trey was deliverin' phone books at that particular moment."

"You and he have a relationship?"

"If'n you mean we was kin through marriage, and then my answer is yes. If'n you mean anything else, then my answer is no."

"He wasn't coming to see you?"

"No sir!"

"Did he know you were here?"

"No sir!"

"Hmm... so you're saying that it is just a coincidence that Trey Dixon delivered phone books to the very area that you secretly ran away to?"

"Yes sir, that's right. I suspect that Trey done delivered a lot of phone books to a lot of other areas. There's a lot a country between Rondo and Chatfield. But I 'spect you already know that."

"You are really a clever girl. You surprise me, Mrs. Dixon... now I think I'm ready to talk to you about a proposition."

"A proposition? What do you mean, Mr. Clement? My client has suffered enough. May I remind you that Mrs. LuCinda Dixon was fleeing for her own life, and that of her son, from the cruelest man I have come to know, albeit through her own words. Her actions were to escape from a life of misery and woe that you and I will never be able to comprehend in all our days... her actions were not illegal. It is unfortunate indeed that Mr. Dixon is now dead, for he truly escaped. He escaped from this earth, never to face justice for what he has done to my client. But my client has not escaped Mr. Dixon, not even in his death. Now because of his cruel and most likely careless life, he, with the help of the Rondo Police Station, seeks to hold this innocent young girl responsible. Think on your proposition, sir!"

Why, I'd never heard such beautiful words, 'cept maybe from the preacher, but I was near to tears... the more I thought of his words...the stronger I felt. I never heard my life summed up like that. Was that all I was, a product of misery and woe? He was right 'bout not being able to escape Him, though. The runnin' was supposed to be for Jay and me. It was just like Him... somehow He took over.

"Well-said, Mr. Pervis. I am sorry for my tactics. I just had to be sure. I am being very frank when I say we have too many pieces of a puzzle. Please hear me out. It seems Mrs. Loma Dixon did report her son missing, but it was her car she was more concerned with. She thought he was driving it. It seems Mrs. Loma Dixon was confused at the time, shall we say. We have several reports of Mr. Dixon being seen at different times during the evening hours, though all accounts point to his driving a dark blue Chevy. He was always seen alone. It was reported that he was actually "heard" not "seen" sometime Saturday evening. All these accounts don't match up. We know that Trey Dixon was out delivering phone books up until Friday night sometime, more likely in the morning hours of May eighth. Where he went after that is unknown. It seems the phone company or their phone book distributors don't keep very good tabs on their personnel. Last but not least, we have the time of death put at sometime Saturday night to Sunday when he was found on the tenth of May. They sent the report on to the state for further investigation. Since we couldn't pinpoint Trey's whereabouts, well, it was a long shot but I just had to be sure."

"This is most unusual. This entire case is very strange... Wilford Dixon's family, their stories... It seems like they have gone to considerable lengths to implicate my client. Does that sound odd to you?"

I knew what Mr. Pervis said 'bout me bein' quiet and all, but I just couldn't help it and I started right in.

"No sir, that don't sound odd to me. Not one bit. It sounds like They are bein' themselves. Shoot, They were all probably drinkin' right along with Him. They were probably even down at Thirsty Creek. Somebody probably got mad at someone for somethin' and everyone went their separate ways. What I come to understand, being away for a while, is this: what seems odd or unnatural to you is just a way of life for someone else. See, my problem was that I kept tryin' to make some kinda sense outta somethin' that just wasn't possible. There was no sense or truth there. There was just no livin' goin' on. Livin' that is the way my Granny raised me to hope for. The only way for me to see this was to take m'self out of it all together."

I didn't know if I was makin' any sense at all, but Mr. Pervis helped some.

"I think I understand. You see things from a different perspective now that you're physically and somewhat emotionally removed from the situation. Their life was your life. You knew it was not what you wanted, so you had to extricate yourself from the old and put on the new. I see. Detective Frye, Mr. Clement, we're thinking on this too much. It is the way it is."

I didn't rightly know what he said, but if'n it was 'bout bein' born again, leavin' the bonds of Egypt behind like the children of Israel, well then Amen.

"What is your proposition, sir?"

"Well, now Mr. Pervis, thanks to Mrs. Dixon, I think we'll be able to come to some agreement."

## CHAPTER 6
## Exodus

Sula, Jay and me were on our way to Bowler to see my Granny. *Lord please let her live 'til I get there.* I could hardly believe it! I was excited and scared at the same time. It would be a six-hour drive 'ccordin' to the map. I hated for Sula to bear that burden of mine, but she said she was glad to do it. She said she needed to get out of the house for a good spell anyhow. This would give her somethin' to talk 'bout at the diner for weeks on end. *Lord, I don't know how you placed this here woman in my path, but I thank you kindly.*

Jay saw so many things. Why, he just kept his eyes open wide and took it all in. There were so many farms, especially dairy farms. Every time we come upon a herd a cows, why, we started sayin' the next herd is yours or the next herd is Sula's. It was fun. I was enjoyin' the game until the next herd a cows was mine. It was rainin' some and as we come over the top of the hill, why, that herd a cows was all standin' under the same tree for shelter. The problem was, only one of the cows was gettin' sheltered from the rain. Stupid cows! Why were the cows all facin' the same way together when they weren't sheltered from the rain? It would have to be my herd. Sula musta figured somethin' was botherin' me.

"You know, LuCinda, I'm mighty proud of you."

"Me?"

"Yes Ma'am, I am."

*She called me ma'am.*

"You see, you're movin' on with your life. Even though you got to get through a few more rough spots afore you can move forward, you're movin' on just the same. Now take those cows back there. Sometimes folks are like cows. They follow the cow that has the bell around its neck 'cause that's how they were raised. Whatever bell rings the loudest, why, that's where they go, hither and yon. It doesn't matter to them. Sometimes it leads them to food and shelter. But sometimes it leads them to be hangin' out in the rain. They don't know any better. But, now, I bet you didn't see the one cow I saw?"

"No Ma'am, just the cows 'round the tree."

Now, see I didn't think you did. There was one cow just a sittin' there in the cover of the whole woods. She knew better. She didn't follow the rest. She's still got to face the rain. Maybe even thunder and lightenin' if it comes, but the Lord will help her get to where she needs to get to. He cares for even the tiniest sparrow... remember that, Cinda."

I could see what she was gettin' at. I smiled and nodded.

"Thank you, Sula."

She was right about the thunder and lightenin'. There it was ahead of us. We pulled off at a little motel to stay the night. Sula and Jay went on to the diner attached to the motel, while I went to the room to get it ready for us to sleep.

"Bring ya back a hamburger and an Orange Crush."

Jay seemed to accept Sula just fine. I sure hoped he'd remember Granny though.

The room was nice. There were two beds and a bath and not much else. A small davenport and the tiniest little kitchenette I ever did see. They advertised a TV, but they didn't say that it was in the motel office.

I ran some extra warm bath water, but not before I cleaned the tub. I needed to think some. Now, if I got it all straight, Mr. Clement was goin' back to Rondo. The police would issue a statement 'bout Will's death bein' an accident. That's all they pretty much had to go on, anyway. They would make it clear that no one was a suspect, 'specially me. Mr. Pervis and his man would go to Rondo and keep on workin' to get me free and clear of Wilford and His family. This meant divorce. Mr. Pervis would start the proceedins to get the homestead free and clear too. This meant we would sell the place. Since Granny wasn't any better, why, the homestead would be no place for her to live. Home or not, I wasn't goin' back to live. Then the hard part would come, I would have to go back to Rondo. I would pack up the homestead and stay there 'til… well I didn't know when. Mr. Clement and Mr. Pervis seemed to think the guilty party would show his face somehow, if there was a guilty party at all. Either way, someone had to pack up Granny's things and it was best if it were me, since she couldn't, that is.

Jay barely finished his pancakes when Sula pushed us on out the door.

"Come on now. Let's get movin'. We got us less than half a day's drive. We'll be in Bowler before suppertime."

Jay was all excited to get in the truck again. He wanted to see more animals.

"Cows! Horses! Pigs! All mine."

It was a pleasure to look on so much greenery. There was farm after farm. You just got to 'preciate those farm folks. Why, I liked to garden some, but I thought farmin' would be somethin' I couldn't do. There's a lot of work to it. Oh, I didn't mind work, it's just that havin' a farm seemed like you and the earth got to be one somehow. Each of ya tied together. I loved to weed and look on my garden so clean...unspoiled...nothin' to hurt it. I couldn't imagine havin' a whole farm to tend, to keep clean of the things that can hurt it. I wondered if that's how God felt sometimes. He must get tired of pullin' weeds too. I guess he didn't want anything to hurt us either. Somehow we had to help ourselves whilst men of God showed us the way, like Moses. Humph... couldn't be that easy. It sure seemed like there was more to it than that.

My head hurt, so I started thinkin' on Sula. She sure has showed me a lot a ways. There wasn't 'nother person like her that I knew. Oh, she was strong like Granny, but in a different way. Granny tried to help me all my life, but she was thinkin' Maw was doin' right by us. She sure was wrong 'bout that. Then there was Wilford. I know she tried to steer me clear a Him, but I was so dumb! Yet, even though I dug m'self a pit, as Maw would say, Granny was still there to guide me along. Now Sula was doin' the same thing. I felt bad for all that Sula had done, when all she started out doin' was givin' me and Jay a warm place to stay.

I thought on her, how she looked and carried herself. Sula was just as pretty as could be. She had dark auburn hair with a tinge of red. That was the color she said it was. I never heard of it before. She wore her hair up most times. She was always dressed proper. She wore real pretty dresses, jewelry, and heels. Her nails were painted too, but even though she looked real refined, boy could she could be sassy! I hadn't known her long, but she never seemed to be sad. She was alone in her big ol' twin home.

I had only been in Sula's parlor a few times. There was fine paintins, hurricane lamps, and flowers. There were settin' chairs with their backs covered with little lace doilies. It was a room that was so dignified and ladylike. There were pictures everywhere. Sula said she like bein' 'round people and pictures was one way of doin' that. There was one lone picture on top of the fireplace mantle. It was a picture of her and her husband, Robert Cantrell. She liked to say his whole name when she talked 'bout him. They never had any children, but Sula made her peace with God 'bout that. Robert Cantrell went off to war and never come back. He didn't have to go 'cause he was older when the war broke out. But Sula said that bein' the patriotic man he was, why, no one could hold him back. She'd been a widow for a while and now here she was drivin' me and Jay up to Bowler to see my Granny.

"Sula? Can I ask you a question?"

"Sure enough, Cinda, 'cause I know you won't ask anything foolish."

"Why did you take me and Jay in the way you did? You know, that night at Maude's Café?"

"That's an easy one. I just took one look at you and Jay comin' off that bus, walkin' toward Maude's, why, I just knew you were good people. I think I told you I know people. I can tell good people from bad people just like that! I think it's a gift from God. Since I couldn't have children, why, this here is one of the gifts He gave me. Now I saw you and Jay walk into Maude's. Jay looked so tired and you... why, you looked so scared. You both looked like orphans, scared orphans. Did I ever tell you why I went to Maude's that night?"

"No Ma'am, I don't think you ever did."

"Well now, I was tired that evenin', but I sure had a hankerin' for liver and onions. You see, Maudie makes a mess of liver and onions on Fridays. One never knows which Fridays, but it's Fridays just the same. Anyhow, I got to thinkin' on how tired I was and thinkin' on them liver and onions...well, I was goin' back and forth with myself when a voice said to me, 'Sula, you bess get down to Maude's, she'll be needin' you!' It was just like that. So, I got dressed up and drove on down to Maudie's. I had my fill of liver and onions, and I got to talkin' to Maude. I musta asked her too many times if she needed my help 'cause the last time I asked her, she said, 'If'n you ask me one more time, it's gonna be the same, NO!'"

"Just then the red eye pulled up. I saw people gettin' off. Then I saw you and Jay. I watched you both walk up to Maude's Café all wide-eyed. I thought, now there are good people. I watched you eat. You were obviously scared silly, the way you kept lookin' around like someone was chasin' ya. Yet you still minded how Jay was feelin'. You tried to make him feel at ease even though you weren't. I said to myself, 'They're the ones who need your help, Sula.' So I got up and walked on over to you and started talkin'. I don't even know what I was gonna talk about. All I knew was that I needed to help you and Jay. That's all I knew."

I smiled at Sula.

"I can't ever thank you enough for that kindness. It's meant so much..."

"Now, you just stop right there. I ain't the only one who's given here... let's stop afore we both start cryin' like some blubberin' old women. Why, I won't even be able to see the road any. You take a rest like Jay here, and we'll be in Bowler in no time. Rest now."

"We're here! Y'all wake up now, we're here. We're here before supper just like I said. I got the directions and everything. We're just a few blocks away."

I woke up to Sula's excitement. I had seen that we were at a gas station just inside of town. I sat up to freshen myself a bit. Jay was already awake, slurpin' on a lollipop. Sula!

We pulled up to a little one-story white building. Land sakes! If that was a hospital, where'd they put the patients? There was a sign tucked inside a pretty flowerbed. It read: Bowler Community Hospital and Nursing Home. I sure was surprised to see that there was more to the building once we were inside. I asked a nice lady for directions to the ladies room and to my Granny's room.

"Why sure, welcome. The ladies room is just down the hall, see right there? And, your loved on is on the Nursing Home side. That'll be down the hall to the left, room number 107. Just follow the signs."

"When did they put my Granny in the nursing home?"

"Can't rightly say when, dearie. Some time this week, I think. To be sure, ask one of the nurses you see, okay?"

Sula, Jay and me walked down the hall real slow after we freshened up. I didn't know how it was gonna be. Would she be able to talk? Would she know me? Jay? I sure hoped Mercy was there too. I had one day to visit with Granny before we had to get back on the road again. How did you pack what seemed like a whole lifetime in one day?

"Now Cinda, try not to let on none if your Granny ain't what you expect. Try to be happy to see her. Think on Jay."

I walked into the room and I saw her right away. My, she looked so tiny. Her hair was so white. Her eyes were closed, and she looked real peaceful like. Mercy was sittin' next to her, sleepin' in the chair. They sure did look alike. If it weren't for those big old hoop earrings in Mercy's ear, you might say they were identical.

"Granny? Granny, it's Cinda. I'm here. I'm sorry it took so long to get here. Jay's here too. Jay come on and say hello to Granny."

Jay stood by me but wouldn't budge any. Mercy woke up and smiled at us. Sula went right over and started talkin' to her. Granny moved her head toward where I was standin' but didn't open her eyes. After a bit she started smilin' but didn't open her eyes.

"I think she's knows you, Cinda. I think she does. She hasn't opened her eyes for a few days now. It's her heart. It just gave out. She moves her head from time to time and smiles. Just like she's doin' right now. That's what she does. She doesn't look like she's in any pain, Cinda. Be grateful."

I don't know what happened to me, but just as Mercy said, "Be grateful," why I just started cryin'. Mercy come up to me and held me. I couldn't talk. I just kept thinkin' at how ungrateful I had been toward this great woman lyin' there so helpless.

"It'll be all right, Cinda. Your Granny, my sister, is tired. It's gonna be hard..."

Mercy seemed a might choked up too. She was the only sister Granny had left. Earlier that year, Granny thought Mercy was gonna leave her first. But she stayed by her the whole time and saw her through it. Now, it was Granny.

I pulled m'self together and found a brush by Granny's bed. I brushed her hair and held her hand. I didn't know what else to do. Sula and Jay went for a walk, since Jay was so edgy in the room, lookin' at Granny and all. Mercy took her leave, since it was gettin' late in the evenin'.

"My neighbor's comin' to get me in a little while. Now, you stay as long as you like. I got some good old hominy on the stove for you to eat. How long can you stay?"

"Only one night, I'm afraid. I got to get back and take care of some business. You know, Will died and it's... well it's a mess."

"I heard, child. I heard."

"Did Granny know? I mean does she know about anything that's goin' on back in Frog Creek?"

"No, no she doesn't... but she thought somethin' was gonna happen. Not like what happened to Wilford. No, she knew that you were gonna 'get free.' I suspect that involved Wilford, but she was thinkin' more on you. That's what she said when she came to visit me. She thought it was gonna be your time soon enough. We can talk later, if you like. I better start walkin' toward the front of this here hospital; my neighbor will be here soon."

As I saw Mercy leave, I watched her walk so slow. She was a might more fragile than Granny... why did Granny have to get sick?

Later on when the nurse came in, I helped her get Granny ready for bed. It was pure pleasure for me to help her that way. The nurse seemed grateful too. After we got Granny all situated, I got the brush out again and gently went through her hair. She liked to brush her hair a lot. "Till my scalp gets red," she'd say.

For the first time in my life, I couldn't think on any one thing. I just kept thinkin' 'bout Granny and her life. Every now and then I'd get all choked up thinkin' 'bout life without her. I started talkin' to her 'bout my life and what I was goin' to do.

"I'm plannin' on goin' back to Frog Creek just as soon as we leave here tomorrow, Granny. I gotta get back and pack up the house. You know the homestead? If'n you get outta here, why, we gotta find us a new place to live. I know you'll be sad to leave but, well... things bein' the way they are, it's best if we leave. Now, I'm not sure how to say this but, I'm divorcin' Wilford. I'm breaking free, Granny. I want you to know that it was you that gave me the strength to do this. It was you..."

I started cryin' all over 'gain. I just didn't see no sense in tellin' her that Wilford was dead and me in trouble with the law for a bit. If'n she could hear me, it was gonna be good. I put my head down on her bed and held her hand. That was the way the nurse found us a little while later.

"Visiting hours are over. Excuse me, but visiting hours are over. I'm sorry, but you'll have to leave."

I kissed Granny so long, wasn't gonna say goodbye. I told her that I would see her in the mornin' before I left for Frog Creek. She never did open her eyes. She looked like she was sleepin' real peaceful like. I guess she would sleep peaceful. I didn't know a nobler lady than my Granny. She never hurt anybody. All I ever seen her do was give. She gave people food, shelter and clothes when they needed it. She even gave people a piece of her mind if she felt they needed that, too!

I found Sula and Jay sittin' outside by the flower garden. They were enjoyin' the outdoors.

"Sorry if I didn't bring Jay back, Cinda. He looked a might scared, and I didn't want you to feel bad. It's different for children... we walked some, picked some flowers and passed the time away."

"Don't worry, Sula, that's okay. I needed that time to be with Granny and I had it. Thank you for tendin' Jay. We better get on to Mercy's. She's expectin' us for supper. It's late though."

I hadn't been to Mercy's since I was a child, but we managed to find the way all right. Bowler wasn't a big town. It was kinda like Rondo. There were small shops and one big store where you could buy everything you needed, 'cept for groceries. They got their one and only grocery store just a few years back. Afore then, one had to go clear to Spring Valley. Mercy lived in Bowler all her married life. After her husband and son died, why, she couldn't bear to leave. She and Granny exchanged visits until Mercy's health kept her near home.

Mercy and Granny were sisters all right, but they were as different as night and day. Granny liked things a might more simple around her, whilst her dresses and household linens were a tad bit fancy. Granny didn't take to jewelry while her sister did. Mercy, well, the more color she had around her the better. Her decoratin' made up for her simple ways. Jay couldn't take his eyes off'n the train lamp. He looked on one side of the lamp and then the other, tryin' to figure out where the train went. Why, there was a story on every table, shelf and picture arrangement.

After we ate, Sula and Mercy took to talkin' 'bout the old days. They talked on 'bout their men, families, health and what not. Jay and I nestled in real good in the bed we made for ourselves in the livin' room. It was real comfortin' hearin' Mercy and Sula talk on the way they did. I felt so safe and warm that I was sure that I wouldn't have one of them dreams tonight. There's just times when even all our problems can't matter. Times when there is so much history, love and overcomin' all around us that you know it's gonna be safe. It was like my own pillar of fire by night. That night I thanked God for those good women.

Mercy made us a fine breakfast of eggs, mush, bacon ends and skillet toast. Sula went on and on 'bout how Mercy was bein' too good to us. That meant Mercy was puttin' on a feast fit for royalty. Mercy seemed to enjoy the praise.

"I won't be goin' with you all this mornin'. I generally go and visit in the afternoon and stay 'til evenin'. I even take my supper there at the hospital. They've been right nice to me and my sister. I'm not sure how long they're gonna let you stay, Cinda. The mornin' hours are their busy time."

"Oh, I know. I just want to see her one more time before we head back to Frog Creek. I plan to come back just as soon as I get the house packed up and all the papers signed...it's just that I don't know when that will be."

"Don't be hard on yourself, Cinda. My sister is tired. She was happy for you when she came. I don't know why. All I know is that she made her peace with Frog Creek and you. I could sense it. Like I said, she's tired. Her heart just gave out. That's what the doctor said the night I brought her in. She's looked as peaceful then as she does now. That's how I know she's made her peace. Don't be delayin' her, Cinda. Sula will tell you."

I really didn't understand what Mercy was sayin'. What I had in my head was to say "see ya later" to Granny, get back to Rondo, pack up and come back to figure out what I was gonna do next. I didn't even talk my plans over with anyone, not even Sula. I guessed it wasn't like I was with Him anymore. I didn't have to plan it all out in my head afore hand, all secret like... I guess I had a long way to go afore I was really rid a Him.

Jay and Sula stayed with the truck to get it ready for travelin'. The nurses were workin' on Granny when I got there. They got her all washed for the day. She had on a new gown and all. Why, they even brushed her hair. I sat next to Granny and told her all my plans. I stroked her hair and arms. As soon as I felt m'self ready to cry, I stood up.

"Granny, I gotta get goin'. I'm gonna pack up the homestead. I'll probably sell off what I think we don't need.

I hope you don't mind any. I guess it's time I took some responsibility for things bein' the way they are. I'm not sure how to do that, though... I'll be back just as soon as I can. I gave Mercy the number 'gain on how to reach me, just in case. There are some things I gotta take care of. I don't know how long I will be. I ain't asked... I mean... the Lord willin', we'll see one another 'gain. Please hear me, I love you so much. I don't know where I would be if'n you didn't help me and show me the way. I'm sorry for all the heartache I caused you. Please hear me..."

Just then Granny smiled, turned her head towards me like she was listenin' all the while. She never did open up her eyes.

When I came outta the hospital, Sula and Jay were in the truck all right, but Sula was in the passenger seat.

"Sula, what's goin' on?"

"Now look here. The way I see it, you gotta learn how to drive. It's high time you started. Now we got us a straight shot to Rondo, so get in."

"I declare, Sula, it ain't safe. Why, I ain't had any practicin' or nothin'... I can't..."

"How you do think I learned? Besides, I'm right beside you."

I started it up like Sula said and did exactly what she said. I don't think I ever paid as much attention to anything afore in my life. I was scared. I ain't ever had that much power before. Why, what if I was to get us in an accident?

"See, you're doin' just fine. See, even Jay is enjoyin' the ride."

Sure enough, he was smilin' and lookin' out the window like he had no cares at all. I sure wished he could remember Granny.

I had to get used to the brakes and the gas pedal. Sula had been braggin' on her truck, sayin' how it could drive itself. It wasn't so. 'Bout the time we got further into farmin' country, I was startin' to like drivin'.

"You know, Sula, I could get to like this here drivin'. It's not so bad."

Just then a truck full of hay came right up behind me. I got scared all over again.

"Sula?"

"Now, just slow up a bit. That old fool is tryin' to push you, don't you let him."

I took my foot off the gas pedal like she said, and the man gave me a loud honk.

"Just let him stew back there. If he wants to pass, why, it's a free country."

"Sula, why don't I pull over and let him go by?"

"Well, that's one way of handlin' it, I guess... but you think you can pull over on gravel?"

"I don't see why not."

Gravel ain't like the highway, no sir. I managed to keep it on the road though. We slid a bit, but it wasn't bad. I pulled over, and the truck just whizzed by us. Sula looked a little scared if I do say so myself.

"You all right, Sula?"

"Yes Ma'am. I surely am. You know you are drivin' like you done it before. I'm right proud of you. Now let's get movin'."

I drove 'bout half way and I asked Sula if she wanted to drive for a spell. I felt a little sick. I felt like I was gonna hurl. Thank goodness there was a gas station comin' up. I pulled us into a gas station, and I went to the ladies room right away. Splashin' cool water on me helped some. I figured drivin', concentratin' so hard on keepin' us on the road, made me sick.

"You all right? You do look a little pale. I guess drivin' was too much, huh?"

"I don't know? I just felt sick... maybe a cool drink will help some, too."

"Cinda? You ain't expecting, are ya?"

"What?"

I never thought on such a thing. Could I be? *Oh Lord, how could this be?* I couldn't be pregnant now. I saw a bench off the side of the station and sat down.

"Cinda, now try and think. When did you last have your time?"

"I don't know. I ... just can't be! Sula, I don't want to be pregnant. I don't want another baby from Him! I mean, I love Jay, but now, I could never love this baby the way I love Jay, not now. Oh Sula..."

"There, there, you just let it all out."

"Oh, Sula, no... please no!"

"Shh... Now listen to me. We all have been there one way or another. We can be filled with love one minute and turn into a bear the next. We can want the moon and stars and give it all up for someone who loves us and respects us. We can love someone who doesn't love us and still rise up to our responsibilities, even though our hearts are broken so much we think we will never love again. If it is to be, Grandma Sula will be here."

Sula drove the rest of the way to Rondo. I just couldn't bring myself to talk. I felt like such fool. What was I thinkin'? How was I gonna live now? I never felt so down on myself. Even after He would say hurtful things to me, I would manage to find some spark of life in me. I had to. I had Jay. Now, I felt so helpless. I couldn't think of a baby inside me, when so much anger and despair filled my heart and mind. Sula musta known that I was not in a talkin' mood. She sang songs and played "I Spy" with Jay. That is, until he fell asleep.

"Cinda? Rondo is just up ahead. You all right to talk some? We gotta make us a plan. Now, I telephoned Mr. Pervis's office in Chatfield and left his secretary a message. I called whilst you were tryin' to calm down. Anyhow, I told her to tell him that we'd be in Rondo in the afternoon sometime and maybe we should meet in the local diner. You all right with that?"

"Won't that get people talkin'?"

"Cinda, girl, they're gonna talk just as soon as they find out you're in town. Let's hope Mr. Clement did his job like he said he was gonna do. I sure don't like that man, and I don't trust him none either. Sometimes you just gotta grab the bull by the horn and meet him face on. You know what I'm sayin'?"

"Yes Ma'am, I do. I probably coulda done it before..."

I couldn't say it. I just couldn't get it out. Sula kept on.

"Mr. Pervis said he'd check with his secretary today and knew to expect us in Rondo. He wanted us to go to the bank right off. It'll be all right. One thing at a time for now, okay?"

"Yes, Ma'am, I guess that's how it's gotta be. Please don't tell Mr. Pervis or anyone 'bout me bein'... you know."

We pulled into town in the late afternoon. We stopped at the diner to see if we could find Mr. Pervis and his man. Now, Shirley's Diner was nothin' like Maude's. Shirley's husband was the one who ran the diner. He named it Shirley's 'cause he thought that would make people come in more than if the diner had his name on it. His name was Ernie. I think he was right. He was a cook in the army and did all of the cookin' for the diner. Ernie dressed and talked like he was still in the army too. Shirley ran the register and took orders. She liked to visit with people and seemed real nice, at first. She was too rough for me. I heard tell Ernie met Shirley whilst he was on one of them furloughs. She was workin' in a bar off base, and they fell in love. She talked like a man but got hurt real easy. And if anyone got on her bad side, look out. They were matched perfectly for one another; that's what I heard, anyway.

I don't know how it happened, but we found Mr. Pervis in the diner. It sure was good to see him. He was settin' at one of the yellow tables in the back. It was a funny color for a table in a diner, especially when the booths and stools at the counter were red. The diner wasn't real full, so that helped some. I held on to Jay's hand real tight. Shirley and Ernie were there drinkin' coffee at the counter, visitin' with some people I didn't recognize. Thank the Lord for that! The booths were filled with some younger kids, a family and a couple of farmers. Mr. Pervis directed us to a table toward the back.

"Hello, ladies, I hope you had a good trip? It's good to see you safe and sound. I must say I was worried. But I called my secretary this morning and she gave me your message. Thank you."

"Mr. Pervis! You are a sight for this old lady's eyes. It's good to see you, too!"

"Cinda, are you feeling well?"

"I think the trip wore her out, is all. You know, with her Granny and all."

*Sula, what would I do without you?*

"I'm tired is all. I'm glad to be here at last. It was a long trip."

"I hope you found your Granny all right?"

"No sir, she's doin' poorly just like they said. At least I had a chance to see her and talk with her again."

"Oh, well... good. Now, I hate to start right in on business, but that's what we have to do. Okay? Shirley? Could we have some menus please?"

"Well, Mr. Pervis, you do surprise me! You moved right in, huh? I told you diner folks were different. Anyone come up and talk to you? Say on, man, we ain't got all day."

Shirley brought over the menus and some water. She looked at me real puzzled like.

"You know, LuCinda, I don't know you real well, but I'm real sorry 'bout all your troubles. We all are. We got a special on the burger and fries, comes with a drink. I'll give you all some time."

I looked 'round the diner and seen that everyone was lookin' at us. People nodded and went on with their meals or visitin'. Every now and then I could see them starin' at me. I didn't feel awkward at all. It was funny, any other time this would a sent me into a spell for sure.

"Thank you kindly."

I looked 'round the diner and the people nodded back. Sula chimed right in.

"See, didn't I tell ya. Well, maybe some of the credit goes to that man Mr. Clement, huh?"

"Oh, yes. He did all right by you, LuCinda. He made a real nice speech I'm told. He was very clear in the fact that you were sought after by the police department so you could be informed of the tragedy. At least, that's what my man told me. I saved you the paper. Do you want to read it?"

"Not now. I'm just a little stressed right now. You mean no one knows that I left Him? That's why I left, cause of Him."

"No, as far as I can tell, no one is aware of the reason behind your leaving Frog Creek. Well, let's say from what I have heard here in the diner. I believe I have come to know all of Shirley's... I mean Ernie's specials."

"You can be funny, Mr. Pervis, in your own way. Now tell me, when am I gonna meet your "man" and all? I'd kinda like to meet him."

"He'll be here any time now, Sula. He had an appointment at the bank this afternoon, right after lunch."

I thought Mr. Pervis was right funny too, just like Sula said, but I couldn't bring m'self to say so. I just smiled as usual. I think I've always been afraid to say what I was thinkin'. I was afraid of what people would think 'bout me, in public anyway. With Will, it was just best to keep my mouth shut and smile and play dumb.

"Has your man had any luck with that lady at the bank?"

"Yes, I wanted to talk with you about that, LuCinda. Can we wait until we go out to your home in Frog Creek?"

Just then Shirley came and took our orders. I wondered what Mr. Pervis was holdin' back. Why? After all I heard 'bout His doings, what could surprise me now? I seemed hungrier than usual, but I only ate a little. I didn't want to get sick. I didn't want to give anyone the least little suspicion that I might be expectin'. In a little while a man came in wearin' a fine suit and sunglasses.

"That's gotta be your man. I kinda figured he'd be a fancy-dressed man. Is that him?"

"Why yes, Sula. That's him. His name is Percival Jenkins. Allow me to introduce you."

"Hello, everyone."

He took his sunglasses off, spun his chair 'round and sat down. He was smilin' so big. He had nice teeth, too. Sula took to him right off.

"How do, I'm Sula. Sula Cantrell. This here is Cinda and her son Jay."

"It's always a pleasure to meet new people, especially such lovely ladies. Why, you two must be sisters? Am I right?"

"Oooh, do go on, Mr. Jenkins!"

"Call me Percy. That's my undercover name here in Rondo."

He winked just then. Why, he was just funnin' with us, and Sula was goin' right along.

"Do tell, Percy. Why, come sit over here by me... move over, Mr. Pervis. You must be hungry. Where's Shirley?"

"Don't worry; she'll be bringing me the special anytime now."

Percy started lookin' 'round, and sure enough there came Shirley with the day's special, burger and fries.

"Here you go now, Percy. Let me know if you got room for pie. How you all doin'? Is everything okay?"

We all thanked Shirley. By now, people were used to seein' us all together there in the diner, so they went on with their own talk. I felt a little more relieved.

"Percy has been working real hard here in Rondo. He has gained the trust of most folks. Anything to report, Percy?"

"Why yes, sir. I got me a date with one Miss Priscilla Dalton tonight. We're going to the Kat Club for dinner and dancing. It's my last week in town. I've been talking to her for a few days now. I'm here on business and got to get back to the big city."

Percy winked again.

"Good work, Percy. After lunch, I wonder if LuCinda and I could go into the bank. Jay should go with us. There are some papers that we do need to sign, LuCinda. The bank manager assured me that they would be ready by three o'clock this afternoon."

"That's nice you all got assignments. What's mine?"

Sula looked a might upset 'bout not bein' needed.

"Don't you worry, Sula. I saved the best for you."

"Say on, Mr. Pervis. I'm all ears!"

"I wonder if you might go around the various stores and buy whatever you and LuCinda might need while you're staying at her Grandmother's home for the next few days. Be sure to say that you're a relative that has come to stay with LuCinda while she ties up loose ends here in Rondo. Sula, I will have to ask you to… uh..."

Mr. Pervis was at a loss for words.

"I think I know what you're gonna say, Mr. Pervis. Keep my opinions to myself? Is that it?"

"Not exactly. I trust that you will know what needs to be said. It's just that people think poorly of the Dixon family. From what I have gathered, and Percy too, it's generally felt that they are not respectable people, shall we say. We don't need to fuel that fire any longer. It's LuCinda that I'm worried about."

"Well, seein' how we both got her best interest at heart, I think I can manage to say what needs to be said."

Mr. Pervis cared 'bout me? Well, I knew he did, but this sounded different to me. It was like he cared about what happened to me after the case was done. I thought he sure would change his mind if he knew I was probably expectin'. For once I didn't smile. I just kept my head down and kept quiet.

Mr. Pervis, Jay and me walked on to the bank, leavin' Sula and Percy to go shoppin'. Percy was showin' Sula where the shops were. Land sakes, I do declare Sula enjoyed the attention she was gettin' from Percy. She liked bein' happy. It was true enough she invited joy into her life, but she truly felt that there were plenty of reasons to be gay. It just plain wore me out. I think it's because I knew those happy times were gonna end and when they did, look out!

Rondo was a small town by most people's opinion. As we were walkin' it seemed so different or maybe it was me. For me, the town was just big enough. There were plenty of little shops around. There was a nice bakery, shoe place, barber and what not. I hadn't been inside of most of them. Jay and me spent a considerable amount of time just "window shopping" as they call it. I went into the big department store a few times with Granny. Back when Granny, Maw and I would come to town, we would end our trip with a stop at the diner and get us a hot roast beef dinner. Those were happier times, or maybe there was a might more time to take in the pleasures of a small town?

Walkin' into the bank gave me the shivers all over again. I had that same feelin' when I was runnin' away from Him. Only the feelin' wasn't so strong. We were greeted by the security guard. He kindly directed us to Priscilla.

"Why, I declare! LuCinda? Is that you? You look so different... what are you doin' here?"

"Mrs. Dixon has some papers to sign with the bank manager. I'm Mr. Pervis, her lawyer. Kindly tell Mr. Smith that we've arrived. He's expecting us."

Mr. Pervis grabbed my arm and guided me toward the chairs in the lobby area. He grabbed Jay too. I sure liked that he was takin' charge the way he was. Sometimes a body needs someone to take charge, to lead the way in a proper protectin' way. Not like He did, mind you. He just took over and only cared 'bout His way. I could tell Priscilla was a might insulted by his attention to me and not her. She looked back so much at us that she practically ran into the door to Mr. Smith's office. Once we were inside I felt like I could breathe.

"My, LuCinda, you look wonderful! It's good to see you and Jay safe and sound. I'm sorry to hear about your Granny. She's a fine woman. I can't say that there are many women like her. I have all the papers ready to be signed, Mr. Pervis. I'll call my secretary in to be a witness. One moment..."

I looked at all of the papers that I was supposed to sign. I had no idea what was necessary to get me free and clear of Rondo and Will. I looked at Mr. Pervis. He musta knew that I was overwhelmed.

"We'll sign them one by one, LuCinda. First things first. It won't seem as much that way."

He sounded just like Sula. I closed my eyes. *Lord, I do appreciate these here people you have sent to help me in my journey to be free. But am I ever gonna be able to help m'self without bein' so scared?*

"LuCinda? Are you all right?"

"Yes sir, of course I am. I'm just thinkin' to m'self is all."

As far as I could tell as I looked on those there papers, I signed the DEED to the homestead, account transfer papers, divorce papers, and finally trusteeship papers. I now owned the homestead and had the right to sell it. The Slatters wanted to buy it, and I signed that agreement too. I had 30 days to vacate the premises, but Otto Slatter said I could take all the time I wanted on account of my Granny bein' so nice. I was also the owner of my Granny's accounts, and I had a tidy little sum of money, as Mr. Smith called it. I also had legal rights to decide her affairs, and that made me real sad. I cried a little when I signed that paper, but I got control of m'self again. I signed those divorce papers real quick like. Mr. Pervis said now that Wilford was dead; it would be real easy to get a divorce. I wouldn't even have to go to court.

"Do you need me to go over these papers, LuCinda?"

"No, Mr. Pervis, I understand them just fine."

"Good. I thought you could understand them."

After Mr. Smith's secretary left, he wanted to let me know that my Granny took care of these things before she left. Actually, weeks before she left Rondo to visit her sister in Bowler.

"LuCinda, your Granny worried about you and Jay. She prepared a very clear Last Will and Testament. She knew that Wilford was trying to get the homestead from her. Your Granny laughed, right here in this office, at the very thought of Wilford Dixon owning her homestead. She knew that if she were to die suddenly, it would have happened that way if she didn't draw up a very specific will. Everything was transferred over to you and Jay. If something were to happen to either you or Jay, it would have been given over to her sister. Since her sister's health was in question, why, the entire estate would have been given over to charity.

"The last thing she did was draw up a check for $1,000.00 made out to you. If you ever came in here needing money, it was to be taken from her account, no questions asked. Your Granny was a clever lady. You know, Wilford Dixon came in here one day, and he actually showed me a promissory note with your signature on it? It was money was to be taken from your future hold in the homestead. I don't know how he obtained such a note, but I refused to honor it. I do believe that made him quite angry. I told him that if he pursued this claim, I would be forced to turn the matter over to the police. I do believe I upset him. He stormed out of my office, and I never saw him again."

I did remember what Mr. Smith was talkin' 'bout. Will sure was mad. We left there and drove on over to the drive-in. I got me a burger and fries. He said He wasn't hungry. He brought me home and drove off over to see His kin. I didn't see Him 'til the next day.

"Thank you for tellin' me these things Mr. Smith, it helps me 'bout now as I am tryin' to piece a lot of things together. I knew He was tryin' to butter up my Granny and then when that didn't work; He started to write my name... I found some papers with my name written over and over again. To be honest with you, I didn't know that we had any money. I mean, my Granny. She never let on any. I am grateful for all of your help. I don't know if you remember, but the day I left Rondo, and Will, you gave me your number, in case I needed help. I want you to know that it has been with me ever since."

"I'm glad to hear it. You deserve some peace of mind now, LuCinda. I hope you can start to feel that real soon."

As I walked out of the bank, I did feel different. Mr. Smith gave Jay a big ol' toy semi truck for bein' the newest member of the Rondo Bank. I didn't even notice if Priscilla was lookin' on us or not. I didn't care any, and that felt good.

I wanted to walk on over to the police department, but Mr. Pervis reminded me that now was not the time.

"Be patient, LuCinda. There will be time soon enough. I'm sure of it."

We met up with Sula at the Red Owl grocery store. She was fixin' to buy up the entire store!

"Sula, just what do you think we're goin' to do with all this food? Mr. Pervis thinks we're only goin' to be here a few days."

"We could be here a few days to a week, that's what he said. Now, we got to have something to give people should they happen by... to pay their respects or visit."

"Sula, Frog Creek ain't like Chatfield. People aren't so friendly and all."

"Maybe so, but I wouldn't want to be caught short. Now, why don't you show Mr. Pervis how you can drive this here truck. I think I'll ride with Mr. Jenkins. Come on, Jay. You ride with us."

As we drove toward Frog Creek, I felt a little queasy. Mr. Pervis got over feelin' so scared of my drivin'.

"We have to get you a real driver's license, LuCinda. Let's do that right away tomorrow."

"If you think that's proper at this time. I'm not so sure it is, though. I guess it's because you're a man of the law."

I opened my window wide and let the wind hit my face. I felt so warm and tingly. I sure didn't want Mr. Pervis to suspect a thing.

"LuCinda, I hope it's okay that we discuss some important matters?"

"'Bout the case?"

"Uh... what?"

"We are drivin' on the very road that me and Jay took when we left Frog Creek. Pretty soon we'll come up to the tree that I marked so that I could hide our clothes. Somebody took them once... at least, I think someone did. That's why I marked the tree."

Mr. Pervis looked at me kinda puzzled like and started listenin' to me ramble on.

"Right here is the tree."

I stopped the truck and got out. I showed Mr. Pervis my mark. It was a funny black mark I made on the tree. I imagined it was like that of the Passover, meanin' no disrespect. There was my mark. I was goin' to get free of here and that was like my sign to God. I would somehow pay enough of my own dues and one day I would be of better use to him.

"I'm sure this return trip to Rondo is difficult...will be difficult for you, LuCinda. I'm sorry that I didn't realize that... I mean I realized it would be, but I didn't do a very good job of conveying that. I am sorry."

"Thank you for sayin' so, Mr. Pervis. Shall we go?"

Seein' the homestead sent shivers right up my spine and down again. I know how folks say that things look small when you go home after you've been away for a while. But that weren't the case for me. The house looked so big. I could feel some kinda weight settle on my shoulders. It did look old, though. I went to the side door first, but it was locked. It turned out that all of the doors were locked. I reached 'round for the spare key and found it. It was hidden on the first window next to the front door but only worked on the side doors. I walked in to find a mess.

"Someone's been here lookin' for somethin'...wouldn't you say, Mr. Pervis?"

"I know the Rondo Police sent some men over to look for the secret compartment you mentioned during your interview... I had no idea they would leave the place in such disarray."

Some habits are hard to break. I set right out to clean the place up. At first I thought I shouldn't in case I needed to see if some things were missin', but I started cleanin' anyway. I seen Mr. Pervis look through the entire place before he went into the bedroom.

"I hope you don't mind, LuCinda. I've wanted to see this room ever since you told me about this secret compartment, and it piqued my curiosity even more when we found out about the watch discrepancy. I'm just curious how this could have been here and..."

"You go right ahead, Mr. Pervis."

Mr. Pervis was real quiet for a spell. It kinda got me worried for just a bit.

"Are you all right? Mr. Pervis?"

I put the dustpan and broom down right where I was. I walked slowly into the room. I saw Mr. Pervis all crouched over strugglin' to get the cover off.

"I used a pencil to pry it off the first time I saw it. Do you have a pencil?"

"Uh... yes, I do. It's just that I feel like I am intruding on something that is rather personal for you. How do you feel about this?"

"It weren't my secret hidin' place. It doesn't bother me at all."

That's all I said. I couldn't believe it m'self. I said it and I walked away. I wondered why everything that was His couldn't be that way. Why couldn't everything just be that way? I heard a car pull up just then and jumped. Who was I foolin'? I was still scared. I could still feel His terrible presence 'round me even though He wasn't here.

"Cinda, you here girl? We finally made it. There was quite a little scene we had as we were tryin' to leave town."

Sula was all out of breath. She was totin' bags and looked a might tired. Percy was right behind her, but I couldn't see Jay.

"A scene? What do you mean? Is Jay all right?"

"Oh, yes. He's just fine. I think he remembered this place. Why, we pulled up, and he jumped out and ran out back."

I looked out the side door and saw Jay playin' beneath my clothesline. All his little things were there. It wasn't much. There was a pail, shovel, a few cars and some special rocks he found. He managed to find special rocks whenever we were walkin'. I suddenly remembered those walks. Walks to practice runnin' away. Walks to find empty soda pop bottles. I closed my eyes and told m'self that I could get through these next few days.

I forgot all about the groceries and Sula's goings on 'bout a scene. Mr. Pervis and Percy were bringin' in the groceries. I come in on Sula tellin' Mr. Pervis 'bout a lady comin' up to them insistin' that she hold Jay.

"What, someone wanted to hold Jay?"

"Yes Ma'am, that's what I said. So I told her that's nice you want to hold my little man, but I don't know who you are and so you won't. She said her name was Loma Dixon. Why, I remembered what you said, Cinda, so I got all huffy and said it again. I told her if she wanted to hold this here youngin', why, she'd have to talk to you first! That's what I said. I grabbed Jay and Percy here, why, he held the door open for us to the car and we left just like that. Don't worry any, Cinda. It didn't seem to stress Jay none. He was just fine."

At the sound of that woman's name, I declare I felt tired. They'd all be comin' here like before. They'd be tryin' to run my house. They'd...be all... No! This here was my house now. Jay may be her grandson, but I'd be danged if she was gonna take him or try and get her hands on him in any way. Why, she never gave one hoot 'bout him before. I was workin' myself up into a lather all right. Thankfully, Mr. Pervis started talkin'.

"LuCinda, now, I didn't get a chance to talk to you about some important matters. Sula, I expect Percy told you?"

"Yes sir, he did."

"Percy told her what? What's goin' on?"

Percy and Sula started to leave, but I told them not to.

"It seems we're all in this together. I can't imagine what you could possibly say to me that would surprise me now. Just say on. We can talk outside if you like. But first, Sula what was Loma like when you left it?"

"She was stewin' a little, but that didn't last long. You see, well... I'll let Mr. Pervis here tell you why."

Mr. Pervis and I went outside, but Sula and Percy stayed inside. Sula started in on supper. Percy was gettin' ready for his "date" with Priscilla. Mr. Pervis asked him not to leave before they had a chance to compare notes, whatever that meant. I sat on the stump and tried to brace m'self for the next thing. Sometimes things just come one right after 'nother. Jay was playin' in the grass and the dirt all at the same time. Now that's what made me happy, seein' him play and enjoyin' himself. That's the way it was meant to be for children, playin' without a care in the world and enjoyin' nature and feelin' safe.

"What Sula was talking about... with Wilford's family... is that they are unsettled about his death being called an accident. They want more answers. I'm told they come into town every other day, go to the police department and demand to speak to Mr. Clement. Actually, it is Detective Clement. No matter... I think it was just a coincidence that they came into town on the same day you arrived. I'm sorry about Jay. It is interesting that they are unsettled about Wilford's death. Their stories really don't help the situation and well, it's just curious."

"I don't find it so. They're probably just mad 'cause they don't want to accept any of the blame is all. Whenever they get to drinkin' some old stuff starts surfacin'. Just like dead fish in a dyin' bed of water. One thing right after 'nother. It's not strange to me. Someone might side with someone one time and the next time, it's all different. They don't have a real bond with one 'nother. That is, except when they can all agree 'bout one thing— then look out!"

"LuCinda, there's something else. It seems that this Priscilla you put my man on to...she's... uh...you know, there's..."

"I think I understand, Mr. Pervis. She was seein' Will, right?"

"Yes, she had been with him on several occasions at The Kat Club and Sharky's. Percy thinks that it's possible that they were having an affair."

"You didn't mention the Dew Drop Inn."

"What? I'm sorry, I didn't get that."

"That's another little souvenir Will had in his secret hidin' spot. There were matchbooks from the Dew Drop Inn. That was where the night clerk spotted Will on the Friday night I left town, remember?"

"I don't know. Percy didn't mention that. Dew Drop Inn, huh? I will ask him about that as well. LuCinda, I want you to take a good look at this watch."

"Is that Will's watch? The one I gave you?"

"You tell me."

"Looks like it. Why do you want me to look at it?"

"There's an inscription on the back. I don't think there's an easy way to say this... look on the back."

There it was.

"Priscilla? You mean that lady had her name put on His watch? Why would she do a thing like that for? I ... how could I be so dumb?"

"LuCinda, she gave him the same type of watch you did. The watch *is* from her."

"What? I can't believe it! This is so strange. So, the watch the police found was the one I gave Him. He was wearin' the watch I give Him and not hers? That doesn't make any sense. So, did she kill Will? Was she with Him the night it happened? Are the police goin' to put her in jail, like they did me?"

"You know, LuCinda, my job in this case was to prove my client was innocent and that's what I did. I gave this information to the police department and now it's up to them. I did agree to one thing though... please try to hear me out..."

"Well, did you tell her? Cinda, you gonna cooperate just one more time? By the way, supper's ready. Pork chops, fried potatoes and a mess of grits. Come a runnin', Jay! Come on now. Everybody better be hungry... you too, Percy."

Sula's announcement kinda startled me. I almost fell off the stump. I felt like a fool. Mr. Pervis askin' me if I was all right made me think that I musta looked right funny just then.

"Yes, I am fine. Sula just startled me is all. She's got a way of comin' right in when I need her and at times when I don't. What is it you want me to do? Whatever it is, well, it's the least I could do considerin' all this here you done for me and Jay. If I didn't know better, I'd say you done a lot for Sula too."

I felt like cryin' then, but I didn't.

*Hurry baby. We gotta go now. I'll just make this call and we can go. We gotta have someplace to go. Why doesn't he answer? Did I dial right? Oh, there's no time. He's comin' home any time now. Where did I put my bags? It's too late. Where can I hide them?*

*What are you doing? You're so stupid. Get over here! I said come here!*

"NO! Help me! Please... help!"

I woke m'self up. I looked around Granny's old room. I thought I wouldn't have a bad dream if I slept in there. I was wrong. I got out of bed and looked for Jay. He was sound asleep at the foot of the bed. My, that child slept, but he musta been restless. I suppose my dreams don't help any. I was all sweaty. I needed water. There was a light on in the kitchen. Sula was up.

"Sula? Are you awake?"

"Yes, I am. I heard you whimperin' in there like a hurt pup and I got up. I came out here to sit and wait for you. They say you're not supposed to wake someone up who's havin' a nightmare, but I was right close to doin' so."

"You could hear me?"

"Oh, yes Ma'am. I was kinda tossin' and turnin' anyhow."

"I'm sorry. I thought Jay's little bed would be comfortable for you."

"Don't worry any. I miss my own bed, you know. That's all. You been havin' them dreams a lot?"

"Yes Ma'am, I do. Sometimes I can go without havin' one for days and then it comes again. I guess bein' here, thinkin' on all this mess... I think it's gonna take a long time for these here dreams to stop."

"Stick to your real dreams. You hear? Those are what are real. If you're all right, I'm goin' to bed."

"I'm fine. I'll just sit here a spell 'til I relax."

"'Night, Cinda."

"Good night, Sula."

Now that I think on it, I never coulda stayed there without Sula. It woulda been too hard. Mr. Pervis had to go back to Chatfield. He had 'nother case. It's funny how I forgot that he had other work to do besides my case. I felt foolish for thinkin' so much of m'self that I forgot that other people got their lives. What 'bout Sula? Guilt just washed all over me. I needed to think.

The runnin' bath water was good for my nerves. Then I started to think 'bout me bein' pregnant. I remember sittin' with a bunch of women somewhere... where was that? Quiltin'? Was it Granny? Anyhow, they started talkin' 'bout stoppin' their pregnancies. Sit in a hot water bath. Do an extra heavy load of laundry by hand. Make a lot of bread. Ride a horse. Go dancin'. I remember thinkin' what would drive a woman to do such a thing. Now I knew. I always did like the water extra warm. Now I didn't know what to do. I decided to take my same hot bath.

The next mornin' I felt so tired. My back hurt. I was so tense all the time, no wonder. Jay was still sleepin'. Good for him. He's a growin' boy. Sula was fryin' bacon. I could hear a tractor. It was gettin' closer. I got up and looked out the window. There was Otto plowin' up my old garden. I threw on some clothes Sula got me. My, that woman sure did have fancy taste!

"Good mornin', Sula. Did you sleep some?"

"Yes Ma'am, I did after all. How about you?"

"I had to take a bath to calm down. I'm a little nervous 'bout today."

"Well, you sure look good. Say, that outfit suits you. It surely does."

"You think so?"

It was a cowboy style brown pants and a pale blue shirt with matchin' pockets on the pants and shirt the opposite of the other. The buttons on the pants and shirt were mother of pearl, Sula said. I looked like I was goin' out ridin' or somethin'. Nothin' could get me on a horse! I'm scared silly of them.

"I see there's a man diggin' up the dirt in your yard. Do you know him?"

"Oh, sure, that's Otto Slatter. He's the man who bought this here place. He's the patriarch of the Slatters. There are a whole ton of them. If you ain't a Dixon, Jackson, or Lawton, then you're a Slatter."

"He sure looks scruffy. He probably hasn't shaved himself in a while either. Why is it men don't think on themselves? Do they think we like lookin' at scraggly faces? Land sakes! Where's my little man?"

"He's still sleepin', but I suspect this here tractor will get him right up! He loves tractors, trucks and anything with wheels."

I went out onto the porch to greet Otto. I just waved to him. I knew he wouldn't get off his tractor. Otto waved his hat and kept on plowin'. It was kinda late to be plantin' though, but maybe he was just waitin' 'til I signed the papers.

After breakfast, Sula, Jay and me started packin' up Granny's room. There was the old wrought iron bed and the oak dresser with a cloudy mirror attached to it. The lace doilies were still in place. The blue flowered hurricane lamp was on one side of the dresser and a matchin' wash basin and pitcher was on the other side. Granny had little bottles of perfume on a glass tray smack dab in the middle. She only bought Estee Lauder. I'd have to say, emptyin' those drawers was the hardest part of all. There were laced slips and bloomers. There were silk stockins, girdles and night gowns galore. One drawer had a few mementos tucked away inside of it, mostly pictures. There were pictures of her, her sister and other siblings, my grandpa and Maw, Orv and me. It shouldn'ta surprised me none but all this got me to cryin'.

I started on the closet. I handed Sula the clothes from the closet, and she packed them. We did this 'til I couldn't take it no more. It was seein' Granny's most favorite dress and purse that got me almost bawlin'. Sula offered to pack things from there. I set out to take down the pictures and gather up the rugs and blankets.

"This here is all you're gonna pack up? Just this here room?"

"Yes Ma'am. Don't want nothin' else."

"You know there's all the kitchenware, furniture in the bedrooms and living room...why, there's a mess of stuff here. You just gonna leave it?"

"I don't want any of it. I already told Otto he could help himself to the garage and the rest of the house, except Granny's things. Otto seemed right grateful. He's gonna make this his summer home. He could use the things I'm leavin'."

"This won't take any time at all. Let's keep packin'. Now where did I put the rest of those boxes?"

"They're right here. Oh...ow... oh my!"

I reached kinda funny like for those boxes and stopped in my tracks. I grabbed my back and rubbed it. I felt somethin' wet on me.

"You all right? Did you hurt yourself, Cinda?"

"I just reached funny is all. I woke up with a sore back. Here are the boxes. I'll be right back."

I went straight for the bathroom. Sure enough, blood. I was spottin'. What was happenin" to me? Maybe I wasn't really pregnant? Or maybe I was miscarryin'? I'd better not tell Sula just yet 'cause we had us a big day.

We nearly finished packin' up Granny's things. It was nice to think on her after a while. I told Sula stories 'bout this item and that one. I felt like I was handlin' treasures, I told her.

"What time is it, Sula?"

"It's about that time. Now look here, me and Jay will go outside and air out these here rugs and blankets. They need it anyway. While we're doin' that, Priscilla won't be any the wiser. You gonna be able to go through with it? Remember Percy is nearby."

"Yes, I think so. I really don't think she's gonna be so bold as to try and find..."

There was a loud knock at the door. I guess the tractor covered up the sound of the car. Sula and Jay grabbed the rugs and blankets and went outside. I went over to the front door and opened it up real slow like.

"Can I help you?"

"Yes, it's me, Priscilla. I came with some papers for you to sign?"

"I didn't know you were Mr. Smith's secretary now."

"Oh, I'm not. Well, not yet. Anyhow, his real secretary was busy with something important that only she could do and so here I am."

"Come in. Have you ever been here before?"

"No! Why, of course not. Why would I?"

"I meant, had you ever been out this way before. You know, to Frog Creek?"

"Oh, maybe once or twice."

"Come on into the kitchen. I got to read these here papers before I sign them. If we're in the kitchen, I can see Jay whilst he plays."

I started readin' the papers or at least pretendin' to read them. They were just copies of everything I signed the other day. Priscilla sure looked dressed up. She had on the brightest dress I ever did see. Her nails were all red and her hair was just as big as before.

"Oh, you have company! Who's the old lady?"

"*Her* name is Sula. She's my relative on my mother's side. She's come to stay with me whilst I get through all these legal matters."

"You know... I just gotta say you look so different. You look real nice.

I heard you're leavin'. Is that right? Slatters bought the place?"

"My, word does travel fast. Yes, that's right. I'm leavin' just as soon as I get my Granny's things packed up. Otto, why, you see him out there, he's anxious to move in."

"You aren't payin' your respects... guess you heard 'bout me and Will too?"

"Yes, I did. You left him? I mean, that day I saw you at the bank... you was plannin' on leavin' him?"

"Yes, I was and yes I did. Are you surprised?"

"It's just that I... well, I thought you were..."

"Lucky?"

"What?"

"I remember that day I left Rondo, at the bank, you said I was lucky to be with Him. Well, that couldn't have been further from the real truth. Do you mind if I visit with Sula 'bout these here papers? I need to discuss somethin' with her. I'll be outside. Make yourself to home."

"Do you mind if I look around?"

"Surely not. Help yourself."

I had to stop m'self from runnin' out the door. That was one cold woman. She was just like the people Granny used to call the livin' dead. Those people already gave up their souls to the devil and now they's just livin' on the earth tryin' to take other souls down with 'em. Sure enough, that's what she was.

I went over to Sula. I grabbed her hands and held on. I was shakin' a bit.

"How you doin'? Is she in there? Is she lookin' around?"

"Yes Ma'am, I think she is."

We walked behind the rugs so we would be outta her way. So she could think we was talkin' 'bout the papers.

"How long we supposed to stay here, Sula?"

"Percy said for us to give her a good while to look around. He said he would tell her exactly where to look whilst they had dinner. Sure hope he did what he was supposed to. Well, let's talk about something or I'll just bust! I wanna go in there and see what she's doin'. I wanna talk some sense into that girl!"

"Do you think you can? Do you think she cares 'bout anyone except herself? If she did have somethin' to do with His death, why, it's just spooky. She's cold, all right. She's like the walkin' dead or was it the livin' dead? My Granny used to talk 'bout it."

"Livin' dead? I don't know nothin' about that, but I haven't been close enough to her to tell if she's past feelin'. But something about this whole mess just doesn't make sense. I shoulda been a detective. Why I can tell if things are sensible or just plain horse …"

"LuCinda? Is that you behind there?"

I peeked from around the rugs, and there she was. Wilford's sister!

"Cassidy? What are you doin' here? You alone?"

"Yes, I am. Don't want anyone to know I'm here. Can I talk to ya? Just for a minute. I can't stay long."

"Yes, sure. I guess that would be all right. It's just that I got someone here from the bank and well, if you can wait just a bit, I'll talk to you."

"Okay. Can I say hello to Jay? I ain't seen him in a while."

"Sure, but Sula will be here watchin' him."

Sula nodded and started right in talkin' to Cassidy. I couldn't imagine why she was here. It sure was my day for things to happen.

Cassidy was kinda funny. She never really partook in the family doings.

She didn't drink. She didn't chase men. She had some boyfriends or so I heard. She was pregnant once that I knew of but never had a baby. I didn't understand that. Of course, they was all drunk when they started in on her and done told her whole past. I guess I never had a quarrel with her, though she did laugh at me when Will was beatin' on me. I heard tell she made a real big joke 'bout me cryin' afterward, sayin' I sure was dumb to be with someone that beat me up. Why, even a dog knew enough to run away. That was her joke.

I went on in the house. I didn't care if Priscilla found what she was lookin' for or not. I felt all warm and sweat was comin' down my face. I found Priscilla in the front room.

"There you go, I signed all the papers. Oh, I forgot to seal up the envelope like Mr. Smith said. It's not that he doesn't trust you, I'm sure. It's just procedures is all."

"You know, LuCinda... you never struck me as the kind a girl who was ... well, how should I say this... smart. You seemed to be happy with your lot in life. But I guess I was wrong. Guess Willie was too, huh?"

So, He musta talked with her 'bout me bein' so dumb. I was just too dumb to figure out what He was up to. I wonder if He told her how fat I was and how I let m'self go? He musta, why else would she go on 'bout how nice I looked now? I ain't lost any weight... well, I don't think so. I wished I could say somethin' to her to just... shut her up!

"Yes, I guess He was wrong 'bout a lot of things. Bye now."

As she waved at me, I could tell she was either the livin' dead or dumber than a post. I sure didn't tell her off like I wanted to. I supposed it would come to me later. Dang it!

I hurried out the side door to find Sula and Jay. Cassidy was still there too. I could hear Otto revvin' up his tractor like it was stuck on somethin', and there was no sign of Percy. Maybe Percy was gonna follow Priscilla back into Rondo before he came out here?

"I'm finished with the papers I needed to sign. The lady from the bank just left."

Sula and me nodded at one another. Sula kept lookin' at me like she had somethin' to say to me. I started talkin' to Cassidy anyhow.

"I'm gonna help Sula get these here rugs and blankets in the house, and I'll be right out. Besides, Jay's probably ready for lunch."

"That's right! My little man is ready for some lunch. Let's go, Jay, help Sula bring in these here rugs. That's the way. Let's go."

I held the door open for Sula, so I could look back on Cassidy. She seemed quiet, not all riled up none.

"What do you think, Sula? Should I talk to her? I just don't know why she's here."

"I think she has something to tell you that you need to hear."

"Did she say somethin'?"

"No, but I could tell that something is weighin' her down. I think you can talk to her, but what do you think?"

"Huh? Oh, I don't know. There's so much is happenin' to me just now. I feel so warm and my back is ailin' me. I'll just talk to her for a little bit. I don't want to give her the wrong idea, like I care 'bout His family and such. I just want a clean break. That's what I'll do."

Now that I had me a plan, I didn't feel quite so scared 'bout talkin' to Cassidy. I wanted to start the talkin'.

"I guess I kept you waitin' long enough and I don't want to keep you any longer. I am sorry that you lost your brother. But that's all. I know how it feels to lose a brother, so I guess I could feel some for that. I expect you know that I left Wilford. It seems like the whole town knows I left, but the whole town sure don't know why. What is it you want to talk to me 'bout?"

"I wanted to let you know that he took it real hard when you left."

"Who did?"

"Will. Yep, he took it real hard."

"Can't imagine how hard He took it when He was out cattin' 'round on the very day I left."

"I'm talkin' 'bout Saturday, the day after you left. He come over to the house and said you left. You took some things and you weren't around, and he said you finally left."

"What?"

I started to feel uneasy. I really didn't know if I believed her. I started walkin' 'round the yard to hide my uneasiness. I didn't want her to think I cared one bit. Which, of course, I didn't... but I wanted her to know so.

"Yep, he came over to the house in the mornin' and later on in the day. At first I don't think he believed you were gone. By that afternoon and on into the evenin' he knew. He said you musta left 'cause you would sure get a beatin' if you left the house and didn't tell him or come back right away. By nighttime he was even on to tears. That's when I let him have it."

"You did what?"

"I let him have it. I laughed at him so bad— whoo. Feel bad 'bout it now, since he's dead. But at the time, I sure had one on him. I told him he was left by a kid, and she took your kid with her. Anyway, I sure let him have it. Then he got real quiet. He said he thought he was set for life. Yep, that's what he said. Set for life."

"Set for life?"

What? He thought that he was livin' life? Beatin' me. Keepin' me down. He was all right with that? Somehow He thought He was set for life?

"Sure enough. He needed to have somethin' he could control. Be better than. He wasn't doin' nothin'. He had big plans to go to school and be somethin'. Instead he ended up workin' like the rest of those fools. Here he was just like everybody else. Didn't you know that? Anyhow, he thought you loved him."

"Well, Cassidy, it's like you said, even dogs know when to run."

"Whoo, now you tellin' me somethin', you sure enough are! Heh-heh. That's a good one."

"You know, I never did understand that way you all had of bein' so mean. Probably could be tellin' the truth once and a while, but doin' it so mean. I just never did get it."

"Now that's what Maw said. That's why I don't want her to know that I'm here. I got enough grief in my own life without this too. She said you were never really one of us. If you were, you woulda never run off with Jay. If you were one of us, you woulda run off but left Jay. You know, so's you could come back. Well, that's her."

"What about you? Is that all you wanted to tell me?"

"That'a pretty much all I wanted to say. I felt like I had to say that, but now I gotta be true to my brother. You know, like you said. It's too bad he went out drinkin' that Friday night. He felt bad but at the same time he wanted to go the bars, sayin' he was gonna have a good time. After all, it had been a whole week after you had done left. Yeah, the whole family went 'cept me. The next day, no one knew where he was. They all split up after they went to Thirsty Creek. I think Trey, Shiloh, Juniors and Hank went to the Slatter's for more to drink. They were with Will for a while, but he had his sights on some young thing, they said."

That was funny, Priscilla wasn't young. Why, she was older than Will, and He was way older than me. This didn't make sense.

"I hope you told this all to the police, Cassidy. So's they can know the truth and maybe find out what happened."

"Oh, yeah, I did. I told them everything. Maw sure was mad, but I didn't care any. Next thing you know, the Slatter's found him just layin' there. I better get on home before Maw starts wonderin' where I am. I can take her badgerin' for a little while; then it gets right tiresome. I hope to move out again, on my own. It's time for me to move on. I never did fit in with things at home. I guess you know that."

I didn't respond. I felt like we were done. I was done. She said her goodbyes and left the way she came. Past the outhouse, through the woods on the same path I saw Him go down so many times before.

I went inside to find Sula and Jay eatin' lunch. Percy was there too. My, people came and went now, and I didn't even know it. There was a time when I would try to hear everything 'round me. I didn't want Him comin' home without me knowin'. It wasn't like I could do anything 'bout it. It's just that I wanted to know what might be comin'.

"You all right? I told Percy about her wantin' to talk to you. Was I right, did she need to ease her mind?"

"I don't know, Sula. I found some things out, I guess. They were all together like I suspected. They were drinkin' down by Thirsty Creek. Land sakes, it's hot in here... Anyhow, she said somethin' that just doesn't make sense. She said that Will had His sights on some young thing... now, from the way I see it, Priscilla ain't young. I wonder if Priscilla was there. What do you think, Percy? Sula! Ooh, I got such pain in my stomach... Sula?"

# CHAPTER 7
## Pharaoh's Comin'

"Where am I?"

I was awake. My stomach hurt. I couldn't move either. I was so thirsty. I looked around and saw Sula sleepin'.

"Sula?"

"Where am I? What happened? Where's Jay?"

"Sula?"

"Cinda! You're awake! Oh, praise be. Praise be. Girl, how you feelin'? You in much pain? Want me to get the doctor?"

"What happened? I was sittin' at the table, talkin' to you and I don't remember after that... where's Jay?"

"Don't worry about him any. Percy is takin' good care of him. They are in the waitin' room watchin' TV. You're in the hospital, Cinda. Child, you lost the baby and about lost your own life. Why, if Percy wasn't there, I woulda been hard pressed to get you here by myself. You lost a lot of blood and... why... I'll let the doctor tell you the rest. Are you awake?"

"Sula? It's all my fault... I took a hot bath, Sula. God forgive me... I'm so tired."

"Cinda? You ain't makin' sense, girl. You go on a rest. I'm here..."

******

"Can I have some water?"

"Cinda? It's Mr. Pervis. I'm here. Do you want some water?"

"Where's Sula?

"She and Jay haven't come in yet today. I got here as soon as I heard. Here's some water."

My head was so fuzzy. It hurt to sit up. It was Mr. Pervis!

"Thank you for the water. I'm sorry but I just can't have you lookin' at me, Mr. Pervis. I feel so ashamed. I can't explain... please..."

"What do you have to feel ashamed of? Cinda, you were living your life the very best you could. The only problem was Wilford wasn't worthy of it. Do you hear? I need you to know..."

******

"Ow, that hurts!"

"You're awake, good! I'm Nurse Patsy. I have to check on you and see how you're doing. I'm sorry to massage on your stomach like this, but I have to see how things are healing up inside. You stopped bleeding, that's a good sign. Are you hungry?"

"No, just thirsty. Is anyone here? Sula?"

"Yes, Sula is here with your son, Jay. I sent them out of the room while I checked on you. It's time we tried to get you up and washed up. I'll need you to help now. Are you ready?"

"Yes, Ma'am. I'll try. Am I gonna sleep like this all day? What day is it?"

"Why it's May twenty-seventh, and it's a beautiful day outside. You were brought in here two days ago. You're doing just fine, I'd say. The doctor will be in shortly. He can tell you what happened. You know you lost the baby, right?"

"Yes, I know that. I mean, I kinda figured that out."

"Ready, on the count of three we're gonna stand… one, two, three!"

I pulled m'self up, and it felt like my stomach was gonna fall out from beneath me. The pain was almost more than I could bear. I felt so dizzy. She sure was rushin' me.

"You all right? Keep looking straight ahead. I got you. You made it to the chair, ready to try to make it to the bathroom?"

"Yes, I can. As long as we move slowly, I think I can do it."

"If you can make it that far, why, we're going right into the shower. There's a chair inside. You'll feel much better. I'll be with you the entire time. Okay?"

"Yes, I'm okay. A shower would feel good. I have all this here on me... bandages?"

"Yes, only a small incision, considering... You're lucky!"

"I am?"

"Yes, you are. The doctor had to make sure all the baby passed through. You weren't far along, thank goodness. Oh, I'm sorry ... I mean ..."

"It's all right. This here baby was not planned on."

"I see."

I couldn't talk 'bout it no more. If that's what it took, then so be it. I wondered what happened. *Lord, if'n I caused this, then I was truly sorry for the baby's sake only*. I wished I knew if I done it.

The shower did feel good. I felt better to be sure. Sula and Jay came in. Jay was so happy to see me!

"Mama, I see you. I play with Sula and Percy. I watch TV. Can I hold you?"

"Now, Jay, remember what I told you. Your Mama's tummy is right sore. Now be gentle like Sula said."

"Of course you can! Come up here on this old bed."

I cuddled right up with Jay. It sure felt good.

"I expect you're tired. I won't keep Jay here long. Mr. Pervis will look after him whilst you and I visit."

"Mr. Pervis is still here?"

"Yes, he is. He is right concerned about you. He feels bad about the baby and all. He thinks he put too much stress on you. Having Priscilla come out, leaving when he did..."

"It's not his fault, Sula. It's mine. I took a hot bath. I ... I... caused this here to happen."

"What?"

I started cryin' and couldn't stop. Sula grabbed Jay and set him in her chair.

"Now listen here. I don't know exactly what happened, Cinda. But this here wasn't meant to be. The Lord knew it."

"No, I took a hot bath. I didn't want this baby, you know that! I tried to...well I didn't know if it would do anything but I just didn't care. Do you know what I mean?"

"I think I do. So you think 'cause you acted on some old foolish women's tale about how to stop from bein' pregnant, that's why you lost the baby?"

I couldn't talk. I kept my face buried in my hands. I felt so ashamed. I only nodded yes.

"Oh, there, there, child… just let it out. Go on ahead and have it out. Cinda, those are just tales. There ain't any proof in all that! I heard those same things as a young girl. You think you're the only woman who's thought on these things? You listen to Sula now. Do you think you are the only woman who's felt unprepared to be a mother? Especially havin' a baby for some no account man who ain't got the common sense to appreciate what he already has? Think again, girl! Why, it's a complicated thing bein' a woman, let alone a wife and a mother. What you think you did, you did outta fear and I suspect anger."

"Sula, what I tried to do was wrong!"

"Now, I ain't said nothin' about it not bein' right! A little life, just beginnin', why it's innocent and don't know no better. It can't protect itself. It relies on the mama *and* the *daddy*! Why, I'll just let that be between you and God, you hear? As for me, God loves us, Cinda, and He don't need to use no innocent life to punish one person one way or another. This baby ... it just weren't meant to be. No, sir!"

Sula started cryin' right there. *Oh, dear Lord, how could I be so careless?*

"Oh... Sula. I didn't think on you not bein' able to have children...I am so sorry. I wouldn't ever try to hurt you outright like that...I..."

"Don't say on. It's all right. I'm feelin' with ya is all. Women do that for one another— that's a God given right."

We held on to one another and cried. I hadn't done that with Sula before. It felt like I was takin' a shower all over again.

"But, Cinda, this kinda thing will break you...if you let it, that is. Life is complicated. It's gonna take an entire lifetime to break free of all this, don't try to sum it all up in one breath. You hear? Don't try to bring it down to one act or one marriage. The understandin' will come and so will the healin'. All this here involves the acts of so many people makin' lots of choices. Doin' the best they can, well... some people that is. Cinda, all this here will pass, and you'll be stronger in the end. But the wrestle, my girl, is gonna lie with you. The understandin' and the healin's gonna come from inside of you, and that's gonna take a lifetime."

"I trust that you know what you're talkin' 'bout, Sula. I surely do."

"Good morning, ladies! Is it safe to come in?"

"Sure enough. Come in. We are just havin' girl talk is all. Come on in."

"How you feeling, LuCinda? Are you better?"

"Yes, Percy, I am feelin' much better. I want to thank you for helpin' me, and for all you done for Sula and Jay too. Sorry to give everyone such a scare."

"I was scared, but Sula kept me in line. I just followed her orders. Why, do you know she's like a drill sergeant?"

"How you go on. So you ready to go to lunch?"

"Yes Ma'am, I am. Come on, Jay. Percy is going to hold up to his promise and show you how to drive."

"But wait, where you all goin'? What happened to... you know who?"

"That man is just plain wild. Now, you just rest. Things are still sortin' themselves out. Be back later. We're just goin' to the diner. Want something?"

"Oh, I... no I better not. I'm eating liquid foods and some mush."

"Oh, well, okay. I'm gonna have me a hamburger. Enjoy your mush!"

******

"See, I told you she was in here! Didn't I tell you? I heard she nearly died. She was so weak from all the stress she was under."

"Really. My goodness."

I woke up to some soft voices. I looked around, but I didn't see anyone. Nurse Patsy said I wouldn't sleep all day, but that's what I was doin' and now I was hearin' things. Land sakes, what were they givin' me for the pain?

"Oh, are you awake? Can we come in?"

It was Mrs. Parsons and her sister! Why, how did they get in here?

"Uh... I suppose it would be all right... I just woke up. I must look a sight."

"Oh, no, not really, for what you been through, you look good. Doesn't she, Nellie?"

"Why sure enough, Thelma, she does."

"We are so sorry to hear about all of your troubles. You must forgive us— you really must. We didn't know about your husband and all."

At least Thelma was trying to say she was sorry. What did it matter, anyhow? I just couldn't muster up the words, though.

"All my troubles? Sorry for what, exactly?"

"Oh, Cinda or LuCinda, why, when I recognized you, why, I really didn't mean to cause this kinda trouble. I just called my brother and well, one thing led to another and you were brought into jail. Why, I didn't know... I am sorry."

"Is your brother with the Rondo Police Department?"

"Why yes, how did you know?"

"Just a guess."

"I told my brother that I seen someone from out our way and he said who, and well... you know the rest."

"Yes, I do."

"I'm sorry they had to tell you that your husband... well, ex-husband now... why, that he was dead. I had no idea!"

I guess Nellie had been out of the limelight long enough.

"Now Thelma, don't go thinking on yourself. Why, this poor child has been through hell. Sorry to have to use such language, but it's true. Sure is. I heard he beat you. Is that true?"

"Yes, He did."

"And you were running away to save your son and yourself. My, I can't imagine! Now look at you. Why, you're as pale as that sheet."

Nellie took out a handkerchief from her purse and dabbed at her eye. I can't say that I saw a tear though. I nodded and decided not to talk. It seemed like they was doin' all the talkin' anyway. I didn't think they'd miss me.

"Oh, Nellie, you are right. She is pale. You poor thing."

"I'm back and I... oh. You got visitors."

Sula looked surprised. I didn't think I'd seen her look surprised before. Her eyes narrowed up, and she took right over.

"Mrs. Parsons, and yes, well, you'll have to excuse us now. It's time for Cinda to have some broth."

I don't even think Nellie and Thelma knew they were bein' thrown out.

"Thanks for the visit. I'm sure it really helped. I'm sure there are other people in this here hospital for you to cheer up. Bye now."

"How did they get in here?"

"That's what I was wonderin'. Do you think they know 'bout me?"

"No, I don't think so. I threatened the hospital administrator just a bit when we got here. I said I would sue if anyone found out about why you were here. It was your business, and it bess' be kept that way! Besides, this here is still all under police business and they mighta had some clout too."

"Before you start in, Percy has Jay. They went on back to the house to get it ready for you to come home."

"You think I'll be able to get out? That would be nice, but I ain't even seen a doctor yet and..."

"Well, well, speak of the doctor. Here he is. Out late?"

Sula was in a mood!

"No, actually I just delivered a baby."

"You look good for just givin' birth."

"Ha-ha. That's good. My name is Dr. Wilkins, and you must be this young girl's... sister?"

"Why, yes, I am. Her older sister, if you must know. Now how about tellin' us when we can bring her home."

"The nurses tell me you've been up walking, just a bit. You're trying to sit up most of the time. But they tell me that you're still pretty tired, is that right?"

"Yes sir, I am awfully tired. I do feel better though."

"Let's have a look. Mind if she stays here?"

"No, I don't mind."

Sula rolled her eyes and sat down on the chair beside me.

"You were very lucky. The baby wasn't growing in the right place. That's why... the pregnancy ended. You were not very far along, and that's why you're lucky. You lost a fair amount of blood, which is why you're so tired. You have any questions?"

"Why did it end? I mean, why wasn't it growin' right? Could this... could I have..."

The words just wouldn't come. I wanted to plain flat-out ask if a warm bath coulda caused all this to come to an end, but I couldn't say it. Sula piped up.

"She wants to know if there is anything that could have caused this by her doin' something or was it all inside. You know a mother's guilt?"

"Oh, I see. Well, no, there's nothing that you could have done to cause the baby from starting to grow in the wrong place. It all had to do with your insides. Now, I read about some women in your situation. It's entirely possible that some past infections may have lead to scarring. Now, I don't have all that fancy equipment here, mind you. But your case could be similar to others I have read about."

"You said past infections? I don't recall havin' any infections. Wouldn't I know 'bout those?"

"Yes and no. It depends upon the type of infection and where it came from."

"Is it possible that these infections could come from ...?"

I looked at Sula. I knew she would know how to ask. I heard 'bout women gettin' sick after their husbands went off with some loose woman.

"What I mean, Dr. Wilkins is. . .could a woman get one of these infections from a man, if He was seein' other women?"

"Oh, yes, most certainly. I can't say for certain that this is the case for you. Now, Mrs. Dixon, I do have to tell you one more thing. . . I'm late as it is. . . uh; having more children might not be possible. I am sorry."

"Thank you for sayin' so, but I have Jay. Right now, that's all I want."

"I think we can have you out of here in a few more days..."

"A few more days! Why, she ain't doin' nothin' but layin' here as it is. The food is so bland, why, no wonder her blood is poor. She needs real food. And those pills you all are givin' her for pain is just plain makin' her sleepy. If I take her home, I'll make sure she eats and rests. Shoot! If she gets a fever or starts bleedin' I'll bring her back to the hospital. This girl has been through enough. She needs to be around people who love her.

Why, just today some nosy busybodies come in here to visit and woke her up. Now just you think on that!"

Sula was standin' there with her hands on her hips and lookin' like she was ready for round number two. I think Dr. Wilkins gave in because he was late.

On our way home, Sula wanted to stop and pick up a few things at the drug store.

"Now I know I sounded like a know-it-all back there with Dr. Wilkins, but I'm gonna stop here and get some supplies. I don't wanna look like no fool and have you get sick. Sit tight. Be right back."

As I sat in the car, I couldn't help but think on my situation. Could He have brought home an infection like Dr. Wilkins was talkin' 'bout? It sure wouldn't surprise me none. Not so much on Him but on me. Why, the sacrifices I was makin' to get free were startin' to mount up. It was like things were just hedgin' up my way on purpose. Now, Sula said that God didn't punish like that. If it wasn't God, then who was it? Mr. Pervis talked some 'bout people livin' their lives and how then, 'cause of other people's choices, they suffer. It was true; Will was just an evil man, maybe even the livin' dead. He surely had made my life a livin' hell. There is no plainer, truer word for it, though it wasn't so ladylike to say. Was this here a part of life that I had to endure 'cause of Will? 'Cause I trusted Him? I weren't but a kid m'self, so was it my doin'? Maw sure weren't there for me, always gone drinkin'. Granny blamed Maw for my troubles. I guess it was like Sula said, complicated. And it was gonna take me a lifetime to sort it all out and get through it. Sula was for sure 'bout one thing— this here was startin' to break me.

There came Sula totin' a big ol' bag.

"I got us a regular doctor's office in that bag! Now, let's get you home. Well, home for now."

The drive to Frog Creek took a long time. I really was seein' my life pass before my eyes. There was my road, my tree and the bushes I hid some clothes in. It was funny how I was on the road but not. Everything had changed. I hadn't had no word 'bout Granny. I got a real ache in my chest just then. I started cryin'.

"Cinda, you thinkin' about things? There sure is enough to think on. Cinda, when we get back, why, I'll start supper. You got to keep your strength up. Percy threatened to cook without us. I called from the hospital. Mr. Pervis is there too. I told them I was bringin' you home. Now, I told Mr. Pervis and Percy to take it easy on what they tell you. It's all done now, Cinda. You are a free woman. Do you hear? It's gonna be all right in time. It's gonna take time."

"Yes, I figured that out not too long ago. I sure was foolish thinkin' that runnin' away from here was the answer. I thought everything would be better by leavin'."

"Oh, it wasn't foolish, Cinda. It was just the first step, and it was a big one. It took courage to do what you did. Now it's up to you to make it better."

"Yes, Ma'am."

I didn't agree with what I said. I just didn't know how things could get better. How? Where did I begin? There was still Granny. If'n I lost her too, why, that would just do me in. I didn't know how I could stand it.

We pulled up to the homestead. I was so anxious to see Jay, Percy and Mr. Pervis. Sula was dotin' on me.

"Don't move so fast. Don't let Jay jump on ya. Watch your step. Land sakes, I think those men cooked! Smell that? Oh

Lord, let it be something edible. You got to have meat and vegetables."

"Welcome home, mommy!"

"I taught him how to say that, LuCinda."

"Thank you, Percy. Come here, Jay! Come on and hold me."

I held him so tight. He started squirmin' though, and Sula was right there.

"Now Jay, remember what I said, no roughhousin', son. No sir. You go on and roughhouse with Percy."

"Hello, Mr. Pervis. It's good to see you."

"You too, LuCinda. You are looking much better than when I saw you last. I'm sure Sula will have you healthy in no time. I suspect she told you the good news?"

"Yes, well, she told me that I was a free woman. Is that right? I'm just plain LuCinda Jackson if I want?"

"Yes, uh... you know, Jay is still a Dixon, LuCinda. There's plenty of time to decide about that."

"Percy, you have outdone yourself! I didn't know you could cook. My, my, pork chops, sweet potatoes and corn mush. Why, I couldn't have done better myself. Let's see how it tastes. Come on, you all. Let's eat!"

Sula was right; the food at the hospital was bland. The food Percy made tasted real even though it was a might overdone. I think it was good to be back there. I hadn't had such a fun meal since I was... well, since I was at Sula's. Maybe there could be happy times that didn't call for me to think so far back to my childhood times with Granny. I sure hope so.

After dinner, Percy left and said he had "one more item" to tend to. Sure couldn't imagine what was left.

"Now, Mr. Pervis, when am I goin' to hear about Priscilla? What has happened? I really think I'm strong enough to handle the truth."

"Let me get Jay to bed before we get to talkin' on all that. LuCinda, here, take this vitamin. Percy's chops were as dry as skillet toast. The sweet potatoes were all right but that corn mush. Whoo! You know his heart is in the right place. I sure wish I had someone to hitch him up with. He'd be a fair husband. And while we're at it, let's get you all washed up, change those bandages and then we can see about talkin'."

"Why, Nurse Sula, I do believe you know what's best. Come on, Jay."

"Mr. Pervis, don't think I forgot about you. Why don't you make yourself useful and clean up this here kitchen. I can only imagine what that stove looks like after Percy cooked this here meal."

"Yes, Sula. I will make myself useful. As you say, so it shall be, my lady."

"Oooh, Mr. Pervis. You do know how to talk to a lady!"

Jay fell asleep so fast. I declare he seemed like he was growin' up. He seemed to be doin' all right after all this, at least right then. Time was gonna come when he'd have so many questions. I couldn't think on it then.

"Cinda, why don't we sit outside? It's nice enough, and we can hear Jay from out there. Come on, Mr. Pervis, you too. The outside air will do us all some good."

"Sula, you know this is the best part of the day. Have I ever told you how much I like the evenin' time? Well, I do."

I took a deep breath in and looked up to the sky. Mr. Pervis brought out some chairs for us to sit on. He sure was takin' all this in stride, I had to say. He didn't complain at all. I couldn't imagine his other cases were like this one.

"Mr. Pervis, are you glad this case here is nearly over?"

"Oh, yes, I am. It's been very interesting and satisfying. My client's life has been improved significantly in this case. My man Percy has outdone himself, and he shows real promise. I do owe a great deal of thanks to you two ladies as well. Yes, LuCinda, I am glad. Justice will be served in some small measure, but it can never be completely satisfied. I have come to understand this more and more. Nothing can ever bring back what was lost, provided it was good, mind you. I am convinced that justice can never be served in this lifetime. It takes an act of God to make it right. I help to a small degree. Now, if you are ready, we can discuss what has transpired thus far."

"Oh, yes, sir. I am ready to hear it all. Now that I'm a free woman, it will set better with me."

"Priscilla and Percy went to dinner, and Percy let a few things slip out. He acted like he really didn't care about the entire affair since he was leaving town soon anyway. So to remind you, the key items were Wilford's secret hiding spot, the Dew Drop Inn and also the watch. I must say, Priscilla took the bait as if, well, as if she was waiting for it all along. She, as we expected, said she had seen Wilford out before, but never really paid any attention to him. However, she seemed very interested in the hiding spot. She asked a lot of questions of Percy. She didn't seem to be concerned how Percy got his information.

"The day Priscilla brought out the copies from Mr. Smith, he followed her every step. He saw her very clearly pry open the floorboard. She put her hands inside and felt around. She pulled up a few items, but Percy couldn't make out what they were. Later that same day, Mr. Clement sent some men over to her home and requested that she come in for questioning. Initially, she denied any knowledge of Wilford Dixon. However, during the interview, Mr. Clement showed her the engraved watch, which he explained was in your possession the entire time and well... at that point, she broke down crying. So far, she denies any wrongdoing... ah; I mean to say that she denies killing Wilford.

"This evening Percy was needed to clarify his role in the case. He's at the jail right now, hopefully making it even clearer that you were never involved."

"Well, I'll be! We still don't know what happened after all this? Now, that doesn't seem right! If she wasn't involved, then why did she come out here and help herself to the goods? Well, she thought there were goods to be had, anyway. What do you think, Cinda? You all right to talk about it?"

"Is she in jail?"

"Yes, LuCinda, she's being held there until she cooperates. I see I didn't explain it very well. You see, she's not talking. She denies killing Wilford and has sought a lawyer. She has admitted to being with Wilford on a Friday night. There is enough evidence to show that they were regulars on Friday night at the Kat Club and Sharky's. She claims that the last time she saw Wilford, he was alive and laughing."

"Laughin'?"

"Yes, that's what she claims."

"Did she say where they were? Were they at Thirsty Creek?"

"No, she's not saying."

There was somethin' about Priscilla's story that struck me, like lightenin'.

"Didn't Mr. Clement say that Will was lyin' on his back, and it looked like He was diggin' his heels in?"

"Yes, and he also had bruised ribs, a swollen uvula and he was highly intoxicated. What is it? What are you thinking about, Cinda?"

"It's just when she said He was laughin'. I just got an

image in my mind... of Him lyin' there and laughin' at her. I don't know. He laughed at me so many times. I mean, not just havin' fun... no sir, I mean laughin' at me to scorn. Like I was some kinda fool or somethin'. He would laugh at what I said. He would laugh at what I thought, deep thoughts too. He would laugh when I would cry. I guess I believe her. Don't know why, but I believe her."

"Both of you ladies are right about this turn of events not making any sense. Frankly, I am..."

"Did Percy ever say that she and Him were at the Dew Drop Inn?"

"Excuse me, what? Who?"

"You said that there was enough evidence to show that they were together at Sharky's and The Kat Club, but what about the Dew Drop Inn?"

"Uh... no. Neither the night clerk or the day clerk recognized Priscilla as a customer at the Dew Drop Inn."

"Some things are makin' sense to me..."

"Cinda, you think he was playin' on Priscilla? Don't you?"

"Yes, I do, Sula. In fact, I think it was with Daisy Lawton. That's who He was messin' with before. You know, a leopard sure don't change his spots none. See, when Wilford and I was first courtin', why, He'd bring me down to Thirsty Creek. In time He asked me for a picture of m'self and everything. I was such a fool. Anyhow, I think ol' Wilford was settin' His sights on her. That would explain Cassidy talkin' 'bout His lookin' on some young thing. Shoot, she's my age! Poor girl. I wonder if ol' Priscilla got to wonderin' 'bout the Dew Drop Inn. See, I told her that m'self. I told her that He went there. I didn't know it was a motel at the time when I said it."

"Think on that, Mr. Pervis. A woman's scorn, they say.

Why, for all we know, Priscilla caught Wilford in a lie. Sure enough. Why, what about that picture they say is around somewhere? I think Cinda's tellin' you right."

With both Sula and I thinkin' on this, why, Mr. Pervis didn't know what to do. We were both just lookin' at him. Finally, he got up.

"Let me see if I can talk to Mr. Clement and Percy. I'll go inside and call down to the police station right now."

"Cinda?"

"Yes, Sula?"

"I think you are a right smart girl. I truly do. You see people as they are, too. Just like me."

"I don't know 'bout that, Sula. I just know how some folks are 'round here. They're plain, uncomplicated, and think this is all there is. I've been thinkin' on what Cassidy said... tellin' me 'bout Wilford sayin' 'He was set for life.' He thought this here was all there is. Drinkin' with His kin, playin' round and laughin'. Somehow, He thought I would just go on along with His idea of life. He never even knew what was inside of me. He never knew how Granny set my sights higher than this life. I never woulda stayed, Sula. If it wasn't this time, it woulda been later."

"I think you tellin' it like it really is, Cinda. You feelin' all right about this here? I mean, with Priscilla and now maybe this here Daisy Lawton?"

"I do feel bad. I feel bad for them. I can't say that I feel bad that He's dead, though."

I looked up to the sky. How many times did I look up for help? The sky was orange and deep purple. How many bruises did I have that looked the same color of purple? The hills were dark, filled with shadows, just like my past. The breeze was barely there, and it was just how I felt: barely there.

I could smell the earth though, and it smelled good. I looked to where Otto Slatter had plowed up my garden. A funny thing 'bout gardenin', to get the earth all ready to grow, like it was meant to, you had to expose all the dirt underneath. It needs to be dug right up and left vulnerable and bare. I surely knew how the earth felt, 'cause I felt bare. Everything about me was out in the open for all to see. I couldn't say that it felt good. I couldn't say that bein' in a corner felt good, either.

Maybe that's what happened to the children of Israel. Everything had to be turned over. Some folks made it and went on with Moses. Others, why, I bet they lamented over their lives. Should they stay on or face uncertainty? How did they go on? How did I?

"Cinda? I can tell you're thinkin'. There is a lot to think on. Why, you are so young and got so much life ahead of you and yet you have gone through so much. You gotta right to be tired. I hope you remember that only you can make this all here better now. I mean for you. Jay too, 'til he's grown and then it will be his time. You got people who care for you, Cinda. Remember that."

How did she do that? I guess I was so easy to read by bein' all exposed, I mean. I think I like a little cover.

******

The phone rang early the next mornin'. I heard Sula answer it right off. Jay was still sleepin' and I was still so tired. Thank goodness I didn't dream 'bout gettin away. Sula came into the back room. She looked awful sad.

"Cinda? You wake, girl. There's someone on the phone for you from the nursing home. It ain't good news, Cinda."

I got an ache right in the pit of my stomach, and it traveled on up to my chest.

"This is Cinda, is it my Granny?"

The voice on the other end sounded carin' enough, but she was obviously doin' her job.

"I'm sorry to tell you that your grandmother passed away this morning. Her sister asked me to call you because she's too choked up to talk."

"Did she go peaceful like?"

"Oh, yes. We all commented on how peaceful and well... if you don't mind my saying so, content... she always looked peaceful and content."

"Yes, she did look like that when I last saw her. Did she ever wake up?"

"Yes, while one of the nurses was offering her some sips of water the day before, she was reported to have said that she was tired. That was all she said."

"She said she was tired?"

"I'm sorry, yes, that's all she said."

"Oh, I'm not sad 'bout what she said. She's got a right to be tired. Thank you for the call. Could you tell Mercy that I will call her 'bout the arrangements later?"

"Yes, I would be happy to do that for you."

After I hung up the phone, I wanted to cry, I truly did, but the tears wouldn't come. I was in shock, I guess. It seems like I can cry up a storm 'bout most things, but just then, I couldn't. If'n shock was a cushion for what was to come, then I was glad 'bout bein' in shock.

Sula tried to offer condolences and pay her respects, but I was kinda numb. Maybe I was tired too. I was just plain tired of all of that mess. I was tired of runnin', hidin' and pretendin'. Granny was at rest now, but I felt kinda mad. I was mad that she was taken away from me just when I was free. How could that be? Why, she and I could have gone places if we wanted to. We coulda been together like was when I was a child, only now I could have cared for her and helped her. Why now? Why now, when I was nearly free?

"Cinda? I see you need some time. I'll go on and get Jay. Breakfast is ready."

"Yes'm. I'll be right there. I just need a few minutes is all."

I went to the back bedroom. In my mind, it was not her room anymore. Why, I had made plans 'bout the next house we would get. It would be Granny, Jay and me. Why, there would even be a spare room for Sula to come visit. And if Mercy's health held up she could come and stay too. Now... the room seemed strange with all of her things put away. I longed for her smell. I needed somethin' of hers. I looked at the boxes all 'round me. I tore open one of the boxes and then another.

"It's in here somewhere. I know it is. *Please.*"

"Cinda, you all right, girl? I heard some bangin'. What do ya need? Let me help."

"My Granny's yellow hair pin bowl. Do you remember it? Have you seen it?"

"I'll look here, in this box."

I felt so desperate. I needed somethin' to hold on to, somethin' of hers.

"Here it is! Here is the yellow bowl right here."

"Thank you, Sula. I just need to hold onto it for a while."

"Go on, I understand. It helps with the connectin'. I do remember that feelin'."

The tears came easy while I held Granny's yellow bowl, it meant the world to me. I could hold onto the memories another day, right now I needed somethin' real; somethin' that was hers.

"Cinda, maybe this isn't the time, but it is not a coincidence this here is all goin' on right now in your life. When you want to talk, I'll be here. I'll go on back to Jay now. Mr. Pervis was here early this mornin' and went back into town. I suspect he'll be back soon. Go on and take your time."

Oh, I knew it was no coincidence. Why, it was just another thing hedgin' up my way. This was another obstacle for me to get through. It was more pain, sufferin' and sacrificin' that I had to make 'cause I was such a fool! Right then I'd gladly make bricks without straw.

******

I stood over the gravesite. Granny didn't have much say in her final restin' spot. My grandfather was already buried in the Rondo Memorial Gardens Cemetery. Naturally, she wanted to be next to him, and I think she woulda approved of her final restin' place. It was on a gentle rise outside of town with a big old creek runnin' along side of it. There were trees all around, lookin' so noble, just like Granny. It was a good place even if it was in Rondo.

"Sula, didn't you think the funeral was nice?"

"Yes, I surely did. It was a nice service, too. I think it reached out to all folks whatever they believed. It was right nice. The preacher too, why, he was from her own hometown! Now, that was proper. She looked so peaceful and dignified. I would have been proud to know her."

"There's no doubt she woulda loved you too, Sula. Jay was well behaved too. He sure is growin'. Granny would be proud to see him all gentleman-like. He is bein' so brave right now."

"I gotta tell you, Cinda, I do believe she got a chance to see her send off. I think she is right proud."

The funeral was right pretty. There were so many flowers! Why, someone even wanted to pay for a real horse-drawn carriage for my Granny! Mercy couldn't come; her health had taken a turn for the worse. She stayed to home and helped me plan things over the phone.

"I am sorry 'bout Mercy, though. I know it pained her somethin' terrible not to be here."

"Now don't go worryin' about her. They were sisters. She's got her bond with her. I think Mercy was ready to see her sister leave. She didn't want her sufferin' any more. That's how I felt about Robert Cantrell. I didn't want him sufferin' either. That's how you feel when you love someone, Cinda. Love opens a door, wider than this here patch of scenery we're lookin' on, pretty as it is. It runs free, especially at times like this here."

I knew Sula was tryin' to tell me somethin'. I just didn't feel strong enough to hear yet. I missed Granny. I felt cheated outta somethin' that coulda been wonderful. A happiness that I coulda known but was taken from me just like everything else was. I looked for Jay just then.

Mr. Pervis was playin' with Jay. Percy too. Why, they had been so kind to me. They were stickin' with me all this time when there was no need to. The case was over, except for the trial. Sula was stickin' with me too. Shoot, my own Mama never stuck by me through anything and here Sula wasn't even kin. I felt happy just then and that was strange. How could I feel happy one minute and feel like dyin' the next? Sula thought it was the hormones.

"I say it's time to head on back to the house. There will be people droppin' in to pay their respects. Cinda, you ready, girl?"

"Yes Ma'am, I am ready."

"I think we got us a mess a food that will last for weeks. I hope these folks are hungry. People just kept droppin' food off. Why, I ran outta room in the refrigerator. It was nice of Otto to rig up a coolin' device for us. I sure hope he didn't slip any shine in on me whilst I wasn't lookin'!"

Folks came by the rest of the day. Sula had set up tables and chairs inside and out of the house. Percy got the chairs from the church, and Otto donated a bunch of sawhorses and wood for tables. Sula was about to run herself ragged with all the fussin' she did over the tablecloths. They were made outta sheets, but they looked real fine. It was a beautiful day! I expect the sunshine and warm breeze was for Granny. Sula said it was Granny. Maybe if I wasn't so mad I woulda felt that way too.

Even though I was feelin' mad, I kept m'self outside. I needed the space. It got to feelin' tight in the old house. There were a lot of people millin' around. There was someone from each of the families 'round the area. The Jacksons, Lawtons, Slatters, Gilmantons, Gilmans, Pettibones, people from Rondo, people I didn't remember and even the Dixons. I declare that gave me a fright to see the Dixons there. They were actin' all carin'. Shoot, all they ever did was keep me away from my kin. All they did was ... why, the more I thought on them, the madder I got!

"LuCinda, can I talk with you for a moment?"

"Shiloh? Why, I never expected to see you here! You are welcome, that is. Providin' you keep yourself civil."

"I don't want any trouble. I just wanted to say that I... well, I'm real sorry 'bout your Granny. She was a good woman... so much like a lady. You know, all stately and refined. I was the one who felt she shoulda been in a horse-drawn carriage. I wanted you to know that."

"You? You wanted to do that? Why, I don't know what to say. Thank you, I guess. Shiloh, I am confused 'bout you payin' such high respects to my kin. I mean, seein' how you treated me and all."

"Can't say. It's just your Granny was different. She was like how I always thought a lady should be. Anyhow, you were you and she was ... well, she was a lady."

"Shiloh, I was just a kid. Soon I'll be 18, hear? Don't know what you expected from me, but right now, I just don't care. Thank you again for thinkin' so highly of my Granny. She is everything you said she was and more."

I turned on my heels and walked away. Lord, that girl just knew how to rile a person up, even while she was bein' so nice. As long as I lived I would never understand the likes of the Dixons! Mr. Pervis's words came to me just then, like a big ol' lightenin' bolt, remindin' me that Jay was a Dixon. I guess I had to work on that. Maybe one day this would all sort itself out like Sula said.

One by one people came up to me and expressed their condolences. Why, I did wish Granny could hear all this. Why, she'd be a might embarrassed 'bout all this fuss.

"Cinda? It's gettin' toward the end of day, I'm gonna bring all this here inside. It ain't proper to be outside in the evenin' when you're sayin' goodbye to your kin. It just ain't proper. Come on, y'all help me bring all this inside."

Toward the end of day, even Mr. Clement came by the house to pay his respects. Soon as I seen his car pull up, I looked around to see if there would be any trouble. Thankfully, the Dixons was all gone!

"LuCinda Dixon... I mean... Jackson, I am sorry. I was right sorry to hear about your Grandmother. I didn't know her very well, but I hear what the townspeople say and it's all good. Why, I just had to come by and pay my respects."

"Thank you, won't you come inside. We're movin' everything inside now. Does your man want to come in too? Wouldn't he like somethin' to eat?"

Would be just like Mr. Clement to leave a poor old policeman in the car whilst he jawed.

"Uh, no. No thanks. Well, maybe I'll just bring him some cookies or something later."

Sula and Mr. Pervis greeted Mr. Clement. I didn't see Percy. Anyhow, he got a proper greetin'. Sula was the first to ask about Miss Priscilla Dalton.

"So, Clement, how are things shapin' up for you? I trust you're movin' ahead with the case or can't you talk about it? I mean, after all, you were pretty set on LuCinda before and now... well, I wonder if I can ask how things are goin'."

I'd seen Sula take on people she didn't trust before. I always felt kinda bad for them, but I can't say that I felt bad for Mr. Clement.

"Well, now, Mrs. Cantrell, since you brought it up... besides paying my respects on your fine grandmother, LuCinda, I did want to thank you for helping us with the case. Once you had been exonerated, LuCinda, why, there was no obligation to you to help in this matter. But I did want to thank you for the information you gave us. Do I have permission to speak?"

"Say on, Mr. Clement."

Sula suddenly seemed glad to hear from Mr. Clement. I asked to be excused while I tucked Jay in Sula's bed for the time bein'. It had been a long day for him, and I didn't want him hearin' somethin' he shouldn't. I looked at Mr. Pervis, and he gave me a smile but put his head down right away. Land sakes, was there somethin' else I didn't know 'bout?

"Since you are still considered family, why, I feel I can tell you some of the recent events that have occurred. It seems Daisy Lawton was seeing Wilford Dixon. See, her family was against it, but Daisy admits to seeing Wilford on more than one occasion. She would have come forward but she's uh... turns out she's pregnant. There is no easy way to say it, I'm sorry. With Wilford dead, why, the family felt they were cursed or some such thing. Now, this Daisy Lawton says that Wilford was with her 'til about ten o'clock in the evening on Friday the eighth of May. All we got is her family to back her up. Priscilla now has changed her story. She might have heard that Daisy Lawton came forward. Priscilla says that she was with Wilford that night, 'til about eight o'clock. She claims she was going to break if off with him, but he left Sharky's in a hurry and she didn't get a chance to tell him. She followed him out of the bar and found him with Daisy. Daisy claims that Priscilla was angry and calling both of them names. Priscilla claims that Wilford and Daisy drove off together."

"What about Thirsty Creek? All of this seems highly likely, but what about where the body was found?"

"Interesting you should ask that, Mr. Pervis. It seems that on Saturday evening, Priscilla caught up with Wilford at Sharky's. She said he walked away from her and wouldn't talk to her. She saw him leave with his family and heard them say they were going down to Thirsty Creek. Priscilla waited a while and then decided to venture down to Thirsty Creek only to get back the watch that she gave him. Priscilla knew that Wilford wouldn't want a scene in front of his family, so she felt safe in going down there. She parked her car about twenty-five yards back or so. She walked up to a car that she recognized as Wilford's. The car was running with the driver's side door open. Not finding him there she walked on a little further and saw Wilford lying in the road. Priscilla claims that it looked like he fell because of the way he was laying. She didn't see anyone else around. She proceeded to talk to Wilford, but he was so intoxicated that he wasn't making sense. She grabbed the watch off from his wrist and he grabbed at her. She admits to kicking him. She says they argued, but she did most of the talking. As she was leaving, he told her that she was too old for him anyway. He pulled a picture out of his pocket and waved it in front of her. She admits to grabbing the picture and then walking toward the car headlights to see the picture more clearly and then crumpling it up. It was at this time that she noticed the watch there in the headlights, and it wasn't the watch she had given him. She walked back to where Wilford was lying and saw he was trying to get up. She threw his watch somewhere on the road and yelled at him some more. Priscilla still maintains that Wilford was lying on the road laughing at her when she turned to walk toward her car and left."

"Could I ask if the picture was of Daisy, Mr. Clement?"

"Why, yes it was, LuCinda. See, we found a note in that secret hiding spot, which simply said, 'Here's the picture you wanted.' That was all it said. That was of no real help to us until, well... let me get back to my story. When Priscilla heard that Wilford Dixon was found dead, she got scared. Fearing that she might be linked to his death, even though he was still alive when she left, she sent the picture of Daisy that Wilford waved at her to Daisy's mother with a note telling her that Wilford Dixon had been seeing Daisy."

"Is that it?"

"Yes Ma'am, it is. Daisy's family can vouch for her whereabouts. And, well, you know about Wilford's family. I'm sorry, LuCinda, for what happened to you as a result of the first report that was made... it seems that Mrs. Loma Dixon tried to implicate you. The problem was they were all about a week off of their dates and times. You can thank Cassidy Dixon for setting us straight on that. Anyway, they were drinking together at Thristy Creek and then went their separate ways. The last time they saw Wilford he was walking back toward his car. It was the Slatters who told us that the Dixons went up to their place to get more to drink."

"My, my. What do you know? Who woulda guessed all this?"

Sula looked like she was sad that this was all there was. I told her that things were just as they were. We can't make sense outta somethin' when there was no sense to begin with.

"There will there be a trial right Mr. Clement?"

"Oh, yes sir, Mr. Pervis there will be. The family of Wilford Dixon is pushing for answers. I suspect you've heard how they have been down to the station, making such a scene. Well, it's got some people talking. This being an election year, well, we got to make sure the townspeople feel safe. We need to assure the townspeople that everyone is doing their job. As you know, there are still some unanswered questions. For example, who was Wilford Dixon with when he checked into the Dew Drop Inn? Or was he alone? What about the lapse in time from when he was last seen to when he was found?

"To be honest, I don't know that Priscilla will be found guilty of murder. It seems the swollen uvula... that was recorded on the autopsy—well, that was the real cause of death. Wilford Dixon suffocated out there near Thirsty Creek. According to the state medical examiner, a swollen uvula is a rare condition, without some kind of infection, which he did not have. But a swollen uvula is common among those people who drink quite heavily. It's likely he was so drunk that he couldn't get up. By all accounts he tried to get up. Or maybe he passed out and then died. What about the effects of being exposed to the night air? Did that play a role in his death? In any case, I don't think the prosecutor can prove she killed him. No sir, I don't."

While Mr. Clement, Mr. Pervis and Sula talked on 'bout the case and upcoming trial, I sat there stunned. Imagine ol' Will just suffocated out there in the night, all alone. I can't say that I felt bad, just surprised is all. How could someone so mean and down right evil just slip away into the night? It seemed like someone like Him shoulda suffered more.

"Cinda, are you okay? Is this here hard to hear all at once?"

"No, Sula. I mean, I guess I should feel somethin', but I don't. I am surprised that He just laid there and died."

"Why, you heard Mr. Clement. Because he was so drunk that poor fool didn't know what hit him. His throat was probably all blocked... couldn't breathe. Now that's a terrible way to go. Just terrible."

"I suppose it was..."

How could I tell her that I wanted Him to suffer? Cry out in pain. Why, my mind was just thinkin' such evil thoughts. I got up and went outside on the porch. I looked up at the sky. Sure hoped He couldn't see the night sky whilst He was layin' there. Sula came out after me.

"You wouldn't be human if you didn't want that man to suffer. Just like he made you suffer. Is that what you're thinkin' on?"

"Yes'm, and I'm not ashamed of it either. I wanted Him to suffer. Shoot, I knew leavin' Him wouldn't bother Him none. Why, even takin' Jay with me wouldn'ta mattered none to Him. Though I am sure He put on a right pitiful act in front of His kin. Fact was, They never knew just how mean He was to me and to Jay. He never had time for my baby, but I'm sure He put on a big ol' act for all to see. I imagined that I would spend my whole life runnin' from Him and His kin. I figured I would get me a divorce and have to stay away from Frog Creek forever. But now... when I heard that He was dead... why... I didn't believe it. Just didn't believe that somethin' so evil... somethin' I feared so much was gone. At first I wanted to see His body, just to make sure. Now, when it's sunk into my head that He really is dead, why, I find out He just lay down and died."

"Cinda that man suffered. He suffered in life and in death. Oh, he suffered. Don't spend any more time thinkin' on that. It's done."

"What do you mean, 'it's done?'"

"Oh, I know all that happened to ya was hard, but you can stop runnin' now. You don't have to hide. You don't have to pretend. You don't have to be afraid of this here man any more. You're gonna' have a hard enough time tryin' to face up to all this here and move on toward better things. There *are* better things waitin' for you, Cinda. You have to believe that."

"It's hard to face up to things when a body hasn't had much control over their life, Sula."

"Now you do."

"It's not that easy."

"I know that. Like I said, this is gonna take a lifetime of sortin' and lettin' go, but you can live, be happy, hope and dream while you're doin' it."

I couldn't argue with Sula. It would be like arguin' with Granny. No Ma'am, wasn't gonna do it. I done argued with Granny and now I wished I had listened to her every word. I started to feel sorry for m'self. Granny woulda understood my wantin' Him to suffer.

"Now, I'm gonna say this only once, Cinda. You listen to me, you hear? I think you're finally in a listenin' mood. You have made this man and his family larger than life itself. True enough he was as bad as they come. I reckon they don't come much worse than old Wilford Dixon and now he's gone. Why, I would like to give him just one slap upside his head myself for leavin' you thinkin' life is hard, filled with hurt and pain. On the other side, you got your Granny. The Lord be praised she was in your life. Now think on this— you made her larger than life too. Only you think that you can't be anywhere near as kind and loving as she was 'cause what all you had to deal with. Why, I would like to give her one big old hug for leavin' you with thinkin' that there is more to this life than what you have experienced here in Frog Creek. You said so yourself. Now, how you gonna go on from here is up to you. Cinda, they're both gone. You got to let it go."

"Excuse me ladies, Mr. Clement needs to leave... am I interrupting anything?"

"No, we're done out here, we're just talkin'. I'll go inside and say good-bye to Mr. Clement. Are you comin', Cinda?"

"Yes. I should say somethin' kind to him for comin' all the way out here while he's workin'. Oh, and his man needs some food too, Sula."

After Sula gave Mr. Clement his food, there was an awkward moment of silence. We all just stood there lookin' 'round at one another. I figured it was all the feelins we shared with one another over the past few weeks. I felt a might embarrassed 'bout feelin' so unkind toward Mr. Clement. Finally, it was Mr. Clement who broke the silence.

"Good evening ladies. Thanks for the food, too. When

do you think you'll be leaving Frog Creek, LuCinda? Are you going to stay on for the trial?"

"No, I don't intend to stay for the trial. I hope to leave in the next few days."

"I see. You can thank Mr. Pervis here for doing such fine work. You don't have to testify or appear in court. I just thought you would want to see how it all ends. I must say I am surprised that you don't want to be here."

"No, I couldn't. It's just time for me to leave."

"Speakin' of leavin', I'm sure your man is hungry out there. Here, let me walk you outside and make sure this here food gets to where it's intended. Truth is you're so skinny, why, I do think you could eat it up before your man sees it."

I don't think Mr. Clement realized he was just put out. My Sula has got a way. I looked at all of the mess and started right in.

"Let me help with this."

"Oh, Mr. Pervis, you needn't bother any. Why, it helps me to keep busy. When are you leavin', Mr. Pervis? I haven't had time to talk with you today. I'm gonna miss that. I think Jay will too. He's been so used to seein' you and Percy, why, he just won't be satisfied with Sula and me. By the way, where is Percy?"

"He is sound asleep on the sofa in the front room. He deserves a good rest. I am going to leave first thing tomorrow. There are a few things I need to check on in town before I leave... papers. Percy will leave tomorrow too. We've got another case, and we need to be back in Chatfield."

They both were stayin' there tonight. Sula agreed with them. "Just to be safe," she said. There was another long uncomfortable bit of silence. I was going to miss Mr. Pervis.

He'd helped me more than I could say. I was sure his fee wouldn't nearly reflect what I had received from him.

"I can't thank you enough. You know about what Mr. Clement said... me not havin' to appear in court... I just couldn't bear it right now. You've stayed on when you found out my Granny died... You've been such a help to me, why, I just don't know what I'm gonna do without you."

"It was my pleasure, LuCinda. When Sula first called me and told me about your troubles, well, I knew I could trust her judgment and then when I met you... heard you speak... I knew you were innocent. I have gone above what is necessary for a lawyer and his client but... I..."

"Yes?"

"I have allowed myself to get a little too involved. I don't have a family of my own, you know. My practice always kept me just busy enough. It really gave me great pleasure to see this case unfold, seeing you and Jay... and Sula... become like family. Well, I think I took some liberties and included myself in on that. Of course, the case did take a few interesting turns. Yes, I really needed... uh, to be here, I mean. Let's see if you'll still be as grateful when you get my bill, shall we?"

"Now that's funny, and I'm sure I will be just as grateful."

I hugged Mr. Pervis just then. After I done so, why, he looked like a scared rabbit or maybe a deer when it's in the headlights. He backed away and thankfully for both Mr. Pervis and me, Sula walked in.

"Is everything all right in here? You two look a little funny. Like you got caught with your hands in the cookie jar. Heh-heh."

*I looked funny too?*

"Yes, things are just fine, Sula. You know, I have to leave

so early in the morning, maybe I had better say good night to you ladies."

"Sure enough! Leave all this mess here for the 'ladies.' Why, I think I'll just put the food away and leave the dishes 'til mornin'. What do you think, Cinda?"

"Oh, I couldn't leave this until mornin'. You both get your rest, and I'll take care of this. It will do me good to be busy."

After I finished with the dishes and straightened up the kitchen, I checked on Jay. He and Sula were snorin' like bears. Percy was sleepin' so sound, I went over and checked if he was breathin'. Land sakes that man could sleep! I covered him up with a blanket. I walked on back to Granny's old room and stopped by where Mr. Pervis was. I suddenly felt funny 'bout him bein' in the same room I shared, if you can call it that, with Wilford. I kept movin' and shut the door to my room. I rested my body on the door and wondered what I was feelin' 'bout Mr. Pervis.

*Hurry, Jay. Stay by mama. We got to hurry. Where did I put my bags? I need help. What is the number? I can't remember. I have to leave now! Please baby, we gotta go now. I don't think we're goin' to make it this time. He's home. No! Please no, I can't be here anymore.*

I woke m'self up by my hollerin' out. My heart was poundin' so hard. I felt like I could wake up the entire house. I was so sweaty that I had to get out of bed. I sat on some boxes and held my head. I started to cry. I wondered how long those dreams were gonna last. I heard a knock on the door. It was Mr. Pervis.

"LuCinda? Are you all right? I heard you cry or something."

"Yes, I'm all right now. I'm sorry to wake you. I'm fine."

I didn't open the door. I laid my head against it and listened for Mr. Pervis to go back to bed.

The next mornin' Sula was up early! She must have been cookin' up a storm to be that loud. I jumped outta bed and got dressed fast, so I could ask Mr. Pervis somethin' before he left. I found Percy and Mr. Pervis at the table eatin' a mess of eggs, fried potatoes and sausage. Why, Sula even managed to whip up some fruit mix. I greeted Mr. Pervis, Percy and Sula with a big ol' 'Good mornin'!' They all looked a might surprised. Sula was the first to greet me back.

"Why, good mornin', Cinda. My, you look mighty pretty in that jumper. Come on and set down. I hope you got an appetite?"

"Yes, the food is wonderful. I probably won't have to eat another bite until I get to Chatfield."

"Too late, Percy. I done fixed you up some turkey sandwiches."

"Good morning, LuCinda. Are you feeling all right? I mean after last night?"

Mr. Pervis looked concerned, and Sula joined right in.

"Did she have another one of them dreams?"

"Yes, Sula. But I think it was more like a nightmare. Am I right?"

"Yes, Mr. Pervis. But I am fine. Now let's all eat this here food. Sula, you are up early this mornin'!"

"Well now, I couldn't let these here fine gentlemen leave without some nourishment. What would they think? Maybe they'll look kindly on us when they get to calculating their fee. What do you think, Cinda?"

"Now, I don't rightly know, since I have one more request of Mr. Pervis."

"Excuse me? What was that?"

"Can I see her? I mean… can I see Priscilla?"

"What!" Cinda! You can't mean it, girl. Now why would you want to go on and see that... why she's nothin' but a ..."

"Sula, I know what she is and I know what she's done. It's just that I want to talk to her."

"I can see if I can arrange it. She is allowed to have visitors... I don't know if I would advise it, LuCinda."

"Why on this good green earth would you want to see Priscilla? See her in jail, no less."

Sula's question was a good one, and I didn't have the answer.

"I don't know why. I just want to see her and talk to her. I don't rightly know what I want to say to her. Maybe I just need somethin' to help put this all here in its place."

Mr. Pervis looked like he couldn't believe what I was sayin'.

"LuCinda, if she has obtained legal counsel, I would hope that he would not allow her to talk to you. I don't think she will talk to you."

"I'm not on trial. I'm not goin' to be in court at all. I just want to see if she'll talk to me and if she will, then we'll see what happens after that."

Mr. Pervis rubbed his head. He took off his glasses and rubbed his eyes. I never saw his eyes before. His eyes sure looked tired. Percy finally stopped eatin' to tell me what he thought.

"LuCinda. I don't think she's going to have kind words for you. Know what I mean? She could really say some things that you don't want to hear. Oh, I think she'll see you. That would be like her, but you might want to brace yourself for what you hear. Do you really want to put yourself in that position?"

Sula shook her head, got up and took her dish away from the table.

"Okay, I'll see what I can arrange. I'll talk to Mr. Clement. I've got to stop by there anyway. I really don't know what you hope to accomplish, LuCinda."

"Are you askin' or tellin', Mr. Pervis?"

Everyone left quickly after I spoke up. They were actin' all hurt or somethin'. I felt good. I ate just fine.

# CHAPTER 8
## Partin' of the Red Sea

"You sad 'bout this?"

"Oh, sure, I am sad in a strange sorta of way. I mean, I did live here durin' my childhood and then later on. Yet, I'm happy about movin' on. Isn't it funny? I never imagined livin' anywhere but here. I didn't even know much about what lies beyond Frog Creek. I know about other places. I studied them in school. I mighta even imagined that I would travel some place real foreign to anything I knew, but this here is for real."

Sula and I loaded the last of Granny's boxes and furniture into the trailer. Otto helped us with the dresser and mirror. He seemed real grateful for all of the food Sula left him in the freezer. He wished us luck and invited us to see his garden toward harvest time.

"Jay, you ready?"

Jay was runnin' around the house pretendin' to drive Sula's truck. He wasn't gonna come near us 'til Sula said he could drive.

"Land sakes, Sula! You are gonna spoil that child."

"Good! Then you can have him back after I'm done."

"Come by Mama, Jay. Take a look on this here place, Jay. We probably won't be comin' back to Frog Creek."

"Bye, house. Goin' home now."

"What do you know? He thinks he's goin' home. What do you think about that, Sula?"

"That's right, Jay, you goin' to Sula's house for now. We got to get home. There's no tellin' what Mrs. Fortney did to my house whilst I was gone. I can't even think on it."

On our way to Rondo, I tried not to think on my road or my tree or bushes. I tried to look at them like they were all new scenery. It's funny how some people can look at things and never really see them. I guess not everyone relied on a tree and some bushes like I did. As we got close to town, Sula got all serious and stopped playin' with Jay.

"Cinda, you sure you're gonna go through with this here meetin'? It's not too late to turn back. Why, we could leave her some chocolates or a magazine. What do you think about that? I'll buy them, and you can drop them off."

"No Ma'am. I really do think I need to talk with her. Besides, just think of all we'll have to talk about on the ride home."

Sula raised her eyebrows and smiled.

"Sure enough. Why, we could probably talk clean past Chatfield on that! I just sure hope you know what you're doin'."

"It will be all right no matter what happens."

I waved to Sula and Jay as they drove off. Sula gave me one half hour. Said she wanted to get the truck ready and batten down the hatches on the trailer one more time. I walked up the courthouse stairs. I felt lighter the more I walked on. I wondered if that was what goin' to heaven was like.

Once I got inside I asked someone where the visitin' room was for people in the jail. As I walked down the hall, people were lookin' at me kinda funny. I checked my clothes. I had on one of Sula's outfits she picked out for me, a pretty floral skirt with a blouse to match, and this time I wore heels. I felt kinda funny in these clothes, but I don't think that was what people were starin' at me for. Instead of directin' me to the visitin' room, I saw that I was near Mr. Clement's office.

"Hello, LuCinda. I knew you couldn't stay away. I wondered if you would want to come down here and see things for yourself."

Mr. Clement looked all proud of himself for somehow knowin' that I wanted to see Priscilla. It didn't matter to me.

"I can't rightly say anything about what you're talkin' 'bout, but I would like to visit with Miss Dalton. I do believe she is allowed visitors?"

"Yes Ma'am, she is. When Mr. Pervis talked to me the other day, he asked if I would please escort you to the visiting room and I am happy to do so. I am a man of my word. Now, follow me."

The way everyone was starin' at us, I guessed Mr. Clement was a man of a lot of words. He musta told everyone that I would be comin' down to talk with Priscilla. As I walked down that long hallway, though I'd been there before, the courthouse looked different. I never saw the pretty tile that covered the floor or those oil paintins of the city's foundin' fathers that lined up on the wall. It was kinda like they were salutin' me or somethin'. I felt real important just then.

"I informed her this morning that you wanted to visit her, and she accepted. This here will be a private visit. If you'll kindly wait in here, I'll let the jailer know you're here."

"Thank you."

I looked around and saw some mirrors on one side of the wall. A private visit, huh? How anyone could be in law or in trouble with the law was beyond me. It was like bein' in a fish bowl if you were in trouble or fishin' in one if you were the law.

The door opened and in walked Priscilla in handcuffs. I wasn't expectin' that at all. It was like seein' Granny all tiny and white haired in the nursing home for the first time. I didn't understand my connection with Priscilla. Why did I care? Priscilla sat down and looked at me. It wasn't that look that she gave me before. No, this here look was different. It was smug but not as before.

"I am glad that you let me visit you, Priscilla. I can't really tell you why I wanted to visit you, but I knew I wanted to."

"Why, I am surprised you wanted to see me. I figured you just wanted to tell me what you thought of me. You know, tell me off. Put me in my place."

"No, I didn't want to see you to do that. I wasn't sure what you would say to me. After all, you coulda refused my visit, but you didn't."

"Nope. So why are you here?"

"Seein' you in them handcuffs kinda surprised me. But maybe that will help... I mean, I'm not so worried about you tellin' me things about you and Will. I don't want to hear about them. Do you know what I mean?"

"No, I don't."

"Well, look where knowin' Him got you. I guess you don't feel so lucky, huh?"

"Maybe... yeah, I guess you're right."

"Anyhow, I don't have much time. I'll try to speak my piece. When I heard your story 'bout how you last saw Wilford. You know lyin' there and Him laughin'?"

"It's the truth! I didn't kill him! I went there to end things once and for all, and he was so drunk...just laying there. When I told him how he hurt me by taking someone else to the Inn, why, he just laughed at me. Can you believe it?"

"Yes, I can. I don't believe you killed Him. I really don't. There is somethin' about the way you described Him, layin' there and laughin', it struck somethin' inside me. I believe you. Maybe that's what I wanted to tell you... anyhow, that's all I really got to say."

"Thanks, I guess. It seems kinda strange to be talkin' to you. I never thought I would, like this. It's strange that you don't care any... I mean about all his cheatin'."

"No, I can't say that I do now. I can't say 'bout before. I guess I didn't really know. I mighta had ideas, but I was just tryin' to get through each day. In time, I was just lookin' for a way out. Speakin' of which, I hope you find a way out too. I got to be goin'."

"I heard you're movin' away from here. Is that really true?"

Priscilla talked like she didn't want me to leave just yet. Maybe she was just tryin' to say she was sorry in her own way. Maybe she was just lonely. I couldn't say that I felt sorry for her, though.

"Yes, I surely am. I'm leavin' today."

"And you wanted to see me before you left?"

"Yes and no. I did, but if you'da refused my visit, well, that woulda been all right too. The last stop I'm gonna make is at my Granny's grave."

"Oh, yeah... heard about that. She always greeted me real nice when she'd come into the bank. Sorry for what I done to her. You know Will was tryin' to get ahold of your Granny's place and her money too?"

"Yes, I knew that. You were in on that too?"

"Kinda. Will told me about his plans is all. He talked real big about havin' all kinds of money soon. I... helped him with some papers is all. I wanted it all to be so, but I never meant to..."

"Don't say on. It doesn't matter one lick now. I really hope you can get free from all of this here. I'll be sayin' good bye now."

"Goodbye, to you, LuCinda. Good luck. I mean it."

Bein' able to walk out of that there jail made me feel real good. It wasn't 'cause Priscilla was still stuck in there either. It felt good to see her, bearin' no malice towards her and walk on out of the jail. I felt right bad for her bein' in handcuffs. It made me think on how we all bind ourselves up with one thing or another. Take Priscilla. She was in a jail, but she was in handcuffs. Funny, even if she did get free, why, she would have to still deal with this all here. All the townspeople would know her and what she done. Her life would be open for all of Rondo to see... Then it hit me. That's what Sula was tryin' to tell me! Why, that Sula was as wise as Granny. I guess some people's handcuffs were harder to see than others. It must be so. Sula and Jay come up a honkin' to the courthouse. Land sakes, Sula was lettin' Jay drive!

******

"This here is hallowed ground to me, Sula. Jay, I want you to pay your respects too. I don't know when we'll be back here to this grave next. Come on."

We stood there a while, and I started to cry. I wished Granny was there to see that I was free. I was leavin' this here town and movin' on with my life. I wanted what Sula said to be true, that Granny was in the sunshine and the warm breeze. If that were true, then she would never leave me. She would be able to see me. I wished I could tell her that she was my Moses and my Aaron and had helped me to feel closer to God than I ever did. She helped me build bricks without straw. She helped me to face up to this here journey I was makin' outta Egypt. The only riches I was takin' with me were my son and the few widow's mites she managed to save.

"Sula, my Granny ain't here, and I need a hug real bad."

"Glad to fill in. You just let it go. I promise you, each time it's gonna feel better. Sad, but better. 'Cause you'll be doin' better."

"Mr. Smith at the bank said he'd make sure her grave stays kept up. He'd put flowers on every so often. Wasn't that nice of him?"

"Surely was."

"I'm ready to get movin', Sula. We got us a drive ahead of us. I'm anxious to get back to Chatfield. I reckon Jay and I will stay on for a while, 'til I figure out what I'm gonna do next."

"I figured as much and I'm glad of it. Do you wanna drive?"

"Sula! You know I don't have my proper license yet."

"Well, I say you can drive. That's proper license enough. You gotta practice. Now let's go!"

******

"There now, that looks nice."

I stood back and admired my new room. Granny's bedroom set was mine now, and it fit just perfect into Sula's twin home. Actually, it was my home. I'm payin' rent. I even picked me some fresh flowers from Mrs. Fortney's garden in honor of the day. It sure took me a long time to get the courage up to make Granny's things feel like mine. Then Sula said all the stuff belonged to Granny and me. I truly never thought on it like that. So this here was 'ours.'

"Mama, come see. Come see my room."

Sula found a regular bed for Jay. He was fussin' with his room like I was with mine. That sure was cute. He liked havin' his own room and I felt safe lettin' him be by himself. Not to mention all the toys Sula kept findin' for him. She was gonna spoil that child somethin' awful.

"Why Jay, you made a building. It looks just fine, son. It's almost as tall as you are."

"Cinda, where are you at, girl?"

"We're in Jay's room, Sula."

"There you are. Why, look at what Jay built! Jay, you are a smart boy. Yes you are. Now Cinda, all the plans are set for your birthday party. Why, I invited the usual— Mrs. Fortney, the preacher, and Mr. Pervis."

"He's back?"

"Yes, just today. I think I'll invite a few more folks from church. That way we know we can tolerate them for an afternoon, anyway."

"Sula!"

"Oh shoot! You know it's true. Some of those ladies do go on. They hardly leave any time for me to be a proper hostess. Now, I hope you're gonna wear a party dress. I am."

"Yes Ma'am. I picked out a dress at the Mercantile in town."

"The Mercantile? Oh, Cinda. Why didn't you go on up to Maggie's?"

"I did. I just thought I would see if you would get all riled up."

"Now, that ain't funny! I got a little suit for Jay. He's gonna look right dapper."

"Oh, Sula, you shouldn't have. Why, you just keep givin' and givin'. I can hardly keep acceptin' all this here. It's not right."

"Says who?"

"Says me. I can't keep receivin' all the time. It just doesn't feel right. It's like I'm takin' advantage of you or somethin'."

"Are you?"

"Why, no of course not."

"Then who cares?"

There was no sense arguin'.

I was thinkin' on the last party we had, the day after we came back to Chatfield. It was a small gatherin', no Mr. Pervis, just Mrs. Fortney, Sula, Jay, preacher and me. I thought about the preacher. He was nice. He made a speech about me comin' back into the fold and all. He said the same thing the followin' Sunday. Sula said he seemed different. It was like he was comin' into his own. Sula thought he would have his own little church one day.

"I'm glad you invited the preacher. He has really made me and Jay feel welcome. I think he helped me... he softened up some of those ladies. You know, like Mrs. Parsons and those other ladies she sticks with."

"I'd say so. The only thing is that he still does go on and on when he prays. My, my, like we got all day. Doesn't he know that there are some of us who pray and on a regular basis too?"

"There, Jay. My, you look handsome. Cinda, now just look at this here boy. He's lookin' so grown. Now Cinda, you get dressed. Me and Jay will go out and help Mrs. Fortney with the final touches. Do you know that she brought over several vases filled with flowers? She says there's something special 'bout an eighteenth birthday. Go on now."

"Yes Ma'am, I better get dressed. I want to greet the guests as they arrive. Why, I haven't seen Mr. Pervis in a while. Will Percy be comin' too?"

"Yes, they'll both be here. I got someone I want him to meet."

"Who, Mr. Pervis?"

"No, Percy. Why, Mr. Pervis is right nice, but he's kind of a loner. He's always so busy with his law. If there ain't enough business here in Chatfield, why, he goes lookin' for more. Besides, I don't think he's lookin'. It's Percy I think needs marryin'. Why, he's a nice young man, and I think Mrs. Fortney's niece will do him just fine. Ain't you dressed yet?"

I left Sula and Jay, and I walked on back to my room. Everyone was celebratin' my eighteenth birthday, but only I knew that I was celebratin' my deliverin'. Happy Deliverin' Day to me!

I couldn't believe I picked out that dress. It was the prettiest one in Maggie's store. It surely was. Now, I don't know? That dress looked pretty, but it sure looked nicer in the store. Why was that? Maybe it was too much? I was eighteen now. Oh, I don't know... maybe I shoulda picked out the plainer navy blue dress with flowers for buttons. This here had big ol' purple flowers on it. It's a good thing the background was white. Maybe it would tone it down some? It came with a matchin' headscarf, but there was no way I was wearin' that! It had a scoop neck too. I put my hair up kinda in a hurry. I wanted my hair up just like a grownup lady. I took one last look at m'self. Well, this was it.

"Cinda! My, don't you look pretty. Look Mrs. Fortney, why, just lookit here, our Cinda is all grown up. I do think you're missin' something though..."

"Now Sula, if you're talkin' about that dreadful headscarf, why, I'm not gonna wear it. It's too much."

"No, I'm not talkin' about a headscarf. Happy Birthday,

Cinda! It's a little after your birthday, but I wanted to wait until everyone could be here."

"I know, Sula, and that was just fine. You know that. Why, it's a little box. Granny always said the best gifts come in little packages. Oh, Sula! It's beautiful!"

"I told Maggie to push this here dress on you 'cause I thought this here pearl necklace would be perfect with it. Do you mind?"

"Land sakes, no! I love it. I always wanted a pearl necklace. Truly I did. When Jay and I would walk around Rondo after cashin' in our bottles, why, I would walk right past the jewelry store and just look on those pearl earrings and necklaces. I never told anyone that I wanted one, though. Thank you kindly, Sula."

I hugged her so tight.

"Now, don't get me to bawlin'. You'll ruin my mascara. Last thing I want to do is look like some ol' raccoon! Now go on and greet your guests."

Mr. Parsons and his wife were the first to arrive. Shoot, I owed Sula fifty cents. The other church ladies arrived right behind them. There went another fifty cents. I greeted them real proper like I seen Sula do. The ladies commented on how nice I looked, even Mrs. Parsons.

"Cinda, you look absolutely lovely. Doesn't she, ladies? Why, who woulda guessed you were in the hospital just a few weeks ago. My goodness, you're color's almost come back, too."

"Thank you, Mrs. Parsons. You are too kind, I'm sure."

I looked over at Sula. She was watchin' like a hawk. I waved at her to know that she wasn't needed. She told me to give her a sign if Mrs. Parsons was actin' up.

The preacher came next. I went up to him and grabbed both of his hands and held on to them.

"Happy birthday, LuCinda! You look so... happy. Yes, happy."

"Thank you, preacher, I am happy. Welcome to my party and to our home. I am glad you came. I want to thank you for makin' me and Jay feel so welcome. I do think you are the one who helped the church and townspeople look on me kindly 'cause of my past."

"That is my job. I mean, I would have only been too happy to help you even if I wasn't a man of God. You deserve happiness after all you've been through. I am sorry about your grandmother, too. When I heard about it I was up in Mantorville. I couldn't get away; otherwise I would have tried to come."

"Why, I had no idea. Thank you for sayin' so."

He woulda come all that way? Why, I had no idea he was so involved in his people's lives that way. I hardly knew him.

"Preacher, you made it at last. Good. You see our Cinda? She's all grown up and just as pretty as can be!"

The preacher didn't know what to do. He kinda stood there all quiet like, noddin' in agreement. *That Sula!*

"LuCinda?"

"Mr. Pervis! Welcome. I'm glad you could come. I heard you just got back into town. Another case, huh?"

"Yes, another case. I had to cut my trip short, so I could come back in time for this lovely party. Who knows what Sula would have done if I didn't make it back? Happy birthday, LuCinda."

"You mustn't worry about Sula. I would have understood."

"Oh, no, I wanted to come back. I was trying to make a joke, a bad joke, apparently."

"I see."

I smiled. Mr. Pervis makin' a joke, now that surely was outta place.

"You do look wonderful, though."

"Thank you for sayin' so. And you should take a look at Jay. Sula dressed him up in a suit, can you imagine?"

"Why Mr. Pervis, there you are! Where's Percy?"

"He's not here, Sula? Why, I thought he'd beat me here. He heard that you wanted him to meet someone. Maybe he's gotten cold feet?"

"That boy better show up! I got Mrs. Fortney's niece all fired up to meet him too. Now, did you see our Cinda? She's all grown up. She's just as beautiful as can be."

I felt right uncomfortable then with Mr. Pervis lookin' at me and Sula sayin' such things. She did the same thing when she talked to the preacher. If I didn't know better, 'cause she knew all I had been through, why, I would say she was settin' me up instead of Percy. Thankfully, Percy did arrive. Sula made a run straight at him with poor Mrs. Fortney's niece in tow. Sula came over to me after she introduced them to one another.

"There, now I have done my part. The rest is up to them. Now, let's get your cake!"

It was the prettiest cake I had ever seen. It was covered with real purple flowers. Why, I think I matched the cake! Sula, now I knew you were up to somethin'. I hadn't had such a party since I was eight years old. I remember. Granny gave me just what I wanted, a pretty chocolate cake with white and pink flowers on it. I invited the entire neighborhood. I even invited kids that were just passin' by. Maw was all mad.

'You don't even know those kids,' she had said.

'I know. I just want them to have some of my cake. I'm just happy is all.'

'They won't give you any presents. Nothin'.'

'I don't mind. It's all right, Granny, isn't it?'

'If that's what you want.'

Maw just sat there all mad. She made sure those other kids' cakes were smaller than the invited kids' cakes.

"Cinda, make a wish!"

"Oh, I don't know that I could wish for anything more, Sula. Come here, Jay, and help Mama blow out these here candles."

It was the perfect birthday party.

As I was sayin' good-bye to my guests, I noticed that Mr. Pervis was gone. I declare, he didn't even say good-bye? Percy and Mrs. Fortney's niece sure seemed to be hittin' it off. They left together, with Mrs. Fortney right behind them. Sula and Jay were pickin' up all the flowers on the tables. Sula's backyard turned into a garden for just one day. Coulda been Eden, I thought. It was gettin' toward dark... why, I missed the best part of my day. I didn't even notice the settin' sun. Sula put out a bunch of new fangled outside lawn lamps. That's what she called 'em, lawn lamps. The preacher was still here. He started walkin' toward me, and I started to feel a little self-conscious again.

"LuCinda? Can I talk to you?"

"Of course, preacher."

"I wanted to give you my present. I didn't wrap it because it seemed... well, it didn't seem right. God's words aren't meant to be kept hidden."

"Why, it's a brand new Bible! I declare this is the sweetest gift I've ever had. It's all white too! I don't know, seems like I'm gonna have to keep this covered up if'n I want it to stay so nice. Thank you very much."

I hugged the preacher right then! I surprised m'self and him too. He looked like he was blushin'. Could a man blush? I guess they could.

"Thank you for this gift. It sure means a lot to me."

"It's to be read, of course, but I wanted to remind you that we can all be as white and pure as this new Bible, no matter what."

I didn't know what to say. He smiled and nodded. He gave a wave as he left. I showed Sula just as soon as I could.

"See what the preacher gave me! Isn't it lovely?"

"My, that's quite a gift... I'd say he really likes you."

"Oh, Sula. He's just bein' nice is all."

After we cleaned up the party leavins', I gathered up Jay in my arms and went on into the house. I gave Sula one last kiss and hug and thanked her ever so much for givin' me such a wonderful party. I gave Jay a bath even though he was so tired. There was cake all over his suit and him too. He played with the bubbles and was singin' up a storm. As I looked at Jay I wondered if I could ever get married again. I sure wasn't in any hurry, but I wondered if I could really find someone to love. I meant real love, not this first love stuff. I done had all I wanted of that. Sula often commented to me, since we'd been back, that Jay would one day need a daddy. Even though I agreed with her, I sure didn't know how it could happen.

"Bess not be thinkin' on that just yet, huh Jay?"

"Yes, mommy. Can you blow bubbles? I want to blow bubbles. Look, bubbles. Can I have more cake?"

I sat in my new rockin' chair and held Jay. I sang him a lullaby and before I could sing it through again, he was asleep.

I held onto him and thought on my life. I couldn't figure out what to do. I needed to find some way to provide for Jay and me. Granny's nest egg would help me get started, but it would soon run out if I didn't find some way to build it up. I was sure Sula would be willin' to help me but I couldn't rely on her. Why, she'd done too much. I couldn't tell her that 'cause she'd just talk me out of it and find some way to help me. No sir, I couldn't keep takin' from her! That only meant one thing. I would have to leave for a while... maybe go... to school to learn some kinda trade. The thought made me feel all excited. Why not? After all, Mrs. Dawling said I had a good head on my shoulders. I'd have to leave and go to a school somewhere... but where?

I tucked Jay in his bed and kissed him good night. Sure hoped he didn't outgrow me rockin' him too soon, but I expect he would. I checked all the doors, and they were locked. I guess old habits took time to break into new ones. I got a drink of water and saw a package on the table. It was addressed to me.

*Where did this come from?* I was about to go ask Sula, but I figured she'd done enough for one day. I carried it back to my room. After I was all ready for bed I opened it. I guess someone wanted me to find it like this. Why, it was so beautiful! It was a book about the most beautiful and interestin' places in the world. It was full of colored pages of Niagra Falls, the Grand Canyon, the Eiffel Tower, and the Pyramids of Egypt... that's where I stopped. Egypt. Just lookin' at those pyramids made me start cryin'. They had real close up pictures of the pyramids. They weren't so pretty close up. They weren't even, neither. I thought on those bricks, made one by one by slaves, no less. People who were in bondage. Now, I was settin' here lookin' at what they built.

*Who gave me that book?* I looked toward the back 'cause I felt a page outta place. There was a blown up picture of Granny's house in Frog Creek. Why, there was me and Jay with Sula off to the side of the house! *Who took that picture?* I didn't remember anybody takin' pictures... I looked toward the front of the book and saw some words through my teary eyes:

LuCinda,

There are many beautiful and interesting places
all around us, but none more so than those
we find with loved ones along the way.

Always,
"Mr. Pervis"

I guess I never did call him by his proper name, Paul. It seemed right improper bein' my lawyer and all. I just couldn't bring m'self to call him by his given name. No wonder he didn't want to give me this himself. He probably knew I would cry just like I'm doin' now. *Oh, Mr. Pervis, it was so kind of you.*

I grabbed my new Bible in one hand and held my new book in my other one. I felt like I had just been given the world and there wasn't anywhere I couldn't go and anything I couldn't do.

## CHAPTER 9
## On to the Promised Land

Cinda, you hardly touched your breakfast. What's wrong, Maude losin' her touch?

"No Ma'am, these biscuits and gravy are just fine. The eggs are a little runny, but that's okay. No, I was just thinkin' on things is all."

Jay was eatin' his fourth pancake. My goodness that boy sure could eat when he wanted to. He was just smilin' all happy. It didn't seem right me uprootin' him again, now that he felt like he had a home.

"Sula?"

"I know you're fixin' to leave."

"How did you know?"

"I can tell. It's time. It's been nearly a month since we've been back and well, you seem all restless. It's like you don't know what to do with yourself."

"I just want to take Jay and travel a bit. I don't even know where. Well, that's not exactly true. See, we were in the drug store and this paper fell down from off counter. Do you know what it was? Why, it was a brochure about the Grand Canyon. I'd sure like to see that. I'd like Jay to see it too. Besides, there's a school I want to look at along the way."

"A school? Land sakes, Cinda, that's just fine. Oh, I'd say that's just right for you now. Uh... before I get too happy, where is this school?"

"It's up near Mantorville way, the state college."

"Whoo-eee! That's sounds even better. Why, you could come home on the weekends, during holidays, the summer and.... Guess I'm gettin' a bit pushy, aren't I? Don't answer, I know."

"You don't mind?"

"Now why would I mind what's natural?"

"What?"

"It's natural. Land sakes, Cinda, it's natural to want to go and see the world and explore. That's usually how a body leaves their home. I'm just tickled that you feel like you're at home and feelin' some peace. I'd like to think I helped a little with that."

"You surely have, Sula. No doubt about that. I don't want to seem ungrateful or nothin'."

"Are you?"

"What?"

"Are you ungrateful?"

"No, Ma'am. I surely am not."

"Then who cares? Now, you gotta get a car. Don't argue with me on this, Cinda. It's high time you put that proper license to use. I got me a friend up there in Mantorville. He has a used car place on the side of his real business."

"He sells cars on the side? Sula, is that good? I mean, does he know cars?"

"Of course he does. Now, no sense wastin' your Granny's hard earned money on a new car, why, that's just senseless. He'll do ya a good deal. When you fixin' to leave?"

"I was thinkin' 'bout Friday, when the red eye comes through. There's a motel right across from the bus station in Mantorville. I'd stay there through the weekend and see how the town is. Come Monday, I planned on goin' to the college and takin' a tour of the campus. I'd see how I could get in and take it from there. The truth is I was plannin' on gettin' a car somewhere. I'm glad you know someone, Sula. I don't know the first thing 'bout a car and probably woulda bought new."

"It seems funny about us talkin' about you leavin' when this is where I first met you and Jay. It seems like a long time ago."

"Yes Ma'am, it surely does. We've been through a lot, Sula, I don't know how I'm gonna manage without you for a while... I never woulda made it this far without you. You know that?"

"Now, let's just stop this here talk. I don't want to be cryin' in Maudie's in broad daylight. Why, the rumors would just start flyin'. We wouldn't want to go and make that Mrs. Parsons too happy. The truth is there is no such thing as goodbye, unless you never expect to see someone ever again. Ya hear?"

******

The week seemed to go by so fast. I started plannin' on this and that. Land sakes, there was so much to think on, travelin' clothes, hats, coats, bags, and whatnot. Why, I was tired just thinkin' on all the stuff. It was a bittersweet time for me. I was thinkin' on the last time I packed up some bags and left. I told Jay we were goin' to visit the Grand Canyon, and he just lit up like he knew exactly what I was sayin'. I relied quite a bit on that brochure— sure hoped they lived up to their boastin'. Sula done talked me into havin' her see us off at Maudie's. She wanted to make a big deal out of our leavin'. Fact was, the red eye didn't come 'til after ten o'clock at night. Now who's gonna want to stay out that late? Sula finally agreed with me.

The truth was I hated to say good-bye, so long or whatever it was you say to people when you're goin' on a good trip. Mrs.

Fortney knew about my trip, so I expect everybody else in the town did too. She offered her "valise," as she called it. I had to say no thank you to that. It was so old, why, the insides were peelin'.

The preacher came by on Wednesday to say goodbye to Jay and me and wished us a good trip. Now that was real nice. I told him I was plannin' on takin' my Bible with me so's I could read while I was away. He seemed right pleased about that.

"Miss Jackson, when will you be returning?" Is that all right that I call you that?"

"Certainly is. I haven't figured out what to do about Jay yet, but LuCinda Dixon just doesn't sound right anymore. Jay and I will be gone for about two weeks. We're gonna take our time."

"I hear you are thinking about attending college in Mantorville. Is that right?"

"Yes, sir. I want to see the campus first. I'm not in any hurry. I thought about tryin' to get in this fall, but I decided to wait until next fall. I wanted to give Jay and me a chance to settle down a bit before we uproot again."

"My ministry brings me up that way, you know."

"No, I didn't know. Well, not exactly. I knew you went a few different places as you're needed. It seems like you're gone for two weeks at a time?"

"Yes, that's about right. I hope to have my own church in time. Yes, they will provide me with a church and a home. They're usually nice accommodations, you know, should I have a family."

"I guess you should get married first though, huh?"

"Yes, right… of course. Good point. Yes, well enjoy your trip. You certainly have earned some time to... breathe. I've been to the Grand Canyon, and it is a marvel. It's one of God's finest creations. I hope you enjoy your trip. Uh... I had better be going now...I'm late. Farewell, Miss Jackson."

"Thank you. Take care of yourself, preacher."

I couldn't bring m'self to call him by his proper name neither, Joel Thilmann. I stood in the backyard a while, thinkin' on the preacher. I wondered if he was ever lonely. He didn't seem to be. I hoped I didn't embarrass him none by tellin' him he should get married before he has a family.

I started walkin' around. I got to likin' Sula's backyard. There were lots of grand times here. I sat down on her garden swing and just looked up to the sky. There were lots of clouds today, big soft fluffy ones. Now, that would be the way to travel! I could just float here and there. It sure would be easier and cooler too. My, it was hot. That sun was beatin' down. Thank goodness for the clouds and the breeze. It felt good knowin' things had quieted down a bit. Jay was sleepin'. I laid him down in my room 'cause it was cooler there. Sula came out carryin' a big ol' glass of lemonade.

"Did the preacher run off already?"

"Yes, Sula, he seemed like he had an appointment or somethin'."

"Did he say anything in particular?"

"Not really. He just wished me and Jay a nice trip. He asked when we'd be back is all."

There was somethin' in her tone got me to wonderin'. She sat down next to me and gave me a big ol' smile whilst shakin' her head.

"You know somethin' that I don't?"

"No, not really. It's just that I had me a nice visit with him is all and now he's gone. We visited mostly about you."

"'Bout me? What 'bout me?"

"Oh, we weren't talkin' about anything in particular. We were talkin' about this and that. Somehow you came up, and, why, he just went from there. He was askin' if I was gonna miss you and Jay. He was askin' about your plans. It was probably nothin'."

"That's right. It was probably nothin'."

I wondered why the preacher would be askin' 'bout me to Sula? He was a right nice man.

"Well, look who's here! Mr. Pervis, how are you? Why, we ain't had the pleasure of your company for a long time. Come and sit down."

"Hello, Sula and LuCinda. How are you two lovely ladies doing today? I'd say despite this hot weather, why, you ladies look... breezy."

"Oooh, now that's what I was missin', your smooth talkin'. You need to come by more often. Why, that preacher just left, and he doesn't talk as sweet as you do."

"Oh, the preacher came by?"

"Yes he did. He came to visit us both. You need some lemonade. I'll be right back. LuCinda, keep him company and don't let him leave 'til I get back!"

"Did he mention anything, LuCinda?"

"No, just wished me and Jay a nice trip. Why do you ask? Is there somethin' I should know about?"

"Yes, probably. I thought you should see this for yourself. It's over."

Mr. Pervis handed me the Chatfield Bugler. There was an article in the paper about the outcome of Wilford's trial. The title read: "Frog Creek Man Dies of Natural Causes."

"Natural causes?"

"Yes, read on."

"What you all lookin' at? Oh, it's the Chatfield Babbler.

Anything worth readin' in there? Have some lemonade, Mr. Pervis."

"I think you'll be interested in this, Sula. I thought LuCinda might be interested in a particular article on page two. I think the editor of the paper put in on the second page out of respect for you, LuCinda."

"What? The trial is over?"

"Here Sula, you read it."

"Why, don't you want to read it first, Cinda?"

"Not especially. Not right now. I'm still thinkin' on the title."

Sula grabbed the paper out of my hands and started readin'.

"Natural causes? Why, nothin' natural about a man drinkin' and then suffocating to death. Land sakes! It says here that Miss Priscilla Dalton was found not guilty in the murder of Wilford. They talk about his family some, how they was all together that evening. It doesn't say what they were doin' though. Oooh says here that Priscilla was havin' an affair with Wilford and how she is gonna be charged with attempted fraud. What do you know about that? Why, lookit here. Says here a minor was brought in to testify too. I guess we all know who that was. I'm sure the entire town of Frog Creek and Rondo knows too. Yes sir, they go into detail about his swollen uvula and about how he was seen drinkin' heavily Friday night and Saturday too. It says here they ruled out foul play. That's it? Shoot!"

I shook my head and laughed at Sula.

"Land sakes, Sula. You know all there is to know 'bout the entire case, start to finish. How can you say that's it?"

"I don't know it seems like it's missin' something. I can't say."

"There's no paper big enough to print the entire truth of the whole mess. Why, in the end, everyone was just out lookin' to protect themselves. Of course His family isn't gonna say what really happened while they were drinkin'. Fact is, what's missin' is Will's side of the story. And you know what? He wouldn't admit He done anything wrong either. It's like Mr. Pervis said, there is no complete justice in this world. We're all gonna have to wait for God's justice."

I don't know what I said, but either Mr. Pervis or Sula had any more to say about the article in the Chatfield Bugler. We sat there and drank our lemonades and commented on the hot summer day.

"Are you gonna stay to supper Mr. Pervis? I'm makin' my famous ribs. I felt like havin' something sassy tonight. What do you say, care to stay on?"

"I hadn't planned on staying for supper, Sula. Thank you. Are you sure it's no trouble? I leave tomorrow on a trip, and I won't be back for a few days. I won't get to see LuCinda off... so supper would be fine."

"Good! Glad to have you. You know, I invited the preacher to supper too, but he's got to go out of town too. My, you men sure do travel. What you need is a family so you won't be runnin' off so much. That would do it. I'll go check my ribs now. Cinda, you want me to check on Jay?"

"No, thank you. I'll get him. Perhaps Mr. Pervis would like to help you with supper?"

"Sure enough. Come on in. I can't leave you out here by yourself. What kind of hostess would I be? Come on in and make yourself useful."

I watched Mr. Pervis and Sula go on into her kitchen. She sure liked him. She'd kinda taken to likin' the preacher too, despite his long prayers. I sure was gonna miss them all whilst I went travelin'. I thought two weeks should be enough time, but I didn't know for what. Yet it sure did feel like I need some space. While I was walkin' toward the house, I thought on that for a bit. I needed space? Land sakes, I was a free woman and I was away from Frog Creek, and I still needed more space? I wondered if it was space I needed.

Once in my house, I stopped to get some water to put in the 'fridge. My, it was gonna be hot tonight. I could hear Sula and Mr. Pervis talkin' just as plain as could be. It was like they were right in the hallway between me and Sula's house. I craned my neck over and seen that both our kitchen doors was open.

"Sula, is LuCinda really planning on attending college?"

"You heard, huh?"

"Yes, my secretary told me. She says the whole town is buzzing about her plans to go to school and possibly move away."

"That's right. She is plannin' on going to school up in Mantorville. I think it would do her a world of good. Why, she's a right clever girl. I hope you know that."

"Oh, I'm sure of it. She just needs a chance... a chance to explore new things and develop her mind without having to fear."

"That's right. You said a mouthful right there. I'm so happy for her. I truly am. She's thinkin' on going to school next fall."

"Oh... why not this fall? Why is she waiting?"

"She says it's because of Jay. She's afraid the change will be too sudden for him. Truth is I think she needs to get used to the idea too. I think I can help her find a job in the meantime. Why, Maggie always needs help. I heard tell Mr. Gould at the Mercantile wants some hired help."

"Oh, I don't know, Sula. She needs something more challenging than that."

"Have you tried to sell clothes to women?"

"No, Sula. I haven't ever had to sell any kind of merchandise, except maybe myself. As a lawyer, I have to assure people that they can trust me. Remember how hard I had to sell myself to you?"

"Okay, maybe you have a point there. Why, you got something better in mind?"

"Yes, as a matter of fact I do. I could use someone to help me with my record keeping and other similar matters."

"Do tell. Is business that good?"

"Actually, it is. I'm thinking of opening another practice in Mantorville."

"Do tell. Why Mantorville?"

"Oh, mainly because I am just about to finish a case up there, and it seems I've made a good name for myself. In fact, there is only one other lawyer there, and he has his main practice in another town. If I were to open another office there, why, I wouldn't be infringing upon his turf so to speak. The town is big enough and seems to be growing."

"Humph!"

"You disapprove of my opening a practice in Mantorville?"

"No, of you hirin' Cinda. She's made for bigger things and ... a man of your intelligence.... Paul you're old enough to be my son, and I'm gonna talk to you like one. I'm gonna tell you something about Cinda..."

I couldn't hear no more. I walked away. I felt a little ashamed of listenin' in on their conversation. I wondered what Sula was gonna tell him 'bout me. I knew I better get Jay in a hurry and get over there. I rousted Jay, who was sleepin' so sound. I felt bad 'bout gettin' him up. I walked into Sula's totin' Jay.

"You two talkin' 'bout me?"

"Why yes, if you must know. Now, let's get this supper on the table and eat. Come on Jay, you sit by Sula."

We ate dinner in a strong silence. Oh, we talked, but it seemed tense. I decided to tell Mr. Pervis what I thought about his nice present.

"Mr. Pervis, I want to thank you for the nice gift you gave me for my birthday. I haven't had a chance to thank you before, so I'm doin' it now. It is a fine book. I really do enjoy it."

"You gave her a book?"

"Yes, I did, Sula. Ahem, excuse me. Yes, it was a book of beautiful and interesting places, a book about places around the world."

Sula nodded in approval. She smiled at Mr. Pervis like she forgave him for somethin'.

"I especially like the pictures of the pyramids of Egypt. Why, I have even read some of the book to Jay. He sure does like the pictures. Thank you again."

The rest of the dinner went better. I don't know what happened, but I think it had to do with me. After dinner, Sula asked if I would see Mr. Pervis out because she forgot that she was supposed to check on Mrs. Fortney across the street. She took Jay with her.

"I understand you're going to the Grand Canyon. I know you'll enjoy your visit there. I went there some years back with my parents. That was a while ago, a family trip."

"How nice. Do you still see your parents? I mean, I haven't heard you mention them before."

"No, I don't see them as often as I should. Uh... so, you'll be going to school too I hear."

"Land sakes, I think everyone knows what I'm doin'. I guess that comes with the territory, huh? Yes, I hope to go to school. I haven't decided what to study, though. I guess that will come in time. I won't be goin' until next fall, but I guess you heard that too?"

"Actually, I did."

"Well, no sense in makin' small talk. I'm sure you've got to be gettin' home. What, with you travelin' and all."

"I am interested, Cinda. It's just that..."

I butted right in. I just didn't want all this idle chatter. What was the point of it?

"I appreciate your helpin' me with my... Well, what do you know; I don't know what to call all this here. My life? My freedom? I trust you got the payment from Mr. Smith? Was everything all right?"

"Yes, thank you. It was hard billing for my services. I hope Sula didn't think I charged too much?"

"Fact is I never showed her. Sula would have..."

"You two talkin' 'bout me?"

I didn't hear Sula come in.

"Yes, as a matter of fact we were. Come on, Jay. Say good night to Sula and Mr. Pervis."

I left them just standin' there. I didn't know exactly what I was feelin' then, but I sure needed to be alone. I put Jay down for bed and went to my room. I thought on what happened. What was all this here about from the preacher and Mr. Pervis? One gives me a fine white Bible and tells me that I can be just as fine as that Bible. One gives me a fine book with pictures from all over the world and well, doesn't say much else. Were they just bein' nice? Why was Sula actin' so funny? Tellin' me I needed to think 'bout Jay and him havin' a daddy. Why, I sure hoped she don't think I was gonna marry one of those two. Shoot! I'd be an old lady of thirty years before neither one of them got to thinkin' 'bout a wife, let alone it bein' me!

******

*Jay, come on now. We're gonna be late. Where did the time go? Now, where did I put my bags?* Thinkin' that stopped me dead in my tracks. Why, I was sayin' the exact words that I said in my dreams. It kinda gave me the shivers. I scooped up Jay and held him close. I had him in his warm nightclothes so's I could slip him into bed. Sula didn't like it that we were travelin' alone. Just like I figured, she tried to work on me and let her drive us up to Mantorville. But I held my ground and tried to reassure her. She didn't let up until I told her I would call her just as soon as me and Jay got into the motel room. Later on she told me she called the motel just to make sure there would be a room. Why, that Sula! She sure did smile when she learned that I had already called the motel to make arrangements. Why, the lady sounded so nice. She was even gonna meet us at the station so's she could help me 'cause I had Jay.

"You ready, Cinda?"

"Yes Ma'am, I think so. I sure am bringin' a lot of things with me. It sure feels funny. I remember when I came, why, I had me a little brown bag and that was it."

"Come on Jay, you come with me. Now I packed you some sandwiches in this here cooler. You'll need some ice. Land sakes, I wish you'd let me drive you. I'll probably sprout me a few more white hairs and wrinkles 'cause of this. Think on that!"

"Why, you'd still be just as pretty, Sula, and you know it."

"Sure do. But just keep sayin' it. It kinda helps me to hear that every now and again."

Sula let Jay drive the truck and honk the horn. By the time we got to Maude's it was already nine-thirty at night. We unloaded everything onto the street outside of Maudie's. We walked into the diner all sweaty.

"Hey, Maude! How about a couple of Orange Crushes over here? Land sakes, it's hot out."

"Sure enough, Sula. Be right there."

Just then I heard a big old loud screech. It was the red eye!

"It's early! Why, what do you know? That truly surprises me. That old red eye is never early."

"It's just as well, Sula. Jay here will be asleep before you know it. I'll take my Orange Crush with me and you take yours... and we'll still be sharin' them together."

The bus driver came into Maude's and got him self a cool drink. Sula gave him my bags and told him how he could help me and Jay.

"Here you go, here are her bags. Now, they are only goin' as far as Mantorville. There's a lady from the motel that's gonna be meetin' her and her boy. Now you make sure on this, hear?"

Sula followed him all the way to the bus, talkin' at him. I don't think he appreciated it, but he was takin' it all in.

The bus that came from Rondo way pulled up. There were a few people that got off of the bus. Gus, the gas station man came out and directed people some. There was an older couple that got off and went on into Maude's totin' a small suitcase.

Pretty soon, a young girl got off. She was all wide-eyed and had herself two suitcases.

"I'd say there are probably some people that will need someone to talk to. You think?"

"There is always someone that needs talkin' to, Cinda. All we got to do is open our eyes. This is hard for me...oh; I know you'll be back before I know it. I'll hardly have time to have the insides of your house all painted. It was goin' to be a surprise, but I couldn't keep it inside."

"Sula! Why, that's right nice of you. What color you gonna paint it?"

"I thought about pearl white in honor of your birth month. What do you think? You know that wallpaper you were admirin' at the Mercantile? Well, I think I'll put some of that up as well."

"That sounds like it will be real pretty. You don't have to go to all that trouble."

"Shoot, it ain't any trouble at all. It will help me pass the time away whilst you and Jay are gone. Besides, I gotta keep the place up. You take care now, you hear? Call me every chance you get."

"Don't worry, I will. I'm sure you'll be just fine."

"You know, you're gonna have a long time to think on that there bus and while you're drivin' to the Grand Canyon. There will be time to think on things. I think you're gonna come back a changed woman. I surely do. This here journey is gonna be good for you. It will help you gain a new perspective on what matters in life."

Now there was my opportunity, and I just jumped on it.

"And would that have somethin' to do with Mr. Pervis and the preacher? Now I know you been schemin', Sula. Don't think I ain't noticed. Why, those two men are plain set in their ways. I'm just startin' out and I don't know that I'm ready to settle down. I know you think Jay here needs a daddy, and it just so happens that I agree with you. But he has me and you for now and that's just fine with me."

Sula just stood there smilin' at me the whole time I was talkin'. It wasn't like her not to say somethin' after I was goin' on the way I was. I wasn't sure if I should say on.

"You ain't sayin' anything."

"That's right."

"So, you think I'm right?"

"Oh, it's all a part of it."

"What?"

"You know, you're lettin' go real nice. Leavin' and journeyin', why, it's all a part of life. I do believe it is what God intended. Now give me a kiss. I love you both, I truly do. I'll see you real soon. Go on, get on that bus before I start bawlin' right here."

I smiled at Sula and kissed and hugged her real tight. I was still confused 'bout what happened between us. It wasn't like her at all. I found me a seat toward the middle of the bus. Jay nestled in right comfortable like. I was determined to enjoy the ride. Why, even my Orange Crush was still cool. We pulled out of Chatfield, and I gave one last wave to Sula. I was cryin' but just as soon as I thought on her words, I stopped. Leavin' and journeyin' was what God intended. She didn't even comment on my noticin' her schemin' ways. It kinda left me empty.

She knew what I been through more than most. Shoot, more than Granny now that I thought on it. I barely got free of that whole mess, finally found my way through all those obstacles. First gettin' free from Frog Creek and him, miscarryin' a baby, losin' my Granny, some fool policeman thinkin' I was involved in his death to boot; and now she was all set for me to move on? Why? To move on to what? Marriage? Why, I had to figure out m'self! I had to figure a way for me and Jay to live. I had to... think on all this... well, I'll be. It hit me.

The children of Israel had some powerful obstacles to get through. Once they got free from Pharaoh, why, he still tried to hedge up their way. They kept movin' on through the wilderness with Moses leadin' the way, leavin' behind what comforts they had, journeyin' on to the Promised Land. Fact is, they'd fall down, change their ways, only to fall down again, and all the while they were livin', journeyin' to the Promised Land.

Why, Sula, you are seer-like, just like Granny. I was livin'. Always was. I just couldn't see it through all that mist of confusion 'bout m'self and what this here life is 'bout. I always had choices before me. I had help bein' delivered from all this here mess, but I saw now that I helped m'self some too. Now I was mad 'cause I had too many choices in front of me. It was kinda like manna from heaven. I wanted someone to show me the way. Which choice was right? The truth was, all this here was a part of livin'. Just like God intended.

I looked up at the stars in the sky whilst I rested my head on the window of the bus. I thought this could be the best part of my day. All the stars were blinkin' and twinklin'. The stars were so far away and still givin' us light. Each one could be a story in our lives, lightin' the way 'til we got to the next place. I heard tell they were all made up of gases. Some of them were even gone, and we were just seein' the light. Boy, leave it to someone thinkin' too much on this stuff to take the fun out of imaginin' sometimes. No, I'd say this here was all a part of livin'. Nature, what God done made. It was here to help us as we journeyed on our way. To give us time to reflect on what was really important in life. This here was the best part of my day.

The bus stopped just then. I didn't even hear what town we were in. I saw a woman get on with two kids. She kept her head down and sat just across from me and Jay. I smiled at her, but she didn't even acknowledge me. She got her two kids settled down, covered them up with blankets. In the dim lights of the bus, I could tell she had been cryin'. The bus pulled out, and we began our journey again.

"How do, my name is Cinda. I'm travelin' up to Mantorville. I see you got two kids. My son's name is Jay. He's three and a half. I got me some sandwiches, you want some?"

I seen her kids piped up some, and they was lettin' her know they was hungry.

"Sure you don't mind? I didn't have time to prepare nothin' for our trip. I left in a hurry."

I gave each of them a sandwich. The kids seemed mighty grateful, and she did too.

"I got some water if you want. I got some apples too."

"Thank you kindly. Say thank you children. Say thank you to the nice lady."

It seemed like those sandwiches were just what those children needed. Why, they went right to sleep after they ate. She got them all quieted down again and sat down.

"I want to thank you again for the food. Like I said, I didn't get a chance to fix any food. I didn't even think on it. My name is Delphine. This here one by the window is my oldest. His name is Marcus, and the other is Ruby Dee."

"Pleased to meet you and your children. You goin' to Mantorville? You don't have to say if you don't want to. I would understand."

"No, I'll be goin' on further north. I got a sister who lives out near Dentonville way. I'm goin' to stay with her for a while 'til I get myself... well, I don't rightly know... what to say..."

She started cryin'. It was like I could feel her sadness.

"'Til you figure out a plan?"

"Yeah, I didn't know how to say it. I'm sorry for cryin'. I don't want to trouble you none. You seem like you got it nice. Are you goin' travelin'?"

"Yes, Delphine, I am on a journey."

"You're lucky to be on this here bus, travelin'. Goin' some place nice, I bet."

She breathed out a heavy sigh and wiped her eyes.

I remembered what Sula said 'bout there bein' people needin' to talk. All I had to do was open my eyes. Well, sure enough. I could tell she needed help. If nothin' else a good old shoulder to cry on. I wanted to help this here woman, but I didn't know what to say.

"Delphine, I got an ear if you want to talk 'bout what's so sad. I ain't bein' nosy, but I'd sure like to help if I could."

"Sure enough? Why, I just don't see how anyone can understand this here mess I'm in. See, I had to leave my home. It wasn't safe for me and the children no more. Are you sure you wanna hear? A proper lady like you might not want to know 'bout this."

"Delphine, say on. It seems like we got a ways to go on our journey here. Say on."